Near the Hope

JENNIFER DAVIS CAREY

Publisher's Cataloging-in-Publication
From Quality Books

Carey, Jennifer Davis 1956-

Near the hope / by Jennifer Davis Carey.

pages cm

1. Women immigrants–United States–Fiction. 2. West

Indians–United States–Fiction. 3. New York (N.Y.)–

Fiction. 4. Domestic fiction. 5. Bildungsromans.

I. Title.

PS3603.A7413N43 2013 813'.6

QBI13-600148

ISBN: 0989545091
ISBN: 9780989545099

Library of Congress Control Number: 2013913545
Blue Mongoose Publishing
Worcester, Massachusetts

Blue Mongoose Publishing
Worcester, Massachusetts

For the family here, gone, and yet to come.

Acknowledgements

This work would not have been possible without the support and encouragement of family, friends, and colleagues. Special thanks are due to the women in my writing group: Margaret LeRoux, Mary Warbasse, Sue Hegedus, Allison Chisolm-Hansen, and Elizabeth Johnson. Their questions and insights helped to fine-tune the narrative through multiple iterations. Jan Cellucci, Joan Gage, Jan LaVanche Garske, Peter Grigg, George Lamming, and Randal Kenan deserve special acknowledgement for plowing through and making important suggestions on embarrassing early drafts.

A bouquet of thanks goes to Catherine Michelle Adams of Inkslinger Editorial Services whose patience and ability to separate the wheat from the chaff helped me to listen better to Dellie as I wrote her story. Jessamyn Hope of Grub Street, Mat Johnson of the Hurston Wright Writer's Workshop, and Evelina Galang of Vona Voices each have my gratitude for their enthusiasm and willingness to focus on the story and its message, rather than my erratic comma usage.

Thanks are due to writer Paule Marshall whose essay, *The Poets in the Kitchen*, opened my ears once again to the lyricism of West Indian speech and allowed me once again to hear the voices of my grandmother and her sisters.

Not to be overlooked are Michael Neff of Algonquin Writers Workshops whose simple statement "this sounds like a novel" pushed me onto this path, and my friend and fellow author, Vieta Jo Hampton, who shoved me when I needed it.

A special thank you goes to three of my teachers, Marjorie Gill, Eileen Mullen, and Virginia T. Mosca. These dedicated women encouraged my voice and demanded precision and passion in the written word.

And finally, to my family, especially my husband, best friend, and partner, Bob Carey, who helped me to keep my eyes on the finish line.

Near The Hope

Mothers Known and Unknown

Barbados and everywhere, 1909, and always and forever

A woman with flawless skin beat the drum.

They did not know her name. Her children did not know her name. For them, she existed in unnamed corners of memory, beyond youth, beyond childhood, beyond the womb. She was in the place of sound, of feeling, of breath. She gathered and was the shadow at the edge of Maude's vision. She was the word just past the tip of Dellie's tongue. She brushed against Lillian's thoughts. She was May's laugh. She was the gesture they all shared, the walk, the tilt of the head, the smile. She was the music of their silver bracelets.

A host of others dressed in white were with her — their hands, wings of movement; their feet, a blur of dance. She was always there. Always with each of them. She was memory and life, passing down and through them. Her face was like an ebony carving, and she beat the drum and remembered what had passed, what was now, and what was yet to come....

PART ONE
Little England

CHAPTER ONE

The End

Barbados, 1909 and 1910

*T*he great kettles in the sugar house boiled down the cane juice, making the air that wafted across the estate thick and cloying. Dellie looked up, her hand wiping away the sweat that crawled past her straw hat. The breeze that criss-crossed the island swayed the crowns of the palms, yet offered no reprieve from the relentless heat of the Caribbean sun. It was too hot. Dellie exhaled as she stooped down and twisted a handful of bushy weeds from the ground, disturbing a beetle as it made its way through the clots of black earth in the kitchen garden.

"Cal, there's just a bit more. I can finish up." She glanced toward her mother, her eyes taking in the bright red flush that colored the older woman's face.

"Cal. Look here." She paused. "Cal, look at me." Her mother ignored her, standing straight, swaying slightly.

Dellie's voice was tinged with urgency. "Did you hear me? Go in. You need to go into the cool. Your face is…"

The older woman looked around, confused. "What is that sound? That drumming?" Dellie dropped her hoe, stepped toward her mother and touched her arm.

"What sound, I don't hear anything." She shook her mother's arm. "What are you talking about? Cal?" Dellie gasped as she watched her mother press her fingers into her temples, brow ruched in pain.

Dellie's eyes followed her mother's as her head turned toward the path that led to the road. The older woman's eyes were focused, not on the donkey cart laden with cane winding its way to town, but on something else. Dellie raised her hands to shield her eyes against the sun. She followed her mother's gaze to the shimmers of heat that rose from the road. Dellie turned at the sound of her mother's voice. "Phoebe? Phoebe-Ma?" Her mother muttered, tongue thick, "Phoebe-Ma?" and then slumped to the ground.

"Cal, what is happening? What are you seeing? Who are you talking to? There is no one there!" Dellie kneeled, upsetting her basket of thorns and weeds as she moved to cradle her mother. Tendrils of cold fear gathered in her arms and crept toward her hands. "Cal, Cal," she moaned, throat tight, as she rocked back and forth.

Cal stared ahead. "Phoebe. My sweet mother. It has been donkey years since I saw you. Since you've been gone. Phoebe. What are you doing here, your good white dress on?"

Dellie's voice was tight in her throat. "Ah Cal, what are you saying? Mother! What are you saying?" She turned her head toward the sky and pleaded. "No, please don't take her." Her breath caught as her mother reached her hand out, fingers splayed in the air, a soft smile playing across her mouth. "Yes, I am coming."

Dellie moved her head closer to hear the run of words as her mother's voice faded. "It has been so long since I felt your hand upon me. So long. Now?" The older woman's eyebrows rose in a question and her head moved in a weak nod. "You want me to come now? Yes. I am ready. Who are all those lined up behind you? All part of us? All? So beautiful they are…and the drumming. The women drumming."

Her eyelids fluttered and slowly closed.

"Cal, no, no, no. Cal, don't go. Oh Cal!" Her hand tightened around her mother's fingers. "Dear God, not this way. Don't answer me this way, please not this way." Dellie's words slipped into a cry.

———

Cal was dead and there were arrangements to be made.

The End

Dellie stood on the rose-colored verandah overlooking the tenants' compound. Her mother lay out on the bed in the sleeping room. Her little brothers and sisters swirled around her, eyes wet. "Please, God, before the children see me break, let her get here. Let her get here..."

She trained her gaze to the gate and the road beyond and wished her grandmother, M'Ma, the woman who would put order to things, who would wash the dead as she did the just born, to appear, rushing over the rise from the Great House.

It had been so sudden. One minute things were one way. Then Cal crumpled on the garden ground. Everything, *everything* changed, as her mother's last breath joined the breath of breeze. Dellie covered her face with her hands and tilted her face upward, tipping back the tears.

The clean scent of her father Henry's bay rum and his touch on her shoulder pulled her back.

"Dellie-child."

The thickness of her father's voice told all. "Her heart just stop. Like that. Give out. Like her own mother."

"We were working in the garden. Pulling weeds in the garden. That is the last thing my mother was doing..." Tears buried her voice. Her father reached to embrace her.

M'Ma's sharp figure appeared. She reached out and her arms enfolded her son and granddaughter. Dellie breathed in the almond scent of the old woman's coarse, gray hair. She breathed out, holding in check the ice that crept through her body as her grandmother led them inside.

"Henry," M'Ma said, "go to the house. Tell Mr. Chandler. Tell Josh, so he can make the pine box."

Dellie caught the cry in her throat. Her mother. A coffin for her mother.

Henry remained motionless, staring, his face struggling for control.

M'Ma added force to her voice. "Henry, this is your wife here. This is *your* job. Do it. Do it now. Cal needs tending, and no one has time to falter. You must get word to the priest. Get the cooling board set up." She touched his arm and lowered her voice. "You must make the marker." She paused. "And you must tell Mr. and Mrs. Chandler." She shook her head. "Mrs. Chandler will take this hard."

He turned and disappeared to carry out the men's tasks necessary to close Cal's time on earth.

Dellie moved toward the stand next to the bed. The small spray of flowers that Cal picked each day and placed in the room had been upset, the blooms now sat in a pool of water. "I saw her pick these this morning." She turned and ran her finger over the curve of a blossom. "This one. She was waiting for this one to bloom." Her voice trailed as she faced her grandmother. "She was waiting for this one. She told me it would be perfect. That it would bloom today. And see?" She held it up to her grandmother. "I watched her pick it this morning and now she's gone, M'Ma." She looked down and took in her mother's features. Even in death, Cal's skin had a glow like a jar of honey on a sunlit shelf. Dellie's eyes lingered on her mother's high, unlined forehead and followed the outline of hair along her brow as it arched to a peak. She studied the nose and full, chiseled mouth, lips dark as if stained by berries. Dellie's fingertips brushed the halo of hairs, freed now from the head tie that had framed her mother's face when she was working. Her hand went to trace the high curve of her cheekbone and pulled back suddenly, stunned by the coolness of her mother's skin. This body, this woman whose hands she had held, whose breasts she had suckled — whose voice had sung her to sleep and whose soft lips had healed every scrape — was gone, the life already run out from her. She would lie in the ground beneath a small white wooden cross — *Caroline Walker Standard* painted in black block letters on the cross beam — that her husband, head carpenter of the Walker estate, Coventry Hall, would carve to mark her life.

Dellie began to tremble. She wrapped her arms around her body and rocked ever so gently back and forth. "M'Ma, it was so sudden. One minute, and then another. And she was talking to her mother, to Phoebe."

M'Ma's voice was low. "Was her mother come back for her. She is with her now and all the rest gone before us. All the ancestors. God willing, they will come for us too when it is our time." Dellie breathed out, working to settle herself. She felt the softness of her grandmother's touch on her arm.

"Sweet girl. Time to talk to the Lord now Dellie. He, too, can help us bear this."

The old woman's voice wavered as she opened her palms.

"Merciful Father, we bless You and thank You for making the journey home of Your daughter Cal quick. Her light, her sweetness, the memory of what You made her will be with us forever. Guide her children left behind. And be with those who love her now and always in the days ahead." Dellie looked up as her grandmother took in a shuddering breath. Her ears took in the muffled aside to the spirits as the old woman worked to stem the rush of grief. "You know she was to me like a child of my own body. Dear Cal. Take care of her and be with me, with all of us through what is to come." Dellie bowed her head as she heard that always-steady voice quiver and break, leaving only God to make out the words in her grandmother's tears.

Through what is to come. The phrase tripped through Dellie's brain. These children with no mother. Dellie looked at her grandmother and waved her arm toward her four brothers and sisters who milled about aimless, stunned.

"Who will mother them? If I leave now, who, M'Ma? Who?"

———

Dellie and her three sisters Lillian, May, Maude, joined M'Ma around the small body laid flat on the cooling board in the shade of the brush arbor. Dellie brought clean cloths and a pan of water sweetened with rosemary crushed against her hand. Its spicy perfume filled their nostrils. Maude pushed a tendril of her hair, sodden from tears, behind her ear. She took the pan from Dellie, placing it on a small table that M'Ma arranged beside the bier. Lillian, the eldest daughter, unfastened her mother's clothes and began the ritual, the same one that Cal and M'Ma performed when any woman on the estate passed on. They had all witnessed it many times, but this time it was just them, Cal's family performing it for her. The women squeezed the cleansing water over Cal. It flowed down the hands that had worked the soil, fashioned clothes for her children, and prepared meals for her family and for Mr. Chandler's, both in her own house and in the Great House that sat at the top of the hill.

The water poured over a body that had borne and nursed seven children, loved a man, and bled with the moon. The water sanctified the feet that long ago had brought her to Coventry Hall Estate, the Walker land in St. George, but no further. As the stream purified the body, the low murmuring of the women consecrated Cal's soul, and their salt tears bore witness to her life and its mark upon the earth.

The bathing ritual over, M'Ma slid the silver bangles from Cal's arm. Cal had added one with the birth of each girl and had worn the bangles every day, her spirit burnishing each.

M'Ma called each girl in turn.

"Lillian." Her sister reached her arm out. Graceful, contained as ever, Dellie knew though that her heart was tearing. Her wedding coming up and their mother not there.

"Dellie."

She stretched out her arm as her grandmother slid the metal circle over her slender hand. Her fingers traced the geometric design incised into the metal. How many times as a small girl had she begged Cal to let her try them on? "Just one Cal, please, for just a minute?" Back then, she had been struck by the weight of each one, now she was struck by their lightness.

She kept her eyes steady as M'Ma offered Maude and May their legacy each in turn.

The girls stood with their grandmother, each with the bracelet worn in her name circling her wrist. Each would pass it on to her eldest daughter and then her daughter and on and on among those still to come.

Dellie thought about the boys. Deighton already off in Panama. She knew that she would be the one to tell him. What words could she put on paper to bear this news to him?

———

The family ringed Cal's body. Somber prayers mixed with bits of hymns drifted into a low keening. Tears flowed freely, and the women, swaying, filled the place with their memories, single, collective. They saw Cal with Henry when his love was high, her hand softly on his knee; Cal offering a full breast to one of the children as a baby; Cal laughing at some outlandish tale told by one of the House women, Cal sweating as she worked to staunch the bleeding of a worker slashed by the razor-sharp leaves of the cane; Cal's face a knot at one of the mad women's rants. Cal.

On some unspoken cue, Dellie turned and gathered together the washing things. Humming a song, the words shrouded by time, the women stepped outside and at the base of the breadfruit tree poured the water that had cleansed Cal's body. Its roots would draw it in; carry it to its leaves and blossoms, making Cal part of the island. Dellie tilted her head and listened to the rush of the spirits of the old dead Africans, the planters, the long ago Indians, and the lines of workers, white, black, colored, on the breeze. She searched for Cal's voice, new among them.

A clatter of hooves and wheels interrupted them. The women stopped their liturgy and took on the faces expected by the House. Josh, Henry's friend and the Chandler's groom sat in the driver's seat of the black brougham, Mrs. Chandler silhouetted behind him. The horses snorted as he settled them before opening the carriage door and offering the lady of the estate his hand as she stepped down. Dellie scanned the faces of the family. "What is the Mistress doing here?" Dellie considered the mix of feelings that wrestled within her. This woman was Cal's aunt and Cal was her servant. Her servant. Cal was her brother's child. But that was not something anyone was to speak of. Not even today.

The old woman's arrival attracted a crowd of silent observers as workers left their tasks and the tools for repairing fences, shoeing horses, making brooms, patching clothes — the work needed for their own places and for the Great House — around the tenants' compound.

Cal's family gathered quickly and stood in silent respect as Mrs. Eloise Walker Chandler approached. Dellie shifted uncomfortably as her father joined the gathering and fumbled for words.

"Mrs. Chandler. We did not expect your presence...I mean to say..."

Mrs. Chandler kept her eyes straight ahead and with a look from M'Ma, Henry abandoned his sentence. M'Ma guided Coventry Hall's mistress to where Cal lay.

In her eighteen years, Dellie had had little contact with the old woman — just the smell of her perfume left lingering on items sent to be washed or a glimpse from a distance while being assisted into her great carriage, her face obscured by a wide bonnet against the West Indian sun. Now, close enough to study the face, she saw her own mother. She turned to her sisters and brothers, across the range of their skin colors from eggshell to chestnut, the Walker notable somewhere in each of them — in the curve of Maude's ears, the shape of May's brow, the cleft on Byron's chin, the curl of Palley's hair. She thought of the scattering of freckles across her own nose. It was hard for Dellie to imagine that according to Cal and the other House women, the gunmetal gray hair on the woman's head had once been the same red as her own.

Mrs. Chandler left a gathering of white flowers at Cal's side and turned to M'Ma. "Margaret, here take this." She gestured to Josh who stretched out his hand to offer M'Ma a package. "I brought some cloth to use for the shroud. I will send a carriage from the House. I will not have Cal wrapped in some rough Osnaburg and carried in a mule cart."

She turned, her eyes passing across the circle of family without acknowledgement. A cloud of gardenia sprang from Mrs. Chandler's lace handkerchief, ironed by Cal, her lady's maid, as she dabbed her eyes and signaled the groom her readiness to depart.

———

Dellie adjusted the jalousies as the sky took on its night colors — to the left, down-country, the pink tipped silver clouds — to the right, up-country the deepening indigo. Mist was beginning to rise as the land cooled and the chattering of the birds gave way to the steady hum of the night insects. The wake would begin soon. As she looked over the rise and toward the cluster of houses in the lower part of the tenants' compound she could see knots of people making their way up the rise for the vigil. She turned and scanned the viewing room. Everything was in place. Someone had crafted sprays of bay leaf to sit at each end of the coffin. Fresh lace antimacassars covered worn spots on the two good upholstered chairs handed down from Mrs. Chandler years ago. Dellie smoothed the front of her dress.

Alone with her mother, she stroked the woman's hair. Thick, wavy, soft, the touch of it soothed her. She thought of her little sister May, the baby of the girls. May, so little. She still loved to take Cal's comb and brush and fix her mother's hair, weaving it over and under into a long braid that Cal wrapped around the crown of her head. Dellie spied her mother's sewing bag in a corner, its contents spilling over the top. The curved scissors shaped like a crane poked from a side pocket. Dellie muttered under her breath, "It is a crime to put that hair into the ground." She clipped a lock from the soft curve of her mother's neck, folded it into a square of fabric, and placed it deep in her pocket.

Dellie reached to adjust the vermillion corsage that M'Ma had attached to Cal's bodice, the pollen clinging to her fingers. "Cal, you see M'Ma has put the bloom you were waiting for upon your dress." She paused, fixed her mouth, wrapping her mind around the words. "Cal, I prayed that something would come up so that I wouldn't have to keep my promise." Her voice was a sob. "So that I wouldn't have to leave. You told me long ago to never pray for things, just for strength. I didn't listen. And now you're gone." She sagged to the floor.

———

People filed in to pay respects as a sliver of moon rose and Dellie took her turn standing with the family next to the simple box. The first to come were the inhabitants of Taborvilla, the tenant land associated with Coventry Hall. The workers from the fields, the servants from the Great House, and the host of craftsmen and managers whose varieties of work brought profit to the sugar estate, all filed past, offering words of respect or pieces of memory.

Dellie excused herself and followed a clutch of women as they migrated to the front room. A chair beckoned for the night's vigil ahead. Across the room, Maude slipped between her grandmother's knees to have her hair combed. Her grandmother hummed—and brushed, brushed, brushed to work out the tangles. Dellie ached for M'Ma to do the same for her.

A group of women from Workman's Village nodded as they came through the front door and worked their way through the crowd that filled the room. They placed platters on the heavy mahogany table that had been pulled out from its usual place against the wall. The seasoned flying fish, sweet plantain, and mounds of peas and rice, along with pitchers of drinks—all brought by family, friends, and neighbors—would see them through the long night. Dellie shifted uncomfortably as their eyes drifted to the wall behind the table. Her father's image impressed every visitor who entered his house. The immense photographic portrait evoked both dignity and energy—a man seeing things and going places, who presided over the rose-colored chattel house. It made clear Henry's command of this clapboard structure—and of his family—on the rise overlooking the field workers' cottages circling Taborvilla and the sugar works in a place near the district called "the Hope."

Henry had the photograph made when he first built the house. The Bridgetown photographer had promised him something that would hold its own against the paintings of the founders of the Walker dynasty in the Great House. In its gilt wooden frame, wide as a child's arms spread, it commanded the front room. The photographer captured not only his likeness, but something more. With a sleek walking stick in hand, weight on the front foot, full, thick handlebar moustache, and piercing gaze, he was the only one in the tenants' compound ever to have had a photograph made. Its unrelenting presence dominated the room and those in it.

Around the close room, from their positions on the pair of worn, tufted chairs that the family was forbidden to sit on and the benches and chairs crafted by Henry, women's voices rose and fell, fans fluttered.

"Even Mrs. Chandler came down to see her, eyes all red. I heard she is going to provide a carriage from the house. Cal is more family to her than her own people over in St. James."

"Two houses are empty now without her."

"It was *Cal* that was the light in this house."

Dellie sensed a harsh and mean shift in conversation.

As she settled into one of the upholstered chairs, and worked to balance a plate of food on her knees, one of the serrated-tongued women from the House spoke. "What is Henry going to do? All his children leaving. The son, Dite, off to Panama. Lillian heading to New York?" Dellie picked up a pitcher, hoping to turn the conversation by offering to refresh the glasses of bittersweet mauby.

"Well, I guess others will have to raise up the small children. It would break dear Cal's heart to see May, expecially May, and the boys running around unsupervised." Dellie's jaw tightened and M'Ma's humming increased ever so slightly. The women took heed and the conversation shifted again as Dellie stepped outside. She made her way past the cooking shed to the brush arbor with its old hammock slung inside. She lay back, watching the clouds making patterns with the moon, thoughts drifting to a day not long ago. The scene played before her. She and Cal were in the cooking shed, steam rolling from a pot of stew, dogs outside yipping for their share.

"Cal, you want me to put some more water in the pot? The stew looks a bit thick to me."

"No. I have some tomatoes to go in at the last. Their juice will be enough. More water will turn it to gruel." Dellie watched her

12

mother turn and wipe her hands on her apron. When she turned to face her, her brow was a knot. Dellie breathed out and waited for her mother to speak.

"Dellie, I have something to say to you." She took Dellie's chin in her hand and met her eyes. "I want you to leave this place and go to New York. Like your sister is planning to. Like your friend Winnie. Your brother Dite has left this place and gone to Panama but that place is not fit for a woman. But New York now. This Brooklyn that they talk about. Seems like a body could see a way to make it there." A rainbow cluster of birds whisked from one tree to another. "Lillian is going after the wedding. You next."

"But, Cal, I have good work with Miss Crane. She has said my work is impressive. And she has the best shop in town."

"I know, Dellie. She has work for you *now*. But the cane crash will reach her and then what? And your sewing, that is a skill, a true gift you will take with you. Dite is making his way. Lillian and Coleridge have a good plan. I hear your friend Winnie is making a place for herself. And soon to be married, too."

Dellie leaned against the doorframe. "But Lillian and Coleridge have each other and like you said, Winnie has Clemmie." She touched her mother's hand. "New York, Cal. It is like fifty of this place and you hear tales that it is hard living there. That women can end up serving in a House no different from here — or even worse." She paused and lowered her voice. "Ruined and walking the streets."

"You are talking about women with no skill, or no sense, or no family to circle around them." Cal's grip on her arm tightened and her tone became more emphatic. "The future of the family is not here. I know what your father has planned, buying a piece of land and cultivating cane. As if he will be one of the Walkers." She chupsed and shook her head. "Hear me. Chance is opening up elsewhere. Dellie, you have got to go. So do you all. You and the rest have a different kind of chance." She tightened her hand around Dellie's arm but turned her face away. "I can only keep you out of the House for so long, Dellie." Cal looked up at the trees. "And don't think that every ruined woman is walking the streets."

Dellie sucked in her breath and stared at her mother. *Ruined woman.* The memory shot into her head and played itself fast through her brain. *She was a small girl, leaning against the wood*

13

paneling of the dining room where Cal was clearing the dining table from lunch. She had known she shouldn't be there and had tried to make herself invisible. Then too, Cal and M'Ma's warning had echoed in her head: "Never, never go up to the Great House." But Cal hadn't kissed her that morning, hadn't picked her up and rubbed her nose with hers that day before heading off to work for Mrs. Chandler, and on top of that Dite had reduced her to tears with his teasing. Dellie had been missing her mother, and just needed a glimpse of her before she could go back to her games. What she saw though was not what she had expected. Dellie had checked the gasp that rose from deep within her chest. Her eyes opened wide taking in the stiffness that shot through her Cal's body as Mr. Chandler, wobbly after his rum lunch, faced her mother. His yellowed fingers rolled Cal's nipples through the cloth of her dress and his mouth, open like a pond carp, pressed against hers. An expression she had never seen before worked her mother's face. Her gaze hovered on Cal's eyes, tight, pinched shut, and her arms, out at her sides, fingers splayed. Dellie stood, silent, rooted to the spot, every part of her, inside and out, trembling. The old man caught sight of her and made a gesture with his hands, like he was testing the ripeness of a fruit and laughed, deep and throaty. She stared and stepped back as he stumbled onto the verandah and slumped into a wicker chair, his loud snores marking an immediate and drunken sleep.

Dellie watched, eyes like saucers as Cal leaned over the great mahogany credenza and stuffed a napkin into a pitcher of water. She could see her mother in the gilt-edged mirror that filled the expanse of the wall above. She watched Cal as she wrung the water out, brought the cloth to her face and rubbed violently, cleaning her mouth and her face. She'd stood, frozen in place, until Cal looked up. Seeing them both in the reflection, her mother turned sharply, looking right at her, an expression she had never seen on her face. Dellie had backed from her hiding place and fled.

She squeezed her mother's arm and Cal turned to her, an old pain etched into her face. "Even with you working a day or two in town, I can only keep up with excuses for so long. I don't want Mr. Chandler calling for you. Or for Maude. And then for May."

Now Dellie turned her face away. She brushed away a fly that lighted on her arm. "Cal, Pendril and I are planning together. He is going to sea and with no expenses on the ship he will save up. Even if the cane crashes, it won't touch the Great Ones. We have thought it through. Land is changing hands here now. A person could have their own piece of ground here. There is a chance..."

Cal's voice was sharp. "A chance for what? Even for the few who actually do buy some ground despite all the talk." She cast her arm about in a sweeping gesture. "What they get a chance for? A chance for more of *this*? A chance to treat colored and black so? A chance to think you are your own person and find out you are not? The poison runs too deep here. It eventually touches everyone. If you don't leave, it will touch you somehow. Black, white, colored. No matter."

"But you and Henry need my coins to make the rent card, to pay school fees. Even with the meals you can bring down from the House, the price of food is dear. It takes more from us each day."

"We will find a way with the rent card, the school fees. Your M'Ma and I know how to tie up our bellies if we have to. So did my mother. Dellie, this place is part of what I am, of who I am. I know how to live poor, M'Ma knows how to live poor. We've learned to manage the needs of the House. To hold a part of us away so it doesn't touch us. But it will end here. It is not something I want any of you to learn. When Lillian was born and I saw her face, I proclaimed then, 'It stops here.' Your place is somewhere else. So is Maude's. And May's." Cal stopped. "Look at me Dellie. Look at me and hear what I am saying. This island is not the only place a man and woman can make a life. You and Pendril need to see that. Child, I need you to promise me."

"But Cal, it is a part of me too."

"Don't say that. Dellie, I need you to promise me."

The sound of a lizard scuttling up a tree pulled Dellie back. She shifted in the hammock, the rope grazing her ankles. Cal gone. Where did that leave her promise? She churned her fingers through her hair, stood and made her way back to the house.

———

The men had settled outdoors around the verandah to weigh the times. The perfume of jasmine and frangipani was heavy and luxurious. The voice speaking was deep and belonged to someone whom Dellie did not recognize.

"This Panama money is some real money." A tilt of the head and fingers rubbed together.

Dellie sighed. Even at this time, the talk was of leaving, of what was to be had off-island. Dellie thought about her brother. One of his friends had come back and was trying to buy a piece of land. Another had came back, nearly dead from yellow fever and full of tales of air thick with mosquitoes, ankle-deep mud, men dead overnight, men falling dead with shovels or pick axes in their hands. After months he was just barely strong enough to work again on the docks. A different voice pulled her from her thoughts.

"That's right and now a shortage of cane workers is the real result. Every day they are moving more women from the fields to the sugar works to take the men's places, and then asking decent people to cultivate cane. I half expect to see Mr. Chandler himself in the cane field, cutlass in his hand!"

"'Tis true! Ferguson has been telling Miles he needs him in the mill. The man is trained as a blacksmith! I was shocked, man, shocked. He makes it sound like if they don't comply, he is going to pull Miles' rent card and make the man uproot his house!"

"I don't put it past them, desperate as they are to bring in the crop!"

Henry spoke up. "Ferguson threw some carpentry work my way. Off grounds. His pal Simpson is preparing for the harvest and the pressing of his first crop of cane, and when he went to mount the sails, he found the arms all rotted up."

"So, Standard, I take it then, you will not be headed to dig the ditch?"

Dellie moved aside as M'Ma stepped through the tendrils of citronella smoke. Her grandmother cleared her throat. "Henry, they need you to start the testimonial."

He didn't respond.

Dellie touched his shoulder. "Henry, did you hear M'Ma? They need you inside."

His back tightened and his eyes remained on the assembly of men.

"I will come inside in a minute."

Dellie's mouth tightened into a line and she shook her head. Why must it always be necessary for him to play the role of the great man? "Henry, the family will be waiting. Sorry to disturb you."

He stabbed his thigh with one finger. "If you are going any-where on this piece of rock, you need land for your ticket. Excuse me now. I must tend to things inside."

As night gave way to morning they swaddled Cal's small frame in the white, fine linen sent by Mrs. Chandler. At daybreak, the death ritual began anew. The women scrubbed the children and put them in the good clothes lent from the rest of the family. Henry, Josh, and Joe Burroughs carefully placed the feather-light box in the back of Mrs. Chandler's carriage, which had been sent as she had said. It would be a fine, respectable turnout with representatives from every family, black and colored, in Workman's Village and Taborvilla.

Henry barked out orders to the assembly. "The small children next." He pointed to May, Byron, and Palley and directed them where to stand and to be still. He continued, "Next, Lillian, Dellie, then Maude. That's it. Straight now, like you are in His Majesty's Review at school!"

The family began the long walk down the hill. Josh held the reins steady as M'Ma and Henry climbed up and sat together side by side. Dellie watched Henry as he surveyed the scene behind him — the family attired in jacket and tie or in white dresses, the car-riage from the Great House drawn by Mrs. Chandler's horse, not a mule or a donkey. She knew he was pleased at the turn out as it marked not only the regard offered his wife, but that of the family that he headed.

The sun, not midway up on the horizon, cast a golden shimmer on the dust kicked up by the feet of the mourners. Dellie glanced to her left as they approached the crossroads, praying that the obeah woman was not out. A tirade from her would be more than she could bear. She was not to be seen and the heavy clomp, clomp, clomp of the horses' hooves beat steadily, the only sound as the cor-tege rounded the corner. The elevation of St. George's Anglican Church grew in the distance.

Dellie picked out Pendril's unruly hair immediately. Just the sight of him soothed her. He stood at the straightaway where the two roads crossed — one up from St. Michael and My Lord's Hill, the other down from Salisbury and Gun Hill. His friends surrounded him — part of the collection of just-turned men pushing at the seams of the island.

He shifted from foot to foot at the front of a clutch of people, waiting for the right moment to join the procession. As the column approached the crossroads, he stepped forward. His face mirrored her sorrow as he grasped her hand and fell into step beside her.

———

Hours later, spent from burying her mother, what Dellie needed was to sit in silence, alone to collect herself and her thoughts. She made her way to the drying shed. The jars with Cal's gatherings glistened in the sunlight-dappled room. A light smell of rosemary rose as her sleeve brushed a sprig laid out to dry. She pulled out Cal's tall stool and sat, her head leaning on her elbows. A rustle of feet nearby drew her attention. It was Pendril.

"Dellie. I was looking all around for you." He pulled a stool up and sat next to her. "I am sorry. It is the worst." She knew that inside of him was the memory of his own parents and the terrible storm that had torn across the island taking with it houses, trees, crops, and parents. They sat in silence, hands barely touching.

"Pendril, I prayed for a way to stay. To not have to hold to my promise to Cal. How could this be the answer? How? If I had known the answer would come this way…" She covered her face in her hands.

Pendril stood, upsetting the stool. "Take that thought from your mind. Talk sense girl."

Dellie turned to him, her mouth a tight line.

"Ah, Dellie. My own heart." He reached for her and she sank into his arms.

CHAPTER TWO

Near the Hope

Dear Deighton,

I have just taken pen in hand to write you these few lines, hoping that the reaches of them find you as well as they leave me. I am sorry my last letter bore such terrible news. There is nothing of the sort in these pages. We here are all learning to live without Cal. I am almost always home on Sunday and Mondays. I try to get back during the week to help M'Ma with the little ones. Lillian does come back as often as she can, usually to help with the wash. Maudie is some help, but you know she prefers to have her nose in a book, than peel a potato or fill the washbucket. I will not burden you with how much I miss our mother. I know you do also. I did dry a blossom from a spray from the service and am enclosing it for you as a remembrance.

Everyone who has come back says it is rough living in Panama. According to the papers, people are sick from the bites of mosquitoes. Some are maimed in explosions or landslides from digging the hole. Your friend Garret's mother heard from him in the last mail. He put in the 500 days of his contract and plans to make a trip back here with some of his crowd. He says the Panama money is good, but the place makes Barbados seem like The King's Palace. According to him, they pay the white worker in US gold, everyone else in local silver worth half. He also said you got a decent

19

job in a field office because you could show your school certificate. Is this true? We are all very worried.

We are all excited about planning Lillian's wedding. People are laying bets already on the limbo contest that they are expecting. Coleridge and Lillian's plans are coming together about heading to New York. We know your days will not be in and so you will not see them before they leave. Taborvilla is changing, with all of this leaving and the sinking price of cane. It is hard to see where it all is leading.

I have been staying at Eva's sister's place in Bridgetown some days. Miss Crane's shop is able to keep me busy a few days a week. She promises me full time, but that has not come to pass yet. Most people are not having things made new, but altering old things to look new. The folks from the Great Houses are learning to live like us!

The obeah woman is still wild. I wish there were an easy way to by-pass her yard, but no one has found that path yet.

The exhibition is just over, and Henry took Flora, the goat, down for the show. He won several ribbons, and Byron and M'Ma took ten shillings each for their hens and eggs.

Please don't wait to write back. We want to know you are well. Everyone here sends love.

———

The town awoke to the first strains of the day, as Dellie walked across the Careenage from the government building to the line of shops branching out from Lord Nelson's statue. The sun had not yet hinted at the coming heat, as a woman from up-country laid out her wares — fine pottery in every shape and size for storage. A huckster, shoeless, cried out, selling ackees with their rinds wiped clean and shining. Another balanced a jug of mauby on her head, while yet another sorted mangoes arranged on a weathered stand. Each lived hand-to-mouth, day-to-day. That's how it was in "Little England," in "Bimshire," in Barbados, the jewel in His Majesty's Caribbean crown. A small clutch of men at the edge of the delivery alley were well into their game of chance, despite the early hour.

The dock foreman came out from the rickety lean-to that served as his office.

"Back to work, you lazy goats! Back to work! Enough nickin' de dice. This ain' de smoking room at His Majesty's hunting lodge. Break over."

"Dellie-girl!" A familiar voice called from behind her.

She turned.

Pendril waved, sauntering up the street.

She suppressed a smile as he raked his fingers across his head in a hopeless attempt to manage the straight black-black hair that refused to lie flat—the trademark of the English, African, and Bengali blood that his ancestors passed on to him.

"I will walk with you a few steps. My crew is on break just now. I am looking for some shade. I missed you this morning."

"I left early to post a letter to Dite and I promised Lillian a final fitting before the shop opens." For several weeks now, she had found on the doorstep of Miss Crane's shop fabulous blooms—ginger, bougainvillea—left by some unannounced visitor. On other days she found small animals, crafted from mahogany and wrought with precision, their shading and markings in the wood used so that the figures appeared to have life. Pendril. Dellie smiled at the thought.

"You posted a letter to Dite? Any news from him?"

Dellie looked away. "No. Nothing in the last mail either. That makes two in a row that we haven't heard anything. I chided him in this one."

Pendril sighed. "Well, I hear mail handling there is one mass of confusion."

"The whole place seems like a mass of confusion to me. But they keep on packing out."

They turned right and made their way up Prince William Henry Street. The milliner and dry goods shops came into view. The crisp lawn dress and parasol in the window hinted at the goods inside Miss Crane's Fine Dress Shop.

"Pendril. I've got to go. You know Miss Crane likes me here early and the stop at Government House has put me behind."

"And I must head back before the foreman misses me."

The air inside was already close. Dellie flung open the jalousies for relief before settling into her work. A pile of hand and machine sewing waited. The social season would soon arrive with its whirl of events for the merchants and those from the Great Houses, all trying to ride out the fluctuations in the price of sugar. She ran her hand over the pile of fabric. Such finery—silks, laces, brocades for the season of parties up and down the island. A million small stitches necessary to secure the gentry among the gentry. Dellie checked the clock—she could make some progress on clothes for her brothers and sisters before Miss Crane arrived and her day began. The boys, especially, needed new pants and blouses for school. Miss Crane had made it clear that those efforts were to be on Dellie's time—before customers arrived—or after her sewing for the shop was complete. She was also expected to make sure the fitting materials, pins, yardsticks, tape measure, and chalk were in place. And she wasn't to forget to keep the dressing area tidy, the sewing room swept. She also was not to use the remnants without paying. Miss Crane would settle her out weekly. That was fair, wasn't it?

The fine sewing work helped settle Dellie. Just a little more finishing on the seams and the last of the shirts for the boys would be done. Tomorrow she'd alter some skirts for Maude and May, and then start a few more things for the boys. She laid out her work in neat piles.

Well, if she got ahead on the children's sewing, she'd have some things stored up. Absent the tucks and pleating of some of the other school uniforms, the attire for the school in St. George was easy enough. School. She sighed. Another round of fees would be due soon—Maude's fees, along with fees for Byron and May. And for Palley to continue, too. And Henry already having trouble with the rent card. She shook her head. Enough of that. She glanced outside. The angle of the sun told her she'd have just enough time to finish the boys' things before Lillian slipped in for a fitting.

———

The thrum of fingernails on the window of the sewing room drew Dellie's attention. She stood and opened the door for her sister and another woman.

"Ah, Lillian! At last you've come." She smiled. "And Mrs. Green. So good to see you! Come in." She cleared a pile of fabric from a chair for Lillian's soon-to-be mother-in-law, and gestured Lillian toward a stool.

The older woman nodded. "Thank you, Dellie. As early as it is you can still feel the heat building. You girls are lucky with the breeze upon the Hope. Down here in Bridgetown the heat just stays put. But I wanted to see Lillian's gown. With all sons, this is the closest I will get. Plus your sister is already like a daughter."

Lillian smiled then turned to Dellie. "Remember, you thought you should take in the darts in the back a bit. You said to make the bodice more snug?"

"I can at least pin it. Miss Crane shouldn't be here for at least a half hour. But we'll need to listen for her. She'll be apoplectic if she finds you here."

Mrs. Green chupsed. "She represents a whole new category of ridiculous." She tightened her lips and turned her head toward the window. "I will serve as the sentry and let you know if I see her coming."

"Also listen for the front bell. If she comes that way, you'll have to slip out the back. If you see her coming from the direction of the statue, she'll be coming through the garden into this room and you'll need to head out through the front." She turned toward Lillian. "Go slip into the dress and stand on the rise."

Dellie sat down on the chair next to the sewing machine and reached to its side, her fingers feeling for her sewing basket. Her hand found its smooth, sanded wood handles. She had seen it laid out by one of the Bridgetown hucksters soon after she had begun working for Miss Crane. She pulled it out and balanced it on her lap.

"My Dellie! That is quite a beauty." Mrs. Green eyed the basket with a smile. "I just keep my sewing things in an old egg carrier."

"Ah, it is really just a large market basket. But I had never seen one with a pattern like this. The woman who made it comes from up near Speightstown." Its maker had crafted it with care, coiling grass and palm and fashioning it into fantastic swirling patterns of light and dark. Dellie lifted it and ran her fingers around the smooth coils and the lustrous threads inside. "The price was dear. I had to work out a weekly payment plan. Deighton fashioned a riser for me that separates it into two levels — one for fabric and one for notions. "She pointed to a slotted section on top. "He made this for my threads. Cal gave me this fabric for a liner. It ties across the top and keeps things in place."

"Well, Dellie. I have seen your work. That is a basket for an artist. And it does suit you."

The color rose in Dellie's cheeks and she looked at her hands. "Thank you Mrs. Green. I do love to sew."

Lillian stepped from behind the woven screen, the bright white of her gown a counterpoint to the nut brown of her skin. Mrs.

Green gasped taking in the voile and organza creation with high neck and fitted sleeves. "Lillian, it is beautiful. The dress is beautiful. People always say 'she looks like a vision,' but child, you do. The cut of the dress does suit you. And those special flourishes, the lace medallion on the bodice. I've never seen anything like it. You look beautiful."

Lillian turned to the mirror, smoothing the front of the gown. "Dellie, thank you. It truly is beautiful." She examined the fine stitches outlining and embellishing the flowers and leaves woven into the fabric. "Sister, you have outdone yourself."

"Well, it is my gift to you. I wanted it to be something special." She took a step forward and squeezed her sister's hand.

Mrs. Green fingered a row of seed pearls at the wrist. "These are beautiful. So delicate."

"I was able to trade the milliner down the street some fine sewing in exchange for those. But come, we must get to work." She gestured to her sister. "Step up on the riser while I gather some pins. You remembered to put on the same foundation garments you are planning to wear for the wedding? Same shoes?"

Dellie pulled her apron from its hook and slipped it over her neck. She added a fistful of pins to the cushion snapped in a front pocket, slid her curved scissors into her pocket and set to work on her sister's gown. Dellie always left extra room in the dress to accommodate any changes in size—from weight gain from the round of wedding parties, or a swelling womb. Lillian had not changed size at all though, making quick work of the fitting.

"There. How does that feel? Turn around slowly so I can see it from all angles." Dellie stepped back, imagining the dress as it would look as Lillian walked down the aisle and stood before the congregation. Suddenly she thought of Cal. Her mother would miss this. Her eyes filled and she reached for a handkerchief. She watched Lillian's face fall as she read the thoughts etched on her cheeks. It was Mrs. Green who broke the silence. "She'll be there yuh know nuh. Yuh know nuh," she said as she shook her head up and down.

Dellie cleared her throat and gathered herself. "Come now. I must finish and shoo you out before Miss Crane arrives."

The door to the garden had just clicked shut when Miss Crane's perfume announced her arrival. Dellie turned.

"Dellie." The woman trembled with excitement. "Go outside and cut a few nice sprigs from the pink bush to place around here. I want the shop to be just so for Mrs. Applethwaite and her daughters! I got word that they are coming today for their dresses."

Miss Crane shook her head and pursed her lips. "We need to make sure she has a special welcome. In fact, I'll fashion the blossoms into a nosegay that she can take with her. Go, quickly...That way she will remember this shop as gracious. Go, go." She shooed Dellie out the back door.

Dellie took the three steps into the garden and tipped her head up, stretching the muscles of her neck, tight from fussing over the dress. The shop garden was not much bigger than a postage stamp, but somehow Miss Crane managed to coax growth from every available space. A breeze rose and she stretched her arms out to capture its coolness and the fragrance it carried. The sweet note was unmistakable — the freesia was in bloom. Cal's favorite flower. Dellie picked up the clippers from the basket of small garden tools hanging from a tree branch and gathered three stalks, the yellow flowers perfect. She closed her eyes and brought her fingers to her nostrils. At the crunch of Miss Crane's footsteps on the gravel walkway, she turned.

"I cut the ones at their peak, Miss Crane. They'll be nice beside the pink blossoms."

"Ah! Grab a piece of organza ribbon to tie them off!"

Dellie did her best to ignore Miss Crane's pacing. She knew the Applethwaites would arrive in their own time. Wealthy town relations of Mrs. Chandler's people, they were accustomed to accommodations being made for them. The shopkeeper's nerves had mapped out a route and routine inside the shop — straighten the dress hanging on the fitting-room curtain rod, pat the bodice of the one hanging on the mirror, pull the curtains aside to look down the street for the carriage coming from the center of Bridgetown. Dellie rubbed her eyes and concentrated on pinning the collar on the dress for the older of the two girls.

Miss Crane's high-pitched "Good day!" announced the arrival of the Applethwaite party. A chill coursed through Dellie's body. She stood, smoothed her sewing apron, and patted her pockets to assure that her tools — scissors, measuring tape, pins — were all in place. She was prepared to carry out her duty.

Mrs. Applethwaite's presence commanded the small parlor. She took her place in a winged chair, her dark skirt aligning in crisp pleats over her knees and to the floor. Her slate-gray hair was carefully ordered into a bun, with a single, firm, unmoving curl hanging before each ear. A pair of spectacles on a gold chain adorned her robust bosom. Had the King been recruiting woman generals, Mrs. Georgina Applethwaite would have been commissioned.

A barely perceptible flick of the ivory fan in Mrs. Applethwaite's left hand set the room in motion. Miss Crane directed Dellie and the girls into the fitting area while she followed closely behind. The hooks screeched as she yanked closed the curtain separating the two rooms.

"Miss Eugenie, this is your dress." With a flourish, Miss Crane spread the skirt out on the floor while holding the bodice up for her to see. "I've added darts to the top to accommodate your lovely blossoming and added some gathers here…"

Behind them a wail from Annabella interrupted the description.

Dellie checked her reaction as the older daughter pulled a dress from its hanger, separating a basted cuff from its sleeve.

"This is my dress? It looks just like what I wore last year! You promised me something different!" Her eyes were narrow and her face red.

Miss Crane passed the look on to Dellie.

"Miss, let me help you put it on," Dellie offered. "Perhaps once you…"

Miss Crane cut her a look. "Let me help you. You see I've re-arranged the bodice and skirt, changed the neckline, and changed the trim…"

"But the fabric is the still the same!" The tears welled in her eyes. "People will think I'm just one of the poor relations. I have a fiancé. What will his people think? His people are merchants! They will think that I am just…a…farmer's…"

Dellie turned her eyes toward the window. Outside, a breeze danced across the leaves.

The crack and swoosh of her fan announced Mrs. Applethwaite before the curtain pulled aside. In a low voice that somehow no one had to strain to hear, she announced, "Enough!"

She placed her glasses on her nose and examined every inch and yard of the dress.

"She is right. This event is most important for her. She must continue to make the best possible impression. Miss Crane, take some fabric left from Eugenie's dress." The younger girl's eyes widened. "And combine the two. That should make something different enough for each of them."

Another wail from Annabella shook the room. "I can't look like Eugenie! And Papa promised!"

"But I did not!"

Silence.

In the garden Miss Crane kept Mrs. Applethwaite supplied with tea and biscuits while Dellie refit the girls. She had in mind a way to outfit Annabella with a fitted doublet and new skirt trimmed with fabric from her sister's dress. She would have to take a new round of measurements of both the girls and the fabric. That required her concentration, but having to listen to the older girl's monologue required her strength.

"Eugenie, you don't understand! If I don't look my finest, I'll never get anywhere. I could be like cousin Violet, no husband, and rattling around the house playing the piano all day, and caring for her drooling uncle! Or worse, married to someone that has to sell their land, like the Chandlers." Dellie willed herself not to look up. The girl on the rise picked up a length of fabric and held it to her face. "This does indeed suit my color! What do you think, Eugenie? Eugenie! I am talking to you!"

With no response from her sister, she turned her attention to Dellie who knelt at her hem, mouth full of pins. Annabella stamped her foot making Dellie jump. The young woman glared at her. "I *said*, shorter!"

"I am going to stay here late today, Miss Crane, if you don't mind. To finish these things for my brothers."

"Not *too* late. The lights cost money!"

Hours later, Dellie folded her work, turned out the kerosene lamps, and closed the shop. The bustle of the day had faded and the drapery of Caribbean darkness had fallen. She listened to the town settling down for the night. All the hucksters had left, and the dockworkers had finished their hauling and scraping. Quiet. The only activity was aboard one of Harrison's ships, her crew readying her for leaving next week.

She nearly stepped on a flower left next to the old boot-scrape as she turned to lock the shop door. She bent to pick it up. It was hibiscus, redolent of cinnamon. Her fingers traced the edges of the blossom, intense red drifting to a lighter pink and back to crimson at the very center. She fingered the clean stickiness of the pistil rising from its center. It was cloaked in fern, like a lace shawl, hugging it, caressing it. Someone had carefully tied flower and fern together with a slim vine, twisting and turning it about the bloom and leaf like a small, green grass snake. Her eyes took in the miracle in her hand and something in her unfolded. She could hear Pendril's voice in her head. "You like what I brought you?"

Dellie walked up the sloped planks leading to the top of Chamberlain Bridge. She loved this time, needed it, alone, to be with the spirits of the island, and to settle herself. From this vantage point she could see for miles. Barbados — Bim — stuck out in the sea. Closest landfall stretched 100 miles west. Bim — where somewhere past memory ancestors were dragged from Africa as a sacrifice to the cane crop.

The glow of the sky caught her eye and she looked up. She remembered a story Henry had told her about the pictures made by the stars in the sky. She found the Dipper — the schoolmaster had called it that. Her father had called it something else, but what? She remembered part of the story and her father's voice filling her with wonder as they looked up at the velvet darkness. How did it go? Something about a woman's gossamer veil as she walked away from her lover. Her eyes followed its edge to the Pole Star. That was part of the story, but she couldn't remember what. She gazed at its brightness. That star was steady, constant, fixed, as the others journeyed across the sky. She exhaled slowly. It was the star that men of the sea used to find their way. The same star led men home after their journeys across God's sphere. Home to India, home to England, home to Barbados, home to Africa, home to...

She crossed the bridge to the inner harbor. It was late; the only sounds, her own footfall, and the kiss of waves. A rhythmic movement caught her eye a few yards ahead. It was Herbert the fiddler, who knew everybody that passed through Bridgetown, and offered each a greeting by name. A fixture in Bridgetown as long as anyone could remember, he could play only one tune. He had many lyrics, but just one set of notes, one melody, one set of intervals, chords, finger placements. But it didn't matter. Here, on this island, one tune was more than sufficient.

"Dellie, I can tell you need a song. What you want tuh hear?"

She smiled and touched the old man's arm. "You play, Herbert. I have already got the words." The old man's bow caressed the strings, luring out a melody as old as the island. The music floated into the night and through the chambers of Dellie's heart. The deep, slow strains tugged forth memories. Herself as a little girl jumping over the foam at the edge of the sea on an outing to Worthing, Henry and Cal ahead, obscured by the dazzling sun. The strings droned and there she was, working with Cal in her shed, grinding flower blossoms for their sweet oil. Dellie knew the spirits of the island and she watched as they rose in wisps surrounding her, caressing her. She breathed in and the breath of the island became part of her. She breathed out, and her breath became part of the island. Herbert played on, the tempo *andante* and memories fluttered across her mind — she, Maude and Lillian chasing a lizard with a grass snare. The melody moved to a minor key and she pictured the front room at Eva's, the sewing teacher, girls like her sewing samplers, dresses, fanciful purses. Herbert's fingers caressed the strings, the air he played light, like the fluttering of wings, and she was under a star-apple tree at Taborvilla with Pendril. Herbert's tune was lush and aching and suddenly there was Cal, her concerns about Dellie and the House etched on her face. It pulled Pendril's image from Dellie's heart. Her thought rested on her own image, her broad African nose covered with smooth skin the color of toffee, sprinkled with freckles. Pendril had said her red hair looked like a crown of flame.

It was too late by hours to hitch a ride to the Hope, and home, so she turned around and headed toward Eva's sister's to spend the night.

———

Morning dew still clung to patches of grass as Dellie made her way across Trafalgar Square in search of a ride upcountry. She smiled as she caught sight of a donkey cart and its driver. Only one person on the island had a hat shaped like that and pants that baggy. And only one person on the island didn't care how loudly he sang off-key. She would be lucky to catch a ride with Cuffee, a friend of Henry's from down at Workman's.

His face broke into a smile as he caught sight of her. "Dellie-girl, you don't even have to ask. For sure, I will give you a ride. I'll drop you at St. George. You can walk the rest of the way up to the Hope."

Dellie settled in for the lazy ride into the hills. She wouldn't have to answer a lot of questions or make a lot of conversation. Cuffee would do most of the talking. She placed the package with the boys' clothes carefully on the bed of the cart, making a pillow under her feet, leaned back against some sacks, and tilted her head up to catch the early morning sun.

"So, Dellie, how is the business going?"

"Busy."

"Busy? He laughed. Tell me, who is doing de buying? De people are putting together their wardrobes for Panama?"

"Mostly the merchant people and the folks in the shipping business buying."

"Dat fuh truth," Cuffee mused. "Ah. I forgot. Dey have got their money saved all over God's earth. Poor don't reach them. And dese shippers, they are spreading their savings into new things. It is de rest of us who live and die by this place. Even de old families, de Great Ones live by de cane. Tings get worse round here every day. The young men all leaving, the old ones can't find work. And soon they will charge yuh, dear too, fuh breathing the air. Yuh hear about Durant and his old woman? Couldn't pay the rent card and Ferguson threaten to ship him off! It is a crime. They have been on that spot of dirt since God formed it."

Dellie shifted at the mention of the rent card. If it hadn't been for her sewing money, Henry's last card wouldn't have been paid either.

Cuffee continued. "So Durant and his woman are just one step from de almshouse. Hoping their boy gets back from Panama before de next card due. Have yuh heard from Dite lately? Soon dis place will just be de sick, de old, and dose in short pants..."

Dellie's eyes began to droop.

"Dellie, Dellie!" Cuffee was nudging her awake. "Dellie, en that Dite's friend Pendril over there by de Church gate? He is a long way from St. Michael!"

Dellie's eyes rested on a man with a gaudily wrapped box in his hands.

Cuffee tapped Dellie's shoulder. "Well, I will leave yuh here. Maybe yuh will catch yuh grandmother on de way from de morning service. Tell yuh father I say howdy. Here."

He handed her a bundle wrapped in brown paper. "Don't forget yuh package."

"Good day, Mr. Clarke, and thank you. I'll be sure to tell Henry you said hello." She grabbed her straw hat, climbed out of the wagon, and trained her attention on Pendril.

He sauntered over; faded shirt washed and pressed smooth, pants cuffed at the bottom to hide the tattered edge. A grin lit up his face.

"Dellie! What are you doing here? I thought you came back last night! I would have ridden up with you!"

"I stayed late at Miss Crane's to sew some things. I didn't expect to see you though."

Pendril's grin grew wider. "I thought we might go calling on your father today."

She raised her eyebrows.

"Yes, that's right, Miss Standard, I thought we might call on your father. I brought him some biscuits. I think we are ready to tell him of our plans. Make it official."

She smoothed her hair and replaced her hat on her head. She reached to squeeze his hand. "Yes, enough time has passed since Cal..." She didn't finish the sentence. "I know he will think it is a good plan. Anything that will keep us here and by the way he sees it, to get a piece a land. We must be firm though. This is *our* plan not *his*."

"True, but it will help the family. You'll be here to help with the children and when I come back with some money saved, we can look at some pieces of ground. Who knows? Maybe even the one he has talked about. Make our life here in this district upon the Hope."

They began the walk up toward Taborvilla. The breeze from the hills teased the ribbon on Dellie's straw hat and lapped at the frayed edges of Pendril's shirt. Around them the variegated green patches, the pale green of the young cane pushing through the deep brown soil, the deeper shinier green of the banana groves, the wild colors—flame red, orange, pink— showed God in a glorious mood.

As they reached the crest of the first rise, Dellie looked into the obeah woman's yard.

Her place, at the spot where the two roads met, was rough, even by the standards of the poorest of the island. Boards lay askew, yard unswept, while rangy chickens futilely scratched in the dirt. Scattered about was the detritus of the island's castes. Old churns, seamstress dummies, broken wagon wheels, buckets, tubs, and farm implements flaky with rust competed for space. The scattered artifacts bore the history of the island and of the empire. An old infantry sword told one story. A register bearing names, ages, and dates documented another. A chaise on a carpet of weeds, its moldering stuffing spilling through split brocade, relayed a footnote. A dead tree hung with ancient, crumbling chemists bottles commanded one end of the yard and held its secrets close. Next to it stood an array of old boards fashioned into a shelter. It was hard to imagine how it remained standing; it appeared to lean both left and right in an endless struggle for shade cast by an old tree heavy with bees. Dellie had heard whisperings of neighbors creeping through the gate in the dark of night, seeking a charm, a chant, or a potion after hope had left them.

Dellie sucked one deep breath and straightened her shoulders to steel herself. The obeah woman had been there for all of the collective memory of the district, and yet no one could recall her given or family name. The old women of the Hope remembered her as ancient even when they were girls. Small, with quick birdlike movements, a body thin and dry like desiccated cane stalks, she was known all up and abroad the region. Always chased from the grounds of the Great House and the tenant lands, she hovered on the fringe of the poor and the poorest. Picking through the leavings of the island's various peoples, she clothed herself in a host of strange outfits — hats once stylish, handed down from the Great House to a favorite maid or cook, and then discarded after years of wear or odd pieces of uniform from Combermere or Harrison's College. From time to time, lace gloves from some long-ago garden party were coupled with a gunnysack, cut to accommodate head and arms. A delegation from St. George's Church had been sent once to try to improve her situation. They were driven off with curses and threats. Her tirades against the Standard family were epic and awe-inspiring in their creativity and venom.

There she sat next to her gate on an overturned sugar cask, picking at the frayed edge of her apron. Dellie nodded in acknowledgement of her gaze and was startled by the strength of the voice emanating from the ancient frame.

"Even a dog can bark, Miss Standard! Yuh back again from yuh fancy job in Bridgetown! They give yuh their scraps in yuh package? You will be de only one left! All de rest leaving. What is holding yuh up? Or yuh want dead in yuh yard like yuh mother? Or to be some knock-about woman? Yuh hear me, Dellie Standard? I hear you are staying." She pointed to a stack of flaking leather account ledgers. I'll be sure to inscribe your name then in the Roster of the Ruined. Maybe next to your mother." She laughed—deep and guttural.

Dellie breathed out as Pendril instinctively wrapped his arm around her shoulder.

"Come, let's go. Walk. Let's go. Turn your head this way. She is mad." He guided her up the hill. The old woman's voice faded behind them.

———

The orange flowers of the flamboyant tree were in a riot of bloom in the center of the yard. Dellie spotted Henry and Josh slapping dominoes in its apron of shade. She called out to her father. He turned toward her voice. "Dellie-girl! Good to have you home!"

Dellie saw a crease appear on Henry's brow as he stared at Pendril. He had little regard for those with South Asian blood on the Island—too dark, too foreign. Before he could let slip the derogatory term, *doogla*, she made the introductions.

"Henry, this man is Coleridge's cousin, Pendril Stoute. He is one of the Green clan. He will soon be one of Lillian's relations. You've heard Dite speak of him."

Pendril extended his hand. "I am glad to meet you finally, sir. Dite has spoken often of his family over the years."

Dellie tilted her head up as her father surveyed Pendril head to toe. His eyes narrowed as he noted shirt, pants, shoes, and the darkness of his skin. "The Green clan, you say? They are a wide group, I see." She ignored her father's glance in her direction. "Well, sit down, man! So you are one of Dite's friends? You ain't gone off to Panama to dig the ditch?"

"I thought about it, yes, sir, but I have got my own plan."

"You are going to New York then?"

"No, sir. I am trained as a cook. I plan to go to sea with one of the merchant ship lines. My man, Lane, is going, too. We'll see some of the world. Then settle. Maybe even buy a piece of land up in this district."

Henry leaned forward toward Pendril, his eyes hooded in conspiracy. "Now that *is* a plan! Good pay, no rent out at sea. You can save up faster. Buy land sooner. I have got my eye on a piece of this Taborvilla land to claim with some money for when these children of mine come back. I hear Mr. Chandler say he wants to sell. Good crop land and a good flat place for a wall house. Standard land it will be."

Dellie moved her fingers across the brim of her hat. Her jaw tightened.

Josh inhaled deeply. "But you and I have heard this all before, man."

"I know, but who would have thought that this Panama talk meant something? Who would have thought that digging a hole in some backwater behind God's face could fill your pockets with money? Some them no counts from down Workman's are actually sending back money and buying up good land from these old Houses that broke up. I thought it was another version of Demarara gold. Another way to waste your time and spoil your back. When Dite comes home, I plan to pace off a piece of ground with him, and figure just how much we can start with."

Pendril leaned in to catch each word.

Josh chupsed, sucking his teeth with derision. "Henry, man, I see too many of these children not wanting to come back. Holder's boy over in New York is now married. Cumberbatch and his wife own land in New York... They are surely not coming back. And the ones going to Panama don't always come back except in a box. I am sorry to say it. I know your Dite is there—my boy too. But it is God's truth."

Henry narrowed his eyes. "I know, but *think*. The Parris boy just bought a plot upon Free Hill. When my children see the piece of land I have picked out, it will make them want to come back. The spot is sweet."

Josh chupsed softly, shaking his head. "Well, man. Enough talk." He placed a domino on the table, took the win and shot a grin at Henry. "I am off." He slapped his hands on his thighs, stood and walked toward the work shed.

Dellie caught Pendril's gaze. A flutter of Clive's wings drew their attention. Henry turned and the squawk of the parrot re-opened the conversation.

"I am teaching him to talk."

Henry pulled some broken bits of biscuit from his pocket and offered one to the bird. "I am teaching him the children's names. Hear. 'Say, 'Del-lie, Del-lie,'" he commanded the bird.

"Cane," croaked the bird with a flutter of its wings.

Dellie shook her head and cleared her throat. "Henry. We have something to talk with you about." She turned to Pendril and squeezed his hand as he relayed their plans.

He ran his fingers through his black hair and lifted his chin as he finished. "And so, Mr. Standard, your daughter and I are planning to get married. We plan to stay here. Here in Bim. We wanted you to know, but we will not be public about this until after Lillian's wedding. She must have her day."

Henry straightened his shoulders, the smile on his face brightened. Dellie could see his mind working. "So the two families will be doubly joined. Two sisters marrying two cousins. And this branch will be staying on the rock. Come into the house. We must find something for a toast."

CHAPTER THREE

This Man and This Woman

G uests began arriving the previous evening, swelling the
population of the small villages in St. George, of the tenants'
compound belonging to Coventry Hall, and of the rum
shops of Workman's Village throughout the district. None wanted
to miss the ceremony uniting two of the island's most populous
clans—the Greens and the Standards. Dellie's crinkly red hair,
forced into curls, wilted at the back of her head as she stood next to
the bride in the nave. She shifted her eyes from the priest to scan the
crowd. The congregation fidgeted, handkerchiefs long past dabbing,
now swabbing sweat from faces. A few matrons with prime seats at
the end of a pew fluttered their fans to signal their annoyance at the
priest's utter disregard for the gathering heat.

It was clear, however, that Rev. Father Williams had been planning for this day as both an opportunity to display his skills in oratory and to capture the souls of those usually absent from services.
He regaled them with florid cadences and gestures punctuated with
considered pauses and stares at certain scandalous pairings among
the gathering. In his recitation on the importance of marriage, he

narrated the story of Jesus' miracle at the wedding in Cana, the fidelity of the late Queen Victoria to her late husband, the royal consort Prince Albert, and then proceeded into a lengthy commentary on how the blush about Tess's name could have been averted had she been virtuously wed. He continued with how the fortunes of Catherine and Heathcliff, along with those of Jane and Rochester, would have been different had they been properly joined.

Most only half-listened, considering more closely the attire of neighbors, noting who had arrived with whom, speculating about who was likely to leave with whom, and pondering what the wedding spread might include. Not one among the guests recalled any couple in the region, married or not, with the names of Jane and Rochester. And Tess? Who would lay such a name upon a body? Surely, not even the people from Scotland District. Dellie, forgetting the decorum required of the bride's sister, wondered aloud to no one in particular who Catherine and Heathcliff were—perhaps people from up in St. Lucy? She caught her grandmother's look and silenced herself.

At the utterance of "I now pronounce you man and wife," some of the less pious members of the congregation did not wait for the recessional but, rather, burst through the mahogany doors of St. George's Church in search of a breeze.

Outside, above the tolling of the great bell, the music of Lillian's laugh drew her attention and Dellie turned to watch her sister and the groom, Coleridge, receive good wishes from one cluster of guests after another. She felt a hand on her arm and turned.

"Pendril! There you are! Look at you." She shook her head and laughed. "Come, bend your head down. Your hair is licking up. You look like the wild man from Borneo." She reached over and raked her fingers through the unruly mass on his head.

"Dellie, stop fussing."

She felt her neck grow hot as he took her hand away and kissed her palm.

From somewhere, notes drifted on the air. Heads turned as a group of men in silken shirts of sky blue, yellow, and soft green rounded the corner adjacent to the stone edifice of the church. A man walking on stilts led them, shaking a ribbon-dressed tambourine. A cheer went up at the first of the tunes from the banjo, flute, drum, and guitar that would lead them back up the hill to Taborvilla and into the night's revels. Pendril turned to Dellie. "A tuk band!

How did they commission it when it's not even near Christmas? Be with me for the procession! He stroked her cheek. "One day Miss Standard, we will have a day like this." Dellie smiled, elated at the thought.

Ahead the bride and groom linked arms and moved from the church, her left hand holding up her skirt to save it from the dust of the road, his right waving his hat in time. They began a step of their own creation — one, two, three, four, five, clap, step, snap. Dellie and Pendril followed with variations on the theme. Behind them paraded the mass of guests.

The music led them up the hill and to the crossroads. Left: the plateau to Taborvilla and the workers' section; right: the rise to the Great House of the sugar estate, standing in full possession of the crest of land called, "the Hope."

There was no way to avoid it. Unless you wanted to risk cutting through a cane field, or veer well out of your way, the only road from the church to Taborvilla passed the abode of the obeah woman.

Ahead she was perched on a new acquisition, a splintered sawhorse placed adjacent to her ramshackle fence. Dellie's grip tightened around Pendril's hand.

"Dellie?"

She turned to him, her voice hushed. "The obeah woman is out."

"She won't do anything in front of all these people!"

She pushed down the annoyance at his naiveté and kept her voice steady. "Pendril, she is *mad*, and knows no boundaries. Besides, I think she relishes an audience." Dellie, along with the rest of the wedding party with Taborvilla or Workman's roots, braced herself as the procession approached the blasted gate. The woman hopped from her post and stepped forward, a large cooking pot in hand, and began to cry out.

"I see the whole lot of you out in your finery today! Miss Lillian, I see yuh dressed in wedding white! Ah. That would make you the first in yuh family not to wear a lie. Mr. Chandler know that? And there is Miss High and Mighty with the red hair! Miss Dellie Standard, I hear you are staying, not heading off the rock like the rest. I'll be holding a place then for you yuh know nuh!

Dellie's face reddened. The rest of the wedding party stared ahead, their faces like masks. The mad woman reached into the pot clutched to her chest. Immediately, the band took a swing to the left and did not miss a beat, startling everyone with its military precision, their bodies providing a shield for the party to pass unassailed, and their notes pitched louder to cover up her cries.

"See Dellie, it all worked out." Pendril squeezed her hand.

"This time, but I wouldn't put my coin on that."

"Ah Dellie, there's not always a dark cloud."

"No, not always, but often enough."

CHAPTER FOUR

Kisses Under a Star-Apple Tree

O n the rise above the tenant quarters, where the Standard house stood, tables wobbled from the weight of food and libations. The Great House had contributed two goats from its stock. Friends and neighbors from all around the Hope— Workman's, Free Hill, Harmony Cot, all the way over toe My Lord's Hill—brought variations on peas and rice, yams, fish cakes, and coconut bread. A group of women supervised the making of a vat of cou-cou, fussing over the correct proportions:

"Slice up a little more okra."

"That will make it too thick. You should know that."

"I think it needs another dash or two of hot sauce."

"No, it is fine as is. You two play with it more, you'll spoil it."

They all chupsed, sucking their teeth in a chorus.

Someone's hand-clapping signaled the crowd to circle the bride and groom, cups in hand. M'Ma stood in for Cal as the mother of the bride and began. She closed her eyes for a moment, tipped her cup of rum punch and sprinkled a few drops on the ground for those who had gone already to the ancestors. The flame-colored blossoms on the flamboyant tree that shaded her fluttered in the breeze.

"We are all gathered here today to bless this union of a man and a woman. This coming together of two souls, two sparks of the Greater." Her arms opened wide, embracing the couple, the gathering, the world. She glanced at the sky, the trees, the ground at her feet and drew the life that hummed around them nearer. "May the One Who made us all and Who is with us, part of us, and all around us, bless this union."

The crowd joined together in a wordless hum.

"May they be blessed," M'Ma continued, "with children, and with happiness in all their days..."

Her voice faded and it was the turn of the father of the bride. Henry's voice quivered with feeling.

"May they always have a roof to shelter them..."

Then Dellie: "May they and their own always walk together on a true path..."

And Pendril: "May they know abundance and plenty, may their journeys be safe, and may home be with them wherever their lives take them..."

Lillian would head off to New York with Coleridge in a few weeks. Dellie had watched them make detailed plans for months—considering times of departure, weighing contacts in the States. They went together to the Government House, together to the shipping lines, together to get information from the families of friends already in Brooklyn. Dellie tilted her head back. So many of her pack were gone now or leaving. Off in New York, over in Panama .... So many changes. So much leaving.

Another voice brought her back to the moment. "And may they always have a circle of caring friends and family around them."

The words of blessing were followed by those of another and another and another. Dellie tipped her head and listened to the voices of the spirits whispering in the trees.

———

As the sun headed toward its zenith, Dellie sought a moment of quiet in the shade and headed for the great breadfruit tree that marked the boundary of the plot of land Mr. Chandler had assigned to the family. She heard Clive, Henry's pet parrot,chattering as he observed the goings-on. She could see her father and one of his companions engrossed in some project. With rum as the lubricant, their voices were loud and bold. "And I hear the Grant boy made an offer on a piece of ground. He came back with a pouch full of Panama money and first thing make the offer. We'll see if the House takes it."

"This land is churning all around us. I've been thinking that if these children of mine pool their money, we can find a nice spot. Put up a wall house. Break away from the whim and fortune of the Great House. I raised it with Dite before he left to dig the ditch. I plan on raising it with Lillian — the New York money, I hear, is even better than the Panama. And with Dellie's job in Bridge..."

Dellie's eyebrows shot up.

"That would be sweet. But don't forget man, you must also have enough coin for the implements to work the land, the fees for processing, a donkey and a cart for transporting, and with the price of cane heading down each day..." He checked himself. "Enough of this business talk. You are wedding off your first child, man! It is surely something. Everyone who is anyone turned out for this jump-up."

Henry lifted his hand to quiet him.

Dellie stepped closer and spoke up. "Henry, what is that you are working on?"

"Hush, Dellie-child. I am concentrating. This is top shelf. The best from in town."

Joe Burroughs and Dellie watched Henry measure out several shot glasses of clear liquid from a brown jug and place them in a row. With the hand of a scientist, he alternated adding the liquid and juice into a wide-mouthed jar.

"Man, why are you taking such care? It is just rum punch."

"I got my hands on something special to add to the grandness of the day. It is called 'Mountain Whiskey.' From Simon's Ned. He got it from a sailor docking from the States. You know those American people only tolerate the finest. The sailor said his uncle has been brewing his own private stock in secret for decades on his own land in some place called West Virginia. Said he uses a special recipe handed down. It is made from corn, not cane. Here, smell it."

Dellie stepped forward.

"Not you, child!" Dellie stopped at the finger waggling in her direction. "This is a man's drink." Henry thumped his chest. "Stand back."

Joe put his nose to the flask and took a quick sniff. His head shot up from the vapors. "You can't be planning to drink that! You must be crazy. It'll take the top of your head off!"

"It's fine, man. I mixed it with other things to dilute and calm it. I made some yesterday as a test. Here, try it." He gave his potion a final stir and poured some into a shot glass.

Joe took a cautious sip. As the liquid made its way across his tongue, he shook, like a dog drying its coat. He raised his eyebrows and nodded his head in approval. "It's pretty good." He jumped as its warmth and bite cruised through his body. "You have a name for it yet? Rare Yankee Punch?"

"I'm calling it 'Jump Steady.' I found out yesterday that after you drink it, you jump steady." He lowered his voice. "Quiet about it, though. I'm only sharing it with a select few."

Hours later the sun made its way downward behind the hills. The raucous laughter from the long-awaited limbo contest in full swing in the center of the yard now drew Dellie's attention. Lillian and Coleridge struggled between holding the limbo pole steady and doubling over in laughter as a lanky man made his attempt.

Someone called out, "How are you planning to clear the pole when you can barely stand?"

"I'll be fine." The man careened toward the pole and shook one limb at a time. "The rum does loosen my limbs. I will be the winner. Watch people!" He stood back, eyes moving from ground to pole as he assessed his challenge. He readied his stance — knees bent, arms out to the sides, deep concentration scoring his face — and fell to the ground. The crowd roared.

"Clear him aside." Another contestant stepped forward. "I will show you how this is done." The music started up.

The crowd gave a collective cry of awe as Lane, Pendril's friend, leaned back and slipped under the pole.

"Ah, man, that is nothing!" Pendril challenged Lane, his smile flashing. He stepped up, kicked off his shoes, and without hesitation shimmied under the pole. It was between him and Lane now. The drummer from the tuk band quickened the beat while a few of the men placed side bets on a winner, handicapping the contestants by a variety of criteria: height, length of legs, breadth of feet.

Lane. Pendril. Lane. Pendril. Henry and Josh took over holding the stick to quell any thoughts of favoritism in the crowd. They bent over in tandem, lowering the stick to an elbow's length off the ground. Lane jumped up and down and crossed himself in preparation. The drummer slowed the beat as Lane slipped his knees under the pole. His body quavered. The crowd held its breath, and then sighed its disappointment as Lane's nose touched the pole.

Pendril clapped him on the back. "That's all right, man. I'll be giving lessons later." He signaled the drummer to begin. "There is no way this contest will finish in a draw!" He bent side to side to ready himself, rubbed his hands together, and leaned back, head almost grazing the ground. He made a few jumps forward, knees, thighs, and then his chest glanced the stick. A cry roared up from the crowd as Lane and Pendril collapsed into each other with laughter, clinking glasses of Jump Steady that had somehow found its way to the masses.

———

Dellie stood next to the food table, considering the masterpiece that she and the other women had worked on for weeks, the wedding cake, black with rum and dried fruit. She turned at a snuffling sound near her. Sam, the neighbor's donkey nosed her arm. "I didn't know you were invited. I see you are decked out for the affair." She reached out and adjusted the tiara fashioned from flowers that someone had placed on his head. "Sam, I don't think you realize that you are a *donkey*." She recognized the laugh behind her. Pendril grabbed her hand and led her running up the rise next to Henry's house and away from the crowd. He steered her toward a blossoming star-apple tree with a makeshift bench under it and they sat down side by side.

"Dellie, Dellie." He whispered in her hair. His mouth found hers and they kissed. Her fingers touched the nape of his neck and traced their way into his thick hair. A breeze brought down a shower of petals upon them.

Dellie rose, pulling Pendril from his spot. Her eyes cast over the quilt of colors: pale green of the young cane pushing through the umber soil and a deeper, shinier jade of banana groves that set off the wild colors—flame red, orange, pink, all gilded in the light near the close of day. Birds and monkeys chattered in the trees winding down their daily tasks. Dellie watched Pendril's features soften, the smile moving across his lips as he turned in a circle and took in the view. His voice was low, gentle. "I have walked and walked this island. Seen every hill and every gully, I thought. But I have never seen anything like this spot. You can see almost the entire place from here."

Dellie touched his arm. "When we were girls, my sisters and I would sneak away from our chores and come up here. We'd make up stories about the pictures in the clouds or about the people we could see walking about."

The two watched the jump-up continue below them — a swirl of people, sound, and color.

"We could tell the time by the songs the field workers were singing. Sometimes we played the Queen and her Court. I always wanted it to be a game about Queen Elizabeth. This red hair was good for something then... I was sure to get to be the Queen. And so get the chance to boss Lillian about."

Pendril studied her face; freckles sprinkled on skin the color of an almond shell. "I remember you when you were a girl. The day I first saw you and realized you were Dite's sister. I remember seeing you at the Opening Day Convocation. Seeing you march with the flag, your back straight, head held high, shoes polished. You gave the recitation." He straightened in imitation of her that day. "You were the picture of dignity. I remember thinking I had never seen a girl like that with freckles and hair like flame." His chin quivered, struggling to hold back a smile. "I also had never seen a girl all wound up in a flag, falling to the ground, twisted-twisted with the wind whipping around." He laughed, his grin moving every part of his face.

Dellie pushed him, laughing. "You saw that? You remember that? I had to stand in the corner of the schoolmaster's room for the rest of the day for 'conduct unbecoming that of a girl enrolled in second primary' or some such nonsense on account of it! It wasn't my fault ... the wind took over!"

His voice grew serious. "Yes, Dellie. I remember seeing you, then. Way back when we were in primary. Dellie, you know I have loved you since then."

Her eyes locked on his and her face heated and colored. For so long he had been a fixture of her childhood, just one of Dite's rusty, scruffy friends who teased and chased her friends, teased and chased her sisters, teased and chased her. This last year, though, since they had been keeping company, she had begun to see him as he was: tall and slender, with muscles in his arms and chest from loading barrels on ships.

He pulled her to standing. "You know, Dellie. I have always had a feeling for this region, for the Hope." His hands were gently circling her waist.   "The way you can see all up and abroad across this rock. The sea, it changes colors, changes moods. But this place has something of its own. I think the two us of together can make a life here. Here in the Hope. And it would be close enough to help your family."

Dellie exhaled slowly and listened to the whisper of the palm trees as the island breathed with her. She sat down and listened to Pendril stake his claim. "This island is my home. I want to make my mark *here*. In this place."

He took her hand. "It would be a good life, I think. A good life, for us, together. A piece of ground up here in St. George would please your father so."

"I would be able to help raise up the children, my brothers and sisters. Byron, May, and Palley are not grown yet. Caring for them will be too much for M'Ma.   It is not the promise I made to Cal. But...still." Her voice trailed off as she thought about her mother. If she helped her brothers and sisters that wouldn't be the promise, but it would be fulfilling a different obligation, one that perhaps Cal hadn't contemplated. She held Pendril's hand, gently rubbing his skin between her thumb and forefinger.

CHAPTER FIVE

A Lagoon in the Moonlight

*T*he flow of people on the main road was steady as Dellie stepped onto the dusty marl. She could hear the grinding of the gears in the sugarhouse and the *whack, whack, whack* sound of the mill's sails flying with the wind. She picked up the frustrated command, "*Chee Jock! Chee! Chee, man!,*" of a boy in the distance urging on a recalcitrant donkey laden with cane, along with the rise and fall of the voices of a group of field workers as they used this day to take care of their own business. The sounds she heard were replicated on hundreds of pieces of ground whose borders were marked by a rise, a path, a piece of paper on file in a Bridgetown office, by sweat, and a hope.

A group of women, trays of fruit carefully balanced on their heads, took center stage, walking in a cluster, the refrain of an Anglican hymn reaching its crescendo, their *a cappella* voices in perfect harmony: "*There is a balm in Gilead to make the wounded whole.*" They competed for space on the road with two men riding a cart laden with vegetables and held together by ancient nails, wire, and a prayer. A huddle of young girls laughed and whispered behind

hands held to their mouths as they rushed toward a day of seabath-
ing at Worthing.

Although she was lucky enough to hitch a ride right away, by
the time she arrived at the Green place over in Oistins, the send-off
was in full swing. The hiss and splat of a fillet hitting hot oil drew
her toward a cluster of people around a cooking station set up in
the dollop of shade cast by the limbs of a broad casuarina. A man
beckoned her.

"Step up! You're one of the Standard girls, right? With the red
hair, you must be Dellie. But you Standard girls all have the same
face." He slid his fingers across his cheekbones to make his point.

She laughed. "And you Greens are always smiling."

"And what is there not to smile about this grand day? Here,
take some fish." He thrust a plate in her hand. "We have flying fish,
snapper, dolphin-fish...Over there..." He gestured with his chin.
"Peas and rice and some fancy wax beans, I think."

Dellie filled her plate and glanced around to find her sister. It
was Pendril who found her first.

"Dellie-girl!" He circled his arm around her waist. "I was
waiting for you by the road, but my stomach got the better of me.
Let me replenish my plate once more, and then we will go sit on
the sand." He pointed to her legs. "That is, after you take off
your shoes and your stockings...This isn't St. George Church, yuh
know nuh!"

Dellie laughed and pushed his chest. "Rude man!" She scanned
the cove. "I thought the Standard clan was wide, but Pendril..."

"I know. The Greens must be related by blood, marriage, or declaration of law to a quarter of His Majesty's Barbados. And when
they put the call out, everybody comes." Heedless of any concept
of temperance or decorum he mounded his plate with peas and rice.
Dellie stared. He lifted his head, eyes meeting hers with a question.

"What?"

"Ah, nothing." She struggled to suppress a smile but gave up.
"Pendril, look at your plate."

He glanced down and then back up at her. "What?"

Dellie burst out laughing.

———

"Lillian! Lillian! I have been looking for you!"

The sisters wrapped their arms around each other in a quick embrace. "I have never gone so long without seeing your sweet face!" Dellie pulled back and looked her sister up and down.

"I see you have found Pendril." Lillian nodded in his direction. "Cousin,

I am sorry to tear her away, but I need to talk to my sister." Dellie touched Pendril's hand and followed her sister to a makeshift shelter that someone had fashioned with some fabric and rough wood against a tree. "First, Dellie, take off your shoes and hose. Tie your dress up. You look like you are going to Mass, not to a fish fry!"

Dellie reddened and made an attempt to change the conversation. "The road down from…"

"That's nice, Dellie, but sit down." Lillian's hand guided her to a pair of chairs worn from exposure to the sun and salt air.

"Coleridge and I are heading to Bridgetown day after tomorrow for the quarantine. I said goodbye to the rest of the family when I was up there last Sunday. Let this be our parting. For now. Come, Dellie. Come to Brooklyn. Coleridge and I will have a place for you until you are on your own. I know that you and Pendril are planning otherwise."

Dellie opened her mouth to protest. Lillian raised her hand to silence her and cut her eyes toward the road. "I know you have burdened yourself with the family. But Cal was right. You can come to New York and make the money to get the family out. Get the girls out. Pendril can follow when he finishes his tour at sea. Coleridge is talking to him about the same thing." She gestured in the direction of the road. "Look at all these people walking, walking, walking… You think your feet will carry you any place different here? *Make your plan.* Make your claim on the world before you miss your chance, and your mouth is full of 'used to be and if only.'"

"Lillian, we have another plan."

"A plan that makes no kind of sense. Lillian's eyes were slits. "Cal told you. And now, I am telling you. You made a promise to our mother and you and I both know that her passing gave you the excuse you were waiting for to break that promise."

Dellie's face fell. The truth of Lillian's words made her want to slap her. When she spoke her voice was a near growl. "Lillian. I am not talking about this. I am a woman grown, eighteen years old. I have a job that supports me. A man I am going to marry. It is my life and *I* will choose. Don't vex me. I don't want to spoil the day by fighting with you, Sister."

"Ah, Dellie, I don't want to fight either. But Soul, please remember what I've said. Come. Come anytime. You both can make a life in New York."

Lillian offered a package, wrapped in white tissue and tied with cord. "Dellie, unwrap it. The passage cost less than we thought. I used some of the extra money to buy one for me." She paused. "And one for you, too."

It was a woman's handbag. Dellie ran her hand over it—sturdy, good quality, a deep black leather with a pebbled surface, two straps and a metal buckle.

"Lillian." She squeezed her sister's hand. "It is a fine thing. How?"

Lillian laughed. "You know it is best not to ask that question around here. I got it from someone who knows Simon's Ned. Beyond that, neither of us wants to know. Open it."

Dellie snapped the metal buckle and pulled the sides away from each other. Inside were pockets and slots—places for kerchiefs, important papers, money, change, and other things that required safekeeping or privacy. In the main compartment was a white envelope sealed shut. Dellie made to open it.

Lillian's hand stopped her. "Dellie, wait until you get home. It is some dollars toward your passage. You must come."

———

Pendril's arm again draped about her waist. "Dellie, come down to the beach. We'll go for a walk." The sun signaled the close of the day, turning the surface of the water into a swath of gold brocade. They walked in tandem, feet on a path washed clean by the lap of waves. "I know every grain of sand on this beach. When Lane, Coleridge, and I were boys we used to steal away from school and scamper about here."

"Why does it seem like you and your friends found many an excuse to steal away from school?"

He laughed. "The sea was always calling. Pulling us here or towards the docks. We were not true scholars, like you and your sisters." He gave her a gentle poke. She chupsed in response.

"Long ago, Dite, Coleridge, me, Lane, and some others of our crew made a pact to head off together. To head to sea. To take off from this island and find what lies beyond it. Dite is finding his way in Panama now, Coleridge is headed to America with Lillian, and the rest pulled out. So now, just Lane and I are keeping that pact. They have a call out for men for a ship leaving in three month's time. I believe Lane and I will sign up for that one. It will give us enough time to make the declaration at church and be married." He stopped walking and looked her full in the face. "Yes Dellie?"

She took both his hands in hers and kissed his fingers.

"There is a lagoon just ahead. Just around that cluster of trees."

Dellie felt the warmth of his fingers covering hers, a counterpoint to the chill etching the air as the sun slipped lower. The water ahead shifted from gold to smooth silver. "Look, Dellie." Pendril pointed to the disk of the moon gliding above the horizon. "When we are apart, we will look at the moon and think of each other." He pulled her closer. They rounded a grove of trees and Dellie saw before her a pool of water ringed by fine sand and small rocks. "Dellie." Pendril's voice was low.

Something at their feet caught the cool light of the moon. Pendril bent and picked up a piece of glass, its once jagged edges sandblasted smooth. Its blue was that of the sea once the sun had gained the sky. Dellie watched as he ran a finger around its edge, taking its measure, feeling its texture. She let him lift her hand and open her fingers.

She closed her hand around its coolness.

They walked a few steps, taking in the cool night air and the intoxicating perfume of the night-blooming flowers opening, prodigal, wanton, parts straining for the night birds and moths flitting from one to another.

"Swim with me. The water here is warm, even with the sun going down. There is some kind of ..."

His voice trailed off. Dellie reached behind her head and unfastened a comb, her red hair cascading about her shoulders, her eyes transfixed by Pendril. He slipped from his trousers and shirt. Dellie gasped. She had never seen a grown man unclothed. She reached her hand out—slow, tentative—and traced the small triangle of hair on his breastbone. His chest, his whole body was smooth—taut lines and muscles firm, ready. He stepped closer to her and unbuttoned her dress. She felt it fall from her shoulders and land rumpled about her feet. She held her arms skyward as he lifted her shift above her head. A shiver went through her as a light breeze played across her skin.

She tipped her head sideways as Pendril's long fingers traced the lines of her breast. He took her hand, led her a few steps toward the water. Bumps rose on her arms and she trembled. He cupped his hands to pour the warm water over her neck and shoulders a blessing.

CHAPTER SIX

It Touches Everyone

Dellie shook her head as she grabbed a piece of confetti lying crumpled in the soil. Even these weeks later, despite the cleaning that the whole family had taken part in, she was still finding remnants of the wedding jump-up in the family's yard. Her eyes followed an electric green bird as it flitted across the yard. "Ah Pendril! Look there! Have you ever seen such a bird?"

He looked up to where she pointed. "I think I missed it." His eyes crinkled as they came to rest on a basket fashioned from vines, hugging a spot of shade. "But look there, isn't that your M'Ma's basket?"

Dellie sighed. Somehow M'Ma had left behind the fresh batch of skin creams and lotions that she had made for Mrs. Chandler. Now they sat forlorn and abandoned on a flat stone. Even with the shade from the great trees, Dellie knew that the careful work would be ruined: the creams a soupy mess and the lotion soured under the rising heat. It needed to be carried up to the Great House. She scanned the yard. No one was heading in that direction. She had just enough time for this small task without being late for her sewing lesson over in Sweet Bottom.

"Come, we must hurry if I am to make it to my lesson. Come with me to take this to M'Ma." Dellie picked up the basket and then hesitated. Cal's voice rang in her head.

"Never, *never* go up to the Great House!" It was that message that both her mother and grandmother had drilled into them, leaning face to face with each child. That adjuration flitted through Dellie's mind. She dismissed it with a chupse. "I am a grown woman. A woman working in Bridgetown. Eighteen years old. This is my home. I will go where I will. And beside, Pendril is with me."

She tugged Pendril's arm. "Let's go. *Now.* Hurry. Eva gets frosty if anyone is late for the lesson."

They skirted Mrs. Chandler's flower garden and made their way up the long path, past the bright white lace curtains billowing through the French doors that opened to the garden. They rounded the side of the House toward the cooking shed where M'Ma could be found at this time of day. Dellie, two paces ahead of Pendril, nearly bumped into Mr. Chandler.

"Ah, excuse me." She looked down. "I mean good morning Mr. Chandler."

He touched her chin and lifted her head up. Dellie jumped and took a step back. From the corner of her eye she saw Pendril's eyebrows shoot up.

"Excuse me, sir. I should watch more carefully where I am going." Mr. Chandler looked at her, his bleary eyes moving up and down and coming to rest on her bosom. She lifted the basket higher.

"What have you got gal?" He stepped closer, closing the gap between them.

Pendril stood as if rooted to the spot, his mouth open.

Dellie felt her heart pounding as the long ago memory of his groping Cal gathered at the edge of her brain.

Mr. Chandler stepped to her side, moving closer and putting his face to her hair. Even this early his words were slurred with drink. "You must belong to Cal. You look just like her. Except for the red hair." He dragged his fingers through the sparse hairs on his head pasted flat with sweat. Dellie held her breath, closing herself to the sharp scent of stale rum. He reached for a lock of her hair. "Red hair. Hah! Red hair on one of you. Hmmm." He laughed.

Now, frozen between the past and present she stood as Mr. Chandler's arm circled her waist and he rubbed against her, his hardness thick and hot through the fabric of his trousers. Words running together flashed before her and coursed through her brain. *It stops here. Promise me. I don't want Mr. Chandler calling you or Maude. Or May. Red hair. I'll be holding a place. Just an excuse. Don't think every ruined woman is walking the streets. I'll inscribe your name. Redhair. Come, come anytime. Roster of the Ruined. Promise me. Promise me. Promise me.*

Her eyes were on Pendril. Standing there. Impotent. Not moving. He was not moving, not moving, not moving to throw Chandler to the ground, to kick him, to push him away. Instead there he stood — arms stretched out, fingers splayed out ready, but not able to grasp — what? On his face, the same look that she knew was on her face. The same look that had been on her mother's face that long ago day. Something she knew neither one could bear to see. And something that she feared each of them would see as one looked at the other. Her motions were beyond thought as she pulled away and ran, fast — fast, past Pendril and back down the path, fast past Henry's house, fast past the tenants' quadrangle and into the hills.

The wharf and all of the area by the Careenage and inner harbor were teeming with people. Stevedores, shirtless, loaded last minute cargo and provisions. Families paid the island's two photographers for a last pose in front of Lord Nelson's statue before separating forever. Up-country women presented their wares, one basket in their hands, another poised confidently on their heads. Small boys exchanged money for comfits and glassies as hucksters peeled back snow-white cheesecloth to reveal their delights. Men examined blazing flower corsages for their women, women examined smoothly laid out ribbons for their children.

Dellie stood wearing her good dress, good shoes, and good hat. In her left hand was a carpetbag holding her clothes and the sturdy black leather handbag that Lillian had given her. In a small compartment was the lock of Cal's hair tied into the edge of a handkerchief. Somewhere else, deep in its recesses, a piece of blue beach glass rested. In her right hand she held her sewing basket and the tools that would help her make her way in New York. The whole family circled her as she waited for the skiff that would take her to the boat. M'Ma pressed a satchel into her hand.

"These are letters for Lillian from the women at church. This is some cassava bread for you. I wrapped it well so it will keep. I don't trust them to feed you decent on the boat." The old woman turned away.

Dellie took a step back and scanned the view before her from left to right, stitching every detail into her memory. The crewman manning the small launch offered her his hand. She stepped onto the skiff and turned to view the scene one last time. Her breath caught in her throat as her eyes picked out a figure to her left. It was a man in faded shirt and trousers, standing apart from the throng under a great palm tree, his hand raking back his black, unruly hair.

PART TWO

This Place Now

CHAPTER ONE

Brooklyn

New York, 1910 August

*T*he first thing Dellie noticed was not the pier, the crush of people herded behind ropes, the smell of the harbor, or even the persistent call of gulls.

First, she saw the buildings. All dizzied toward the sky — some wide, some slender, some ornate, some austere. In places, where the light had gained the advantage, it plated the buildings with sheets of silver or gold as they emerged from a belt of fog. Deep gasps from the immigrants on the ferry's deck sounded as one.

Dellie had boarded in Bridgetown, but the vessel had begun its trip in Rio de Janeiro. Passengers disembarking at Ellis Island represented the full mosaic of the Caribbean. Some of her fellow passengers were the first of their families to leave home, whatever that small place might be, to plant themselves here. Others, like her, were meeting family — sisters, brothers, cousins, a friend, or a spouse. She turned from the city and gazed again, curiously, at the mass of people behind her.

She had heard scraps of the stories during her journey:

"We sold the house and with what Hamilton sent me it gave us enough for my passage."

"The price of cane slipping, there was no way to make the numbers work and so we decide to take the Panama money and head to New York."

"Dorothy, here, scored the highest ever in the Parish. They dangle Queen's College in front of her face and snatch it away! So we saved and then up and left."

The launch jolted as it hit the pier.

Suddenly Dellie was frightened. "I have enough in my bag now for a return ticket. Miss Crane would take me back. I could work Henry's plan and the family could buy...." The tug of that abandoned plan pulled at the knot forming in her stomach.

The throng of people pressed her forward. A mass of people from her ferry merged with the mass from another just landed, forming a single host of humanity. Ahead, through a set of doors flung wide, was a massive staircase. There were all manner of persons before her: men with somber arrays of cloth across their shoulders, women with white caps starched to resemble birds wings, children with shoes carved from wood. Dellie's eyes widened as the living, breathing mass entered a colossal room. "Do not stare up like some sort of bumpkin." But she couldn't help herself. The room vaulted upwards and spread out twice, no, three times or more the size of Government House in Bridgetown. Every inch of the grand staircase ahead of her was covered with people. Women carried babies, older children pulled along younger. To the side, men in uniform pressed unceasingly some device that made a clicking sound. Others used chalk to mark the clothing of some—L, F, H. Lillian had told her in a letter what they meant, but she could not now recall the details.

Dellie felt winded both from excitement and the climb. The air was ripe with the smell of bodies unwashed from days or weeks in steerage. A man with a badge directed her to a seat on one of the benches that filled the hall, row upon row upon row. "Sit down, Miss. It will be a while."

Dellie followed his gesture, unable to decipher the rush of vowels and consonants.

She scanned the room and took in hundreds of little dramas. A man, hair slicked back, shoes polished to a high shine, checked and re-checked his documents. A child, face grimy, examined a copper-colored American coin found on the floor. Next to Dellie, a young girl tried to comfort a child crying for a doll lost on the stairs while her mother struggled to create a cocoon of privacy in which to nurse an infant.

A memory of Cal fashioning a puppet from a handkerchief flicked the edge of Dellie's memory. She reached into the carpetbag gripped between her feet, pulled out a swatch of fabric, and caught the child's eye. The sobbing gave way to a snuffling as the child watched the white square of fabric transform into a little puppet. The mother turned and squeezed Dellie's hand.

"Next! 118! Ruth Adele Standard!"

Dellie rose at the call of her name and stood at the agent's desk. She placed her handbag on the marble surface, reached in, snapped open a compartment, and pulled out her papers.

The man's eyes followed his fingers sliding across the words. "Barbados. British citizenship." He made a series of check marks on a sheet of paper. "Occupation?"

"I am a seamstress."

Another series of marks.

"I see you are going to your sister's. What is her address?"

"Excuse me, sir?"

"Where...does...your...sister...live?"

"Ah. It is Bergen Street, Brooklyn, New York. The number is..." She pushed a piece of paper toward him and pointed.

Twenty nine questions in all. Less than three minutes. He rolled a stamp on a pad of ink, pounded it onto a document, and slid it to Dellie. "Next!"

That was it. She was in New York. Dellie stepped through the wide double doors and looked out, then down, surprised by the hardness of the ground on the sole of her shoe.

Somehow she saw them amid the crush of people. Lillian, and Dellie's long-time friend Winifred, were waiting for her.

Arms rushed out and knocked Dellie's hat off her head.

"You are here!"

"'Tis good to lay eyes upon you!"

"Come, we'll take you to your new home!"

Dellie wiped the tears from her eyes. Lillian had changed little in the short time she had been in New York. But Winifred. Dellie looked the woman up and down. Her hair was different. She was plumper, rounder—but there was something else. Something she couldn't put her finger on.

The streams and eddies of people were unending. She heard all manner of language, saw all manner of dress, watched tears flow as families were reunited, and saw travelers like her head out into the city through the massive doors of the terminal.

More amazing to Dellie than the cacophony of New York was the ease of her sister and her friend Winifred within it. Lillian moved to the left, and then right, a part of the rhythm of the packed sidewalk, as if everyone were part of a dance put together by some unseen choreographer. Dellie felt her own clumsiness in comparison. She mumbled quick 'excuse pleases' to soften the annoyed glances from the people she bumped into.

Her mind was aswirl with their questions:

"How is Cuffee doing? Is he still heading back to Workman's on Sundays?" "And Emmeline, are she and M'Ma talking again?"

"I heard Eva has taken a smaller group of girls this time, is that so?"

"Tell me ..." "

Dellie trained her eyes on the women in front of her. "Don't gaze up at the buildings like some bumpkin from up St. Lucy's in Bridgetown for the first time!" she said sternly to herself.

Winnie touched her hand to get her attention. "Dellie, hold your handbag tight against your body like this. There are purse snatchers all around waiting for a person to be distracted. You will mark yourself."

Dellie's brow furrowed. "Winnie, your talk is different! You still sound Bajan, but there is something else now. The way you say words with a 'th'!" You have an accent now, soul!"

Her eyes widened at Lillian's laugh.

"Dellie, remember here in this man's country, you are the one with the accent. Come. No need to linger here. We've got a way to go. Plus it is getting dark a little earlier these days. Let me take that bag."

"And I'll take the sewing basket," added Winnie.

They stripped Dellie of everything but her dark leather handbag. Holding it tight against her body as Winnie said, she followed.

"Dellie, they don't travel here like at home. We will take the trolley over the bridge. That part of the trip is really something!"

At the trolley stop clutches of people stood in small huddles. A man, in hat and fine gloves, paced up and down, impatient for the next set of cars. A high-pitched ping, followed by a metallic whine, signaled the trolley's approach as it rounded the corner and rumbled to the straightaway.

Lillian tugged Dellie's sleeve. "I will put in the money for all three of us. You and Winnie go through and get us seats."

Dellie followed Winnie's lead.

As the trolley began its trip over the bridge, every child turned in his seat. Dellie rose from the wicker seat with the same eagerness as the children. She pressed against the windows of the car doors and trembled with awe. To her right, Winnie pointed out Manhattan— clusters of buildings touching the sky, expanses of trees, a ring of slips and massive piers for boats and steamships. Ahead, to her left, lay Brooklyn. A row of docks and a nest of flat, dark buildings hugged the water. In the distance lay the green of trees, trees, and trees.

Between the shores ran the great East River heading to the sea.

Lillian pointed to a window at the head of the car, next to the trolley man's booth. The women competed with a clutch of children for the best vantage point.

"There, Dellie." Lillian pointed. "There is the warehouse, see, with the words *'Chase and Sanborn'* on the side, where Coleridge works as a clerk. Clemmie works there, too, but on the docks. He was fortunate to get it, given the union. They make a practice of excluding Negro people. I think they don't know how to categorize him. But the business there is importing spices and such from the world over." She pointed to the right to a tall building with a crenellated roof. "And over there..." Her finger singled out a spot near a cluster of trees. "Over there is where I pick up the trolley in the morning and take it uptown to the Brooklyn *Home for Aged Colored People*. Like I wrote to you, a few days each week I help the doctor there, Dr. Fielding, with some of the bookkeeping, and if one of the old ladies is concerned about being examined by a man, I sometimes help him or stand in the room with him."

Winnie touched her arm. "That is the Fulton-Flatbush Storage Company." She pointed to a tall building with an enormous clock tower. "It is at the edge of our neighborhood. If you are ever lost, you can use that to navigate your way home."

Dellie turned to her at the word "home." Winnie looked at her.

"Oh, and by the way, Dellie," Lillian said as she rummaged in her purse. "Here is a key for you."

"A key?

"Yes, for the front door."

Dellie looked at her sister. "Ah, so you are now carrying a key! The first person in the family to have one..." She turned it over in her hand.

———

A procession of identical houses lined Lillian's street. Only the gardens differentiated them: marigolds, dahlias, Rose of Sharon coaxed from 4x4 foot patches of soil by obsessive hands. It was a glowing, late summer day, and Bergen Street was alive — girls playing a game that involved boxes chalked on the sidewalk and a pebble, boys engaged in another that required chalk-drawn boxes and a bottle cap. A group of women juggled babies from hip to hip and haggled with a man in worn coveralls over the price of vegetables displayed in the back of a wooden wagon. A bent old man patched the paint on the wrought-iron fence that demarcated his property. The off-key voice of someone singing drifted from a window high above the street. A rush of questions tumbled from Dellie's mouth:

"Winnie, the streets. All of them are paved?

"Lillian! Is that an automobile up there? Who does it belong to?

"Did I just see a man let a dog *into* a house?

"Lillian! Why are there little fences around the bases of the trees?"

"That." Lillian pointed ahead to a brownstone near the middle of the block. "Is our place. Mrs. Cumberbatch and her husband own it. She lets me tend the garden in front." A flowering vine flanked by a mound of marigolds adorned the gate. "See, Dellie, marigolds now, but I have been in a mind to plant *daffodils*." She laughed. "Daffodils in memory of the schoolmaster! I understand you have to plant them in the fall. So that will be our project in a few weeks."

"So we will get to see them at last!"

Winnie gestured at the trees. "That is right. And, in the fall, don't forget the leaves change color and fall to the ground."

Dellie turned and stopped in her tracks.

"Come, ladies!" Winnie called them back to their task at hand. "These bags with all of Dellie's worldly goods are not light!" Lillian retrieved a key from her pocket, opened a wrought iron gate, stepped down, and unlocked the door leading to the bottom flat she shared with Coleridge. The place was small, with little sunlight. Dellie's eyes took in the pale yellow curtains that Lillian had hung to keep prying eyes from peering in through the street-level windows. A pink oilcloth lay on a table in the center of the room; a handful of fragrant yellow flowers bloomed from a biscuit tin in the middle. There were three rooms: the bedroom that Lillian and Coleridge shared, a large room that served as both kitchen and gathering place, and a smaller room that had once perhaps been a large pantry.

"Dellie, it will be a bit tight, but I don't think you will mind," Lillian said, peeking in alongside Dellie. "Coleridge's cousin moved out to his own place a few weeks ago after being here for a while. He found the space serviceable. We haven't got much. We are saving to buy house. That is the thing to do here in this New York. That's what Mrs. Cumberbatch does. Buy a house, live in one part and rent the rest out. She has her eye on another property besides this one, I hear. I will fix you some food. Peas and rice? Some nice gravy?"

Dellie rested her chin on her hand as Lillian chatted on. "So you say M'Ma sent some letters. We'll deliver them at the next Lodge meeting; that way we don't have to go all around and about. But then again, maybe that would be a good way for you to get your bearings. See who is here and where they live. Start to get a sense..."

Dellie's eyes grew heavy as her body released the tension from the journey.

It was dark when she awoke. She found her shoes off and a throw over her shoulders. Lillian.

The sound of running liquid drew her eyes toward the kitchen. There, a tall, slender man tried to fix himself a cool drink without disturbing her.

"Coleridge!"

He jumped. Then he picked her up and spun her around.

"Coleridge! Coleridge, this city is enough! I don't need to be any dizzier or more confused."

He threw his head back, laughed, and put her down.

"We are glad to have you here safe. It'll do Lillian good to have family around. She has been planning for you since we got here.

She has a program laid out for you to make this place home. I hope you are ready for it!"

"Where is she anyway?"

"She'll be back soon. She went to drop off a sick-basket to someone from the Lodge. Sit down at the table. You didn't finish your food! I'll heat it up for you. You fell asleep fork in your hand! There's a story! If we were home, people would be singing on it. I can hear it now." His voice was off- key, *"Red-haired Dellie, trying to fill her belly..."* He threw his head back and laughed again.

Hours later Coleridge and Lillian headed off to bed. Silence settled through the flat. Dellie unpacked her bags. Lillian had fashioned a makeshift dresser for her of three wooden fruit crates stacked one atop the other. The top one held her undergarments; the center one, her blouses; and the bottom, her skirts. She placed her handbag on the top crate. Two more crates pasted with advertisements for vegetables created a nightstand, on which stood a kerosene lamp and a small clock. "You'll need to keep that wound, Dellie-girl," Coleridge warned. "No work bells clanging here to pace off your day." A narrow bed with smooth sheets and a thin pillow completed her furnishings. She sat down carefully on it and let her eyes roam. Yes, she had done it. She was here. Her life was to be made on *this* island.

She snapped the latch on her handbag and reached inside. She placed her papers with her underthings for safe-keeping. She carefully counted her money. From what Lillian had told her, she could get through for two weeks, maybe a month on what she'd brought. She rummaged deeper, her long fingers finding the small pouch with Cal's hair. Next to it she felt the smooth coolness of the sea glass and sighed. Images tripped through her head — M'Ma bent over a sheet of figures, the obeah woman's ramshackle house, a crimson hibiscus left at the door of Miss Crane's shop. Dellie pulled something warm and smooth from her bag and she was back in Bridgetown on the day she set off. A small boy she had never seen, his hair a halo framing his face, reached out his hand. In it lay a round brown nut with a deep chocolate coloring on one end.

"A cow-eye nut! You are giving it to me?" Dellie's eyes filled and she hugged the child. "You know the story of these? They say they wash all the way over from Africa so that the spirits of the old dead Africans can watch over us over here." She slipped it into her dress pocket.

Outside, the trill of a cat broke the silence. Dellie crept toward the door. She spread her fingers to muffle any sound as she opened it and slipped out into the Brooklyn night. Her eyes adjusted to the darkness as she stood looking up and then down the street. The purring of a cat and the soft slip of fur across her ankles drew her attention. She scooped up the small creature and fingered the collar at its neck.

"Ah, so someone has claimed you, huh, little one? So pretty you are with your sleek little paws and pointy face. And look you have thumbs!" She ran her fingers under its chin. A whisper of a breeze blew through the soft glow from the gas lights lining the block to make tree leaves and night shadows dance together.

She turned as she heard a rustle behind her. Lillian appeared in the doorway.

"Oh," Dellie said, her voice low in deference to the hour. "I didn't mean to wake you. I tried to slip out without making any noise."

Lillian stepped closer, her hand on Dellie's arm. "Don't worry, Soul. I was tossing and turning. And one of the floorboards does creak when anyone steps upon it." She pulled Dellie toward the stoop and gestured for her to sit.

"Dellie." Lillian's voice was soft. "Dellie, you never did say what made you decide to come. You never said what happened between you and Pendril."

Dellie pulled the cat closer and closed her eyes. She worked to still the trembles that shot through her body whenever she thought of that day on the path to the House. She looked up past the trees to a swatch of sky as remnants of clouds floated by.

"Lillian." She swallowed the lump gathering in her throat. "It is over there. All of that is part of the past. Cal was right when she said the poison runs too deep at home. She said it touches everyone. Black, white, colored. Told me that if I stayed it would touch me too. And it did. And it touched Pendril. There is no more to say." She turned to face her sister. "Ever. I am here now. I am here and I will make my way."

"Oh, Soul." They sat together in silence.

The cat squirmed in Dellie's lap. "Go on in sister. It is late. I will be in a moment."

Lillian sighed and stretched. "All right. But don't stay out here too long."

Dellie looked up toward a swatch of sky as her fingers rolled the cow nut in her pocket. She stood still, eyes open, ears tuned eagerly for the presence of the spirits. Her throat tightened. She felt nothing. No rush of sound on the breeze, no wisps rising from the ground. Her voice was a whisper. "Did you not come with me? Not cross the water with me?" She looked at the trees tamed by the small wrought iron fences that ringed them and felt the hardness of the New York cement beneath her feet. She shook her head.

A sliver of cloud passed by and the moon, a thin crescent, beckoned her gaze. Was M'Ma looking at this moon? She felt a rush of tears. Was Pendril? He had told her he would remember her by the moon. She snuggled her face into the bundle in her arms. "Tell me, kitty, do you think he does? Does he remember me still when he sees the moon? Does he remember the night at the lagoon? Should I?" The cat jumped from her arms and slipped away into the darkness.

CHAPTER TWO

A Program of Sorts

Dellie was grateful that Lillian let her sleep. When she made her way to the kitchen the next morning, she found Winnie sitting there. "Dellie, come. Lillian is about doing errands, so I will give you your first lesson on New York. Walk with me over to the grocery store. That is what they call the market here. The place to go in this neighborhood is Iannacci's."

"Is what?"

"Listen, Soul, you will have to learn all manner of speech if you are to live here. Ja nah chi, you say, though it is not spelled anything like that. They are some order of Italians called Sicilians. You will know the store by the cow hanging from the front."

"I see."

"Some places don't like you handling the fruit and vegetables. Mrs. Iannacci not only let you handle it, but helps you pick out the best. Especially the ones a body has never heard of before. Strawberries, cherries, peaches, pears, and such."

They rounded the corner, passing a dry goods store and a butcher. "Stay away from that one." Winnie tilted her head. "Some of the meat in there was slaughtered before God created time. And the owner likes to try to cheat you with his thumb on the scale."

Dellie struggled to pay attention, but it was as if every sense were turned up. Atlantic Avenue Winnie called it. "Easy for us Bajans to remember!" The street was packed with stores on either side — a dairy, the butcher that Winnie didn't like, a shoe maker. Goods choked the sidewalk — she nearly walked into a massive barrel of black floating things.

"Oh, Dellie, watch for the olives!"

Olives? What are olives?

On the street, men in horse-or donkey-drawn carts called out their goods or services. "Knives sharpened! Scissors sharpened!"

"Peas here! Peas here!"

From somewhere, the smell of baking bread poured into the street.

A few steps ahead she saw the brown-and-white cow that hung above the door. *Iannacci and Family, Grocers.* I-a-n-n-a-c-c-i, how could anyone possibly get Ja-nah-chi from that? It took Dellie's eyes a moment to adjust to the indoor light from the morning brightness outside.

"Ah, Mrs. Holder! I had a feeling I would see you today! What can I get you? Sallie!" she called to her son. "Sallie, come help Mrs. Holder pick out her things."

Dellie turned her head. *A boy named Sally?*

"Mrs. Iannacci, I want you to meet my friend Dellie. She has just arrived from home. She is sister to my friend Lillian Green."

"Oh! Welcome, dear!" She grabbed Dellie and hugged her, nearly knocking her off her feet. "Your sister and your friend are two of my best customers! You know when my little Francesca was born, Mrs. Holder here made her a beautiful little white cap. She wore it for her christening."

Dellie leaned in. This was a different kind of New York accent... she pieced together enough words to get the gist of what the woman was saying. The rest she would have to ask Winnie about later.

"Here, Miss Standard, try this." The storekeeper held out a round fragrant fruit. "It's a peach. Taste it."

Dellie put it between her teeth and bit. It released its juice across her tongue. So this America could produce something sweet like this?

Dellie, Lillian, and Coleridge gathered around the small table in Winnie and Clemmie's flat. Lillian spread out a sheaf of papers.

"Winnie and I have been planning for when you came, a program of sorts. We will show you around here first so that you learn this neighborhood, and then each week we will branch out. Take in something new. It will be an adventure for us all."

"I will be looking forward to that. But more than that, I want to understand what people are saying."

Clemmie shook his head. "It took me a few months, even though everyone is supposedly speaking English. It helped that most of the people at *Chase and Sanborn* are native born New Yorkers. So at first I learned just that one kind of accent. But you add the New York talk to the accent of all of these foreigners around here and you get:

"Whaddjasay?

"*Sed jeet yet*?

"Oh. No idint, djue?'"

Dellie drew back. Lillian, Winnie, and Coleridge doubled over in laughter.

Coleridge translated: "'What did you say?' 'Said did you eat yet?' 'Oh. No. I didn't, did you?'"

Dellie sat still, trying to hear the difference. "Sounds the same," she chupsed, making them all laugh the harder. "Well, I am glad I have had the opportunity to entertain you all so." She crossed her arms in front of her.

"Oh, Dellie!" Winnie reached over and squeezed her. "We are just teasing you. Soon you will understand more than you want to."

"That is for sure," said Clemmie with a shake of his head.

Lillian pointed to the kettle. "Winnie, a cup of tea would be so nice right now."

Winnie rose and slipped a coin in the gas slot and fired up the stove. Dellie stared, fascinated. Clemmie put out some cups and a small bowl of sugar. Dellie reached out and lifted a spoonful of fine crystals.

"You use white sugar here? Like in the Great House? Even Mrs. Chandler only serves it for her Horticultural Society meetings."

Winnie's voice was low. "Dellie. It is the only kind they sell here."

Dellie tipped the spoon and watched the crystals spill back into the bowl.

Lillian was true to her word. As the gray light filtered through the curtain, Dellie was shaken awake. "Dellie, Dellie, you wash up first while I make a little something to eat before we leave. I want to show you the neighborhood."

The street was just coming to life as Lillian and Dellie stepped on to the sidewalk. Winnie joined them at the corner.

"Lillian, do I hear singing?" A call and response of high and low voices hung in the air.

"Oh yes, Soul. I forgot to tell you, there's a nuns' convent a few houses down at the corner. When it is quiet in the morning and evening you can hear them singing their prayers."

Dellie paused. "I have never heard anything like it..." She interrupted herself and pulled Lillian's cuff. "Sister, that man there. What is he doing?" A small man in baggy clothes lifted what looked like a bishop's crosier up to a light.

"Oh, he is late today. That is Casey, the lamplighter. Each day he lights the gaslights in the evening, and in the morning he extinguishes them." Lillian chatted on. "See that house across there, number 187, another Bajan family lives there. They are somehow related to the Parris family — you know that wide clan back home near the Glebe. Well, they have two boys and a girl. Nice children. If you ever need someone to run an errand, you can call on them. And next door is where Coleridge and Clemmie's friend Owen Gibson lives. He is an American Negro, what they call a Pullman Car Porter. He works on the railroads and so is away a lot. But he always comes by with tales of what he has seen and news of what is going on in this man's country. The house there, with the shades all up..."

Dellie interrupted. "Lillian, tell me, what is an American Negro? I hear all this talk about them."

Lillian was silent for a moment. "It is hard to explain. But that is what they call colored and black people here. Any people whose forebears are from Africa. No matter what their color."

"Ah, I see. So here we are all the same. Not like home?"

"No, not like home."

Winnie cleared her throat and glanced at Lillian.

"And Dellie. Some of them are not too keen on us being here. We are foreigners to them. A group of scruffy boys threw dirt on me and called me a run of names when I cut through the park the other day. Good thing I couldn't understand a word they were saying."

Lillian shook her head. "But most of them just leave you be. Ignore you."

CHAPTER THREE

Letters

Dellie read it one more time, correcting her punctuation here and there:

Dear Maudie,

I hope this letter finds you as well as the leaving of it finds me. Each day I have tried to start a letter, but have struggled to find the words to describe this place. Everything about it, even the ground under your feet is different. One part of the district that we live in is filled with stores carrying all manner of goods catering to all manner of people. During the day those streets are teeming with people shopping. Another part of the district is filled with row upon row of houses, with rooms stacked one on top of the other. Three or sometimes four families to a house, one on each floor! There must be at least one hundred families living on just our street! Each house here is a wall house, though. Imagine!

So much of it can be overwhelming. I am training myself to focus on just one thing at a time. Sometimes I focus on the tastes, especially of things I have never had before – peaches, maple syrup. Last week, though, Lillian did buy caramels from the milkman. I had not had that taste on my tongue since Cal made them.

On other days I focus on smells – a man selling roasted nuts sometimes pushes a cart around. There is one type he sells – chestnuts, that are sweet, but soft like a potato. The smell of the wood from his cart makes your mouth water. And then there is the scent of the rain here. Maudie, sometimes it rains for one or two days without stopping! Can you believe it?

Sister, there is not enough paper for me to write all that I want to tell you. Besides, I would rather you see for yourself. Don't delay. I will send something toward your passage as soon as I can. Please share this letter with Henry, M'Ma, and the children and tell them I love them.

She carefully addressed the envelope:
Miss Maude Standard
Taborvilla, Near the Hope
St. George, Barbados
BWI

———

The air was crisp one late afternoon on the cusp of fall and summer making it a good time for a walk to the post office. Dellie reached for a wrap when a knock sounded at the door. Dellie looked to the kitchen. Coleridge was still washing up after coming in from work. She answered.

"Oh! Can I help you?"

It was the man Lillian had pointed out when she had first arrived. Since then, Dellie had seen him many times and noticed he seemed to know everyone in the neighborhood — greeting the men with a good morning and the women with a touch of the brim of his hat. She had noticed that he was always finely dressed — dark suit, bright white shirt that contrasted with the deep blue-black of his skin. Often he had another set of clothes slung over his shoulder or carried a small valise.

"Good evening, Ma'am. I am Owen Gibson. I am just dropping off some magazines that I thought..."

Coleridge came to the door. "Owen, man. Come in. Come in."

Dellie stepped aside to let him through.

"Meet my sister-in-law! Owen Gibson, Dellie Standard. Dellie, Owen."

He tipped his head and extended his hand. The palm of his hand was calloused, work-worn, but the back was smooth, nails trimmed, the light half moons at their base a contrast to the darkness of his skin. She caught a whiff of cocoa butter — the same ingredient Cal had used in her recipes. She took note of that. How many men took such care?

At the sound of voices, Lillian emerged from the bedroom. "Welcome, Owen. Sit down. Have a cool drink. I see you have met my sister."

Owen smiled at Dellie.

"Yes, I did. And yes, a cool drink would be very nice."

"I can do better than a cool drink, man. How about a knock of something?" Coleridge rummaged behind a phalanx of tall jars in the cupboard, extracting a bottle with a map of Barbados on its label.

Dellie shot a glance at Lillian.

"I could be persuaded."

Coleridge gestured toward a chair for the guest.

Lillian rolled her eyes and signaled Dellie. The two retreated into Dellie's quarters. Lillian shook her head. "As soon as the rum comes out, you know it will be a long visit. Watch, Clemmie'll be by in a moment. It's as if he has second sight."

"Hush, sister!" Dellie laughed. "So who is this Owen?"

"Like I told you before, what they call a 'Pullman Car Porter.' He rides the trains providing service to the fancy passengers in the sleeping cars. I suppose talking to people comes naturally to him if he has that manner of work."

Dellie pondered that. "Sleeping cars?"

"Yes, Dellie. This nation is so broad that they do have beds and food service on the trains. According to Owen, the workers are American Negro men. When the railroad buys the cars, the servants come with it. Have you ever heard of such an arrangement?"

Dellie's mouth twisted into something near a smirk. "Sounds like Coventry Hall to me. The Estate came to Eloise Walker and Mr. Chandler with the workers all in place, including M'Ma and Cal."

Lillian chupsed. "Dellie, why must you…Oh, never mind. Let's join them. Your letter can wait until tomorrow."

Owen was one of the few American Negroes that anyone from among the small St. George contingent knew. He shared Coleridge and Clement's interest in any type of sport and that was how their friendship began. Now he stopped by from time to time to share Coleridge and Lillian's table. In the time they had known him, he had become not only their friend, but their ambassador to a wider world — the world of the American Negro.

"I know this place is usually full on a Friday. I just came by to drop y'all off some papers I picked up on my run. Got the *Chicago Defender*, you know that one, the Negro paper, and that *Harper's* that the white folks like to read. But maybe I will stay a bit..."

Another knock at the door. Dellie glanced at Lillian.

Clemmie stepped into the kitchen.

Coleridge grinned. "Come in, man! Fire back the acid with us!"

Clemmie pulled up a chair.

The conversation rolled along without a lull. The pace of refilling glasses slowed as Owen's stories, recounting possibilities they had not contemplated and dangers they had not considered, took center stage. Dellie only half listened, immersed instead in the papers now spread on the table. Stories about union organizing, about lynchings, and about a West Indian-looking man named Du Bois trying to develop a program of advancement for colored people filled the first three pages of one issue. Another focused on a man named Washington speaking about learning a trade. Dellie's face was a knot of interest. Dangers, yes, but you could see your way to something else. Another section had stories of weddings, of graduations, of people opening businesses.

Dellie only heard the last part of the sentence, but it was enough to draw her attention.

"...good land in Delaware. That's what I am saving up my money for, to buy a bit of land. I am thinking of opening a small hotel that will serve the Negro people who are traveling. Open it not too far from a rail line or maybe off a major road. Call it the *Blue Nile Hotel*. Got to have the word 'Blue' in it so folks know we are friendly to colored people. That's right." He rapped his hand on the table. "A bit of land and a business to call my own. That's my plan. My dream." He rested his gaze on Dellie.

She trained her gaze on the table cloth. His plan was not much different from her father's.

———

"You're not double-handed, are you?" The little girl's question was urgent.

Dellie bent down to hear her better. "Excuse me?"

"I said, you're not double-handed, are you? You can turn each rope separately? We need someone to turn for us so we can play Double Dutch."

"You show me. I will try." The little girl had the same intensity as May when she needed something.

"Here, like this. You have to turn each rope in a different direction. Some people can't do it. They are double-handed."

"Oh."

"That's it! That's right! Turn for us for just a few minutes! Please!"

Dellie smiled, she used to play this game with her sisters. The tick, tick, tick of the rope on the ground and the song of the girls as they took turns jumping made her smile. So easy was their world.

"My mother made a fancy cake,
How many eggs did it take?
Was it one, two, three, four, five, six, seven..."

She was listening so intently that the letter carrier caught her by surprise.

"Excuse me, miss, you live here, right?"

Dellie nodded.

"Well, I am a little behind schedule. Would you mind saving me a few steps and taking the mail up?"

She turned to see if Mrs. Cumberbatch was at her usual station in the first-floor window. Someone aside from her taking the mail probably broke one of her rules.

"I'll be glad to. I'll be right back, girls."

Dellie flipped through the small stack. Mrs. Cumberbatch always left the mail on a rickety table in the entryway. The first thing each of her renters did when they came home each day was to check the mail for news from home or from a relative digging the hole in Panama.

It was the colors and number of stamps on the envelope that first caught her eye. Then the postmark—Cardiff, Wales. Then the handwriting that she would recognize anywhere. Her hand began to tremble. The name on the front was clear however: Mr. Coleridge Green. Of course Pendril would write to his cousin. There was probably another note inside, though. If there were a note inside for her, then surely it would be alright to open it... She slipped the envelope inside her pocket.

"Sorry, girls. I have to go inside now."

"But we need..."

"Maybe later." The door clicked behind her.

Dellie pulled closed the curtain Coleridge had rigged to afford her some privacy. She sat on the bed, her back resting against the wall. She considered the envelope, then slid her finger under the flap.

My dear cousin Coleridge,

I hope this letter finds you and Lillian thriving in New York. I am posting it as Lane and I head out for a long voyage. Up to this point we have been doing mostly short trips of a week or two up and around the British Islands. Cardiff is a center for coal and much of the cargo is that.

Lane and I are assigned to the same group so we generally travel together. He does some specialized work in the engine room and I, as you know, am a cook. They have me doing baking. The men are from all over His Majesty's kingdom and used to all different manner of food. Everyone though is coming to love a potato, that at least you can recognize. And then there is what passes for meat, along with what passes for a vegetable. As one of the bakers, the bread is the only thing I will vouch for. When we come into port we all go streaming out in search of something that is not gray and that your tongue can taste.

This trip that Lane and I are taking will be for several months all around and about Gibraltar and the northern part of Africa. I will write again when we are in port.

Please give my love to Lillian.

"Please give my love to Lillian?" The thin paper drifted to Dellie's lap as she lifted her hands and covered her eyes. No special note sealed inside for her? Not a mention of her? Not a question about her? Not a word?

She gathered herself, stood, took her leather handbag from the dresser, opened it, and placed the letter deep inside.

CHAPTER FOUR

Sons and Daughters
of Barbados

A month passed. Winnie helped Dellie put her hair up in a way to make her look like a veteran New Yorker.

"Here, try this comb. It is more sophisticated." Winnie shook her head. "Turn around now. She sighed and shook out her hands. Try this." She stepped back to examine her work. "Yes! That's it! Perfect." She passed Dellie a hand mirror.

And with the comb tucking her hair in, back, and up, Dellie hunted for a job.

The sign said, "*Seamstress Wanted.*" But the man shooed Dellie out.

"No, girl. I can't have you foreigners in here taking work from the folks who have been toiling in this nation for all their lives."

Dellie stood wide-eyed, trying to understand a few words in yet another brand of New York accent.

She walked on. It was the same at the next three places. A flurry of words, including "no," she understood that, and then a gesture toward the door.

By the time she worked her way back uptown, it was late afternoon. She turned the corner and found Lillian a few steps ahead, also on her way home.

"So, Dellie? Anything?"

Dellie's face clouded.

"Ah, Soul, don't worry. This is not like home. Not every story has a sad ending. You watch. Something will come up soon."

Dellie had a short list of items — tea, flour, some canned milk — to pick up for Lillian at Ianncci's Grocery before heading home after another day searching for work. As she turned the corner, Winnie approached from the other direction. Dellie waved.

"Ah, Dellie! I haven't seen you in a few days."

"When I get home after walking about all day, I am too tired to move."

"I remember those days. Are you taking some small samples of your work with you?"

"I haven't been, but that is a good idea."

"I will come by and help you choose some things. With your initiation coming up soon, I was planning to come around anyway to talk to you about the Lodge. My committee is responsible for the ceremony. Since I am your sponsor, I want it to be extra-special. Perfect."

"Well, I have been practicing the oath with Lillian."

"That is good. Many trip up on that facing so many people. But I remember you did win the Recitation in school and so are not chilled by an audience."

Dellie cuffed her lightly on the arm. "Soul, do not remind me of that."

Winnie laughed. "Enough of this chatter anyway, I have to gather my things here and head home ...

Mrs. Iannacci appeared from somewhere behind the counter. "Mrs. Holder, I thought I heard your laugh. Good day, Miss Standard. You don't mind if I talk to your friend for a moment?" She took Winnie's arm and gave it a gentle tug. The two huddled by the register while Dellie addressed the small number of items on her list.

She walked down the far aisle examining items and nearly bumped into a step-stool holding a well-built man stocking the upper shelves. "Oh! Excuse me! I'm sorry."

He looked down at her and smiled but said nothing. Mrs. Ianacci called from the register.

"Oh, Miss Standard. That is my husband's brother Gianni, just here from Sicily. He doesn't hear or speak. He had a terrible fever as a boy." She waved her hand in a signal for him to get back to work.

Dellie made her way toward the counter.

Winnie turned. "I was just telling Mrs. Iannacci about the Lodge Initiation. She will need to order the candles and some of the other items special for us. I was also telling her about the oath and your skill at public speaking. Maybe you could recite the oath for her."

Dellie touched her arm. "Winnie. Soul. Please."

Mrs. Iannacci laughed and handed Dellie her package.

"Mrs. Holder, you are only partly through your list and already it is too much to carry. When you finish, I will have Gianni make a delivery to your house. The items for the Lodge ceremony should be here by next week."

The European immigrants had the Settlement House, the American Negroes had the Church—Baptist or AME—the West Indians had the Lodge.

The *Lodge of the Sons and Daughters of Barbados, BWI* and, more recently, of Brooklyn, New York, had been established nearly fifteen years ago in Bridgetown. In Barbados, the mission of the association had been to advance the aims of education and land ownership.

As immigration brought many to New York, another base of operation emerged. The basement of St. Philip's Episcopal Church in Brooklyn served as the meeting place for the Bajans in Brooklyn. Gatherings were generally twice a month: a business meeting on Tuesday evenings to accommodate the domestics in their number who generally had Wednesdays off, and a social gathering one Saturday evening a month at which light refreshments were served.

Dellie was sequestered in preparation for the ceremony. Winnie emerged from the kitchen drying her hands with a fresh towel. "Dellie, I am giving the dress a bleach soak for you. When I am through, you must boil it so it is pristine."

"But, soul, I have other things to do. I must be out looking for a job."

"I know, but this is important. Your formal introduction to the rest of the Bajans. Not everyone is in the Lodge, you know. If you want to meet and associate with decent people, then you must be a member."

"You are sounding like Henry."

"A wise man your father is."

Dellie chupsed.

"And after you have boiled the dress and the water is clear, be sure to pour in some bluing. When it is dry, I will starch and iron it."

Dellie shook her head. "Are you sure that is all?"

———

Dellie stood stock-still in the basement of St. Philip's Church her white dress on, trying not to bring shame upon Winnie with an errant wrinkle. She reached to scratch an itch at the nape of her neck. From somewhere, Winnie appeared.

"Dellie! Dellie, don't move!"

Dellie turned, panic on her face.

"Good heavens, Winnie, what is it!" She turned to her, eyes wide.

"Don't move, you are about to dislodge that comb that I spent hours fixing just so!"

"But I have to scratch my head!"

"I said, don't move. Tell me where, I will do it."

Winnie and Clemmie bustled about the room attending to last minute details. Warned by Winnie not to lean or sit, Dellie stood and watched her friend place a wide- column candle flanked by tapers for each new member on a table at the front of the room. Clemmie removed the chamois wrapping from a bound black book containing the Lodge Rule and Ceremonies and placed it, along with a broken cutlass, on the table. A semi-circle of wooden folding chairs for the new members surrounded the lectern, followed by the rows of seats for the membership.

As the hands of the round clock on the wall approached the hour, the room filled with members dressed in full regalia — dark suits or white dresses adorned with crimson sashes, and loose, red velvet Tudor berets. Seats filled quickly, save for the small semi-circle at the front reserved for the candidates and sponsors. Dellie worked hard not to sweat in the heat of the basement and so send Winnie into a frenzy.

A woman younger than Dellie nudged her. "Ah, look. There is Lodgemaster. He has a fine job at the Post Office, don't you know. And his sister, she helps with the books at the Colored YWCA. Isn't that something?"

The Lodgemaster and his family entered just as the last chair was unfolded. A stern looking man attired in black suit and bright white shirt and collar, Mr. Charles Walcott had served as Lodgemaster since his arrival six years ago. One of the first families to leave the Island for New York, the Walcotts brought with them education and a modest amount of wealth. From one of the more prominent colored families in Bridgetown, his clan generally produced teachers. He served the headmaster of one of the primary divisions in Christchurch, and his sister, Fan, had been a first form teacher back home. A widower since before leaving the Island, Charles was grateful to her for taking the responsibility of helping him to raise his son, Egbert. Now he walked around the room, shaking hands and greeting people. He moved from person to person, one or two words, conversation to conversation.

"Ah, Rupert! How are you? I hear you have found a new job."

"Mr. Selman, I hear your daughter is a fine student. One of the top in her class."

Dellie turned to the young woman. "I have not yet met him. But I know the Walcotts were already accomplished back in Barbados..."

"'Tis true. And see their son there? Egbert? He is quite something, too."

Dellie moved for a clearer view. She saw a well-built young man surrounded by a group of young girls.

"He will be graduating from a New York high school soon. He is bound for a good desk job, for sure. He is good looking, don't you think?"

Dellie's eyes followed him, noting the way his chest puffed out, stretching the front of his shirt.

The conversation ended abruptly as Winnie and Clement approached from across the room with the Lodgemaster and his family.

"Mr. Walcott, as I was saying, today is a special evening for us, sir. Our friend Dellie Standard is being inducted."

Dellie stepped to Winnie's side and smiled, extending her hand. "I am pleased to meet you."

Mr. Walcott's grin was wide. "Child, you look just like your father! Same cheekbones! But you have got your mother's smile."

Fan ordered her brother's son off on an errand, then turned to Dellie. "You are Lillian's sister, then? I believe I had your brother-in-law in school." She laughed. "I should be more accurate and say I had him in school occasionally. But he has become a respectable man. I remember I used to have to send him to the office at least once a month. Taking off with his friends, including your brother, if I am not mistaken, and their two friends Lane and Pendril, to watch the ships at the dock!"

"You taught Pendril?" Her breath quickened and she leaned in closer.

"Well, I would say Pendril was in my class. I heard he is off to sea. I am not surprised — it was always calling him. Every composition he ever wrote made mention of it as I recall."

Dellie's face softened with the chance to talk about him. "Yes, he is in his Majesty's Merchant Service. Coleridge is his cousin you know, and they stay in touch. She felt a creeping heaviness in her chest at the thought of his failure to mention her or to send a greeting to her in his letters.

"Miss Standard?" The Lodgemaster's voice pulled her back to the moment. "You head over there." He gestured toward Winnie. "We should begin soon."

Winnie waved her hand at the cluster of candidates and sponsors. "Time to line up for the processional."

Dellie suppressed a laugh as her friend cut a dreadful look at one of the male candidates struggling with a too tight collar.

Gavel in hand, Mr. Walcott approached the podium. A few light taps and the assembly came to order. "Ladies and gentlemen, we have a full agenda tonight with our business portion followed by new member induction. Let us begin."

A report came from the Education Committee. A woman, Mrs. Dorothea Atherley, not much older than Lillian but with a harried look about her, stood and offered the report. "If anyone is in need of a library card, Miss Fan Walcott and I will be accompanying a group to the St. Edward Street branch to sign up next Wednesday. Interested parties should meet on the steps at ten o'clock and bring a piece of mail addressed to them for identification."

A gray-haired woman, Mrs. Zuleika Elizabeth Williams, provided the report from the Sick Committee: "Mrs. Nell Dolan is making great progress. Baskets and cooked food are still needed at that residence though, until she is fully recovered and back to work. A sign-up sheet is by the door. Remember, there are three children in that house, so ongoing generosity is appreciated. And also we need a vistor there for Thursday afternoons."

Mr. George Sealey stood with the report from the Finance Committee. "The fund will turn next month, and members eleven and twelve on the list will receive disbursements."

Dellie swiveled a bit, picking up a whispered conversation to her left. "The fund turn means that Lenore will be able to finally purchase that bed outright that she has been looking at."

"And I heard that Pearl had opened up an account at the bank, saving for a down-payment."

"Ah really? But I saw..."

A glare from the Lodgemaster brought the conversation to an abrupt end.

Lillian was called upon to offer an additional report. She cleared her throat and began. "We are creating a Health Committee. The first activity will be a talk by Dr. Fielding on health and hygiene for city living. Too many of us, especially children, are seeing him with breathing ailments."

The Lodgemaster approached and stood by her side. "This new committee is most important, and as you heard, a distinguished member of the community will be in our midst. The fall and winter generally take a toll on us who are used to a warmer climate and fresh air, even indoors. I am extending a special invitation for a representative from each household to attend."

Everyone in the Lodge knew what a "special invitation" meant.

"Let us now turn to the induction of new members. Mr. Holder, please."

As Chaplain, Clemmie stood and approached the podium.

"Mr. Lodgemaster and members of the association, the following individuals are presented for membership." He turned to the six newcomers seated in the front semi-circle. "Sponsors, please stand with your candidates as I call their names."

Feet shuffled.

"Gloria Nurse."

A young woman with a headful of dark hair fixed in a bun stood. "Miss Nurse joins our community from Holetown in St. James. She is sponsored by Rosita and Christopher Pilgrim."

Rosita Pilgrim stepped forward and stood next to the initiate. Together they approached the long table to light the ceremonial candle. A round of applause began.

Clemmie raised a hand. "Ladies and gentlemen, please hold your applause until the end when we will salute our new members as a group." He continued with the call of names.

"Miss Amanda Richardson from Venture. She is sponsored by Mildred Poole.

"Mr. Tennyson Ward from Black Rock. He is sponsored by Michael Ford.

"Mr. Stephen Roberts from near Sweet Bottom. Sponsor, Sidney Franklin.

"Mrs. Helena Hewitt from near Drax Hall. Her sponsor is Elizabeth Moore.

"Miss Ruth Adele Standard from Taborvilla, near the Hope. Sponsored by Winifred Holder."

Like those in line before her, at the sound of her name Dellie stepped forward. With a trembling hand, she tipped a slim white candle toward the flame. For an instant, the two flames burned as one as her taper caught the flame from the stout, blue pillar.

Clemmie cleared his throat. "The lighting of the taper from the central candle reminds us all of the common history that we share, and of the individual light that we are to bring into the world. The two represent our common purpose and our individual agency. It reminds us that we are each separate, and yet one together as West Indians, as Bajans, as members of the Lodge of the Sons and Daughters of Barbados." He paused and addressed the sponsors. "We must thank the sponsors for their support of the new members in preparing them for this moment. They may now return to their places. Initiates, please remain standing for the oath. Raise your right hands."

Dellie locked eyes with Winnie as Clemmie gave the signal to begin. She suppressed the urge to chupse as Winnie signaled to hold her shoulders back.

"I do solemnly promise to bear my allegiance to the Lodge of the Sons and Daughters of Barbados, West Indies and Brooklyn, New York. I promise to uphold its regulations, support its members, and at all times bear

myself in such a manner as will bring honor and respect to the residents of Barbados, both current and former."

As each stepped forward, head slightly bent, the Lodgemaster placed a crimson sash about their shoulders and a matching velvet cap upon their head. Clement closed the ceremony with a blessing.

"Merciful Father, please watch over our new members as they embark upon life in this new land. Let them attain their dreams, and those of all who went before them. And in all things, let them do Your work as You see fit to charge them. Amen."

The applause of the assembly was thunderous.

The members swarmed around the new initiates.

"Dellie, I could use your help on the Sick Committee!"

"Think about the Social Committee. Will you?"

Winnie intervened, her arms around Dellie's shoulders. "I am claiming her right now." She laughed. "Anyone who has seen her sewing knows her place is working with Robes and Regalia."

Dellie made her way to the refreshment table. Her throat was parched from the closeness of the room. Lillian grabbed her elbow. "Come with me. I want you to meet someone."

"Lillian, let me get a cup of punch."

"No, now before he leaves."

"What? Before who leaves?"

"Listen, I want you to meet Tennyson Ward. He is one of the new initiates. Just arrived from Black Rock."

"Oh, I met him." Dellie pulled toward the punch bowl.

"But have you had the chance to talk to him? He is a decent man. From a good family. Friends of the Greens.

"Lillian. Enough."

Lillian held her arm tight. Dellie removed her sister's hand from her arm.

"Lillian, did you hear me? I said *enough*."

CHAPTER FIVE

Standout

Late Fall and Winter 1910

Winnie offered Dellie a lead that she got from her own job sewing at a small shop in Brooklyn Heights but it didn't pan out. Lillian rose with her to help prepare for another day searching for work.

"Dellie, let me help with your hair. I will try pulling it more tightly, giving you a bun at the back of your head. That should make you look older. Maybe that will help. People will take you more seriously."

"Careful not to make me look like Mrs. Applethwaite."

"Hah! I should think not. We don't want to cause people to flee...There now. Let me see you altogether."

Dellie stepped back. "What do you think? I picked up this shirt-waist at a second hand store over on Atlantic Avenue. I noticed that the women here do wear such things with their skirts."

"You look fine." Lillian's eyes ran over Dellie up and down. "Here, though, lift your foot up. Let me run a rag around that shoe again before you go."

Dellie drummed her fingers on the kitchen table as Lillian fussed.

"Sister, I must go. I must catch a trolley. Winnie says I must be at *Abraham and Straus* downtown to meet the head of alterations. I must arrive before his day takes over, and he is too busy to see me. Now, let me leave."

She was discharged with a peck on the cheek.

The morning light was soft and the dark bones of the trees made silhouettes against the gray sky. The air was chilly every day now. She made her way to the trolley stop and waited with other riders who shifted from foot to foot to keep warm. The trolley lumbered along above the street sending out a shower of sparks as it slowed to a stop. Dellie ascended the steps, put her coin in the slot, and took a seat. She glanced around at her fellow riders — some still caught, at this early hour, between sleep and wakefulness.

The streets of downtown Brooklyn were alive with people. Men strode forth in dark suits, mothers clutched handbags and the hands of children. A few newcomers, marked by their tentative steps, ventured the steps of the bank that marked the beginning of the borough's major retail district. Dellie stood and slid to the door. The next stop was hers.

Abraham and Straus, Brooklyn's largest store, took up a full block of the downtown shopping district. Dellie craned her neck upward gazing at the number of floors. "Every shop in Bridgetown could fit in here." She crossed the street and made her way to the front vestibule of wood and glass. Mannequins in a tableau of stylish women in a soda shop filled the windows on either side. Dellie paused. Some sitting, some standing, they appeared almost alive. "Maude will never believe this." She leaned closer, her finger tips on the glass.

"Miss! Fingers off the glass, please!" A bent old man shot her an annoyed look and wiped the window with a damp rag.

"Oh, sir, I am sorry. I didn't mean to make more work for you."

The man shook his rag.

"But if you work here, perhaps you could tell me where I can find Mr. Ames' office. He is head of tailoring and alterations."

"Miss, that is not my line of work. But if you go in and head to the right, the lady at the information desk can tell you."

Dellie struggled to keep her eyes straight ahead and resist the distraction of the fantastic displays of goods to either side. The information desk was easy to find. A smiling young woman sitting on a raised chair gave her directions. "Oh, sure. Just go right through millinery, all the way to the back and down a short flight of stairs. Once you are down the stairs, go left, then right. His office is right there."

Dellie made her way through the growing crowds, willing her eyes away from the polished display cases and the parade of hats, jewelry, and dresses. Electric fixtures cast pools of light and the massive sales floor glowed as dozens of shoppers buzzed about. The place was like an indoor festival.

"Imagine working here!" Her heart thumped with excitement.

The hum of machines directed Dellie. She headed down the short staircase. Pipes ran across the ceiling. Pegs holding threads of all hues covered one wall, bins of buttons sorted by size and color lined one part of the hallway, cubbies with notions—interfacing, hooks and eyes, bias tape—commanded another. Above the hum of a bank of machines came the laughter and chatter of women. At the end of the hallway, just as the woman at the information desk said, was Mr. Ames' office—his name in gold lettering on frosted glass.

Dellie knocked.

"Come in."

She stepped through the door. A bell jingled and a man with a finely trimmed graying beard stepped out from an inner office. Dellie extended her hand.

He did not return the gesture; she let her hand slip to her side.

"Good morning, sir." Winnie had told her to be sure to use the name of the shop when she introduced herself. "My friend at *Corinne's Dress Shop* suggested that I come here. I am a seamstress and I hear that you are hiring additional people for the holidays."

"*Corinne's* is a fine shop. Many of our clients shop there also. I will tell you, however, that we have had many inquiries regarding seamstress work."

"I have had considerable experience, though, sir. Sewing at a shop in Bridgetown that catered to…"

"Well, you are welcome to fill out an application, but as I said, we have lots of applicants." He handed her a sheet with questions, and a pen. His hand directed her to a seat. "There is a wire basket just outside the door on a table. You can leave it there when you are finished."

Dellie placed the application on top of a stack of others. She knew she would never hear from the man again. She would have to think of something else.

The alternative that she had been avoiding thinking of loomed ahead of her. Daywork. There were whispers among the Lodge women and St. Philip's congregation about what that entailed. Almost every one of the island women, particularly the single ones, had bent to that, at one point or another, to see them through. That venture was marked by tales of scrubbing floors on hands and knees in midsummer heat, of hanging damp clothes and sheets on a line in ice-cold weather, inadequate lunches, and short-changed pay envelopes. Each day in that world was a coin toss.

Back at home, Dellie countered Winnie and Lillian's objections.

"M'Ma scrubbed the floor in the Great House."

"But, Dellie, she knew the people and they knew her! She wasn't walking into some stranger's house! And even then... "

"Winnie, you mean to say you yourself never hung damp clothes on the line for the Great House?"

"That was laundry that was brought home to do. Not in the House, as you well know. And Dellie, not in cold that *bites* you. *Bites you,* I say!"

They tried to convince her otherwise. "You know we will take care of you till you find something suitable..."

"Lillian, you know we need to be sending money back to bring the others. Long ago I ran out of what I came with. I came here planning to take care of myself. I will do daywork until I can find something more suitable. It will not be forever. I have made my decision."

———

The hands registered five o'clock in the morning. Before it began its nervous jangling, Dellie reached over and flicked the switch on the clock beside her bed. She gathered her covering about her. "Lillian was right, the cold does bite you." She swiftly pulled on a pair of thick, woolen socks and padded to the bath to wash in water not approaching warm. She charged herself with a cup of hot tea and buttered bread, bundled into coat, hat, and gloves, and headed onto the street.

The gray-tipped clouds promised a sunrise as she trudged, hunched against the cold, to the corner of Myrtle Avenue and Washington Park at the edge of Fort Greene Park. The first of the employers would be arriving soon. The most affluent families sent a servant to the pick. Others of lesser means came by themselves to do the haggling for a woman to clean their house for a day in preparation for a special event, or to fill in for their regular "girl," absent due to illness or some concern in her own family.

Dellie looked at the other women assembled for the standout. All the same, all like her—somber clothing stitched for utility and nothing more, black lisle stockings, hats pulled low against the early morning damp, and a brown bag holding rough work shoes. Some carried a parcel with some sort of food. Lillian had a made her a small lunch after issuing her a stern reminder, "The decent employers will provide a fresh meal, soup or something else hot; those less so will maybe give you cheese, a slice of white bread, and a glass of cold milk. It's best to carry your own bit of something to see you through the day and make sure your stomach doesn't turn."

Dellie scanned the knots of women. The American Negro women huddled in one group, the West Indian women in another. Among the West Indians she noticed the sorting by island and, among those from Barbados, an even further sorting—a clutch of women from Black Rock, a huddle from Apple Hall. Dellie found the group from Gun Hill. With their quiet murmuring and dark clothing, the host of them resembled nuns of some obscure sect gathering to perform some hidden ritual.

They passed on crucial information.

"Stay away from the Graysons if you can. There is a leering boy in that house."

"The Fosters will offer you a single boiled egg and sip of milk and call that a meal before sending you back on your hands and knees to scrub their stairs."

When the first prospective employer drew up, the women fanned out, leaving some consistent, unspoken distance between them; affording each some privacy as she negotiated the price of the strength of her arms, the fee for her attention to the details of dirt, dust, and cobwebs, against her need that day for a few raw-mouthed coins.

Finally, a woman said to her, "Come."

"The Barnetts will be having their holiday party soon. We need an extra pair of hands to get ready. My name is Deirdre." Her voice was lilting and her nervous energy reminded Dellie of Maude, as did her bright chatter that filled the time in the short walk to the mansion on the hill. The flutter in Dellie's stomach waned.

The Barnett home was one of three limestone-fronted houses in an area adjacent to a small park. Dellie and the parlor maid made their way through the servants' entrance under the stairs.

"Wait here. I'll be back with Mrs. Miller. She is the head house-keeper." Dellie took off her hat and gloves, leaned against the wall, and changed into an old pair of work shoes that Winnie had found for her. Barely a moment later, the young parlor maid returned accompanied by the housekeeper, no doubt, notebook in hand.

"Here's the day girl, Ma'am."

The housekeeper slipped her half glasses onto her nose and looked Dellie over.

"Put your hands out, please."

"Excuse me, Ma'am?"

"Your hands, put them before you."

Dellie complied.

"She seems clean enough."

Dellie swallowed hard and held her tongue.

The housekeeper pulled a pen from a chain lanyard around her neck. She turned to the little parlor maid. "Deirdre, have her scrub the front hall floor and steps, and then polish the woodwork. All of it. Then report back to me when she has completed it. And don't you be running your mouth to her the whole time. This isn't the sewing circle."

No, it wasn't. Dellie's mouth was grim.

As temporary day help, she did not have the license to enter areas beyond the kitchen or laundry room. As a "day girl" she was only privy to the muffled sounds of the Barnetts' presence — laughter, the tinkling of china or silver, the rustle of drapery — or sometimes a whiff of perfume. As a "day girl" and not white, she was not admitted to the camaraderie of the regular staff either. She was there only to fill in.

It was the same at her next ten placements. She never worked at the same place more than three days running. Her hours and tasks — scrubbing floors, scrubbing sheets, shoveling coal — generally dictated by a list in the hands of a housekeeper, the head of the permanent staff, with roots in Northern or Western Europe. She was not Miss Standard, not even Dellie, but rather generally addressed as, "you there."

———

Dellie counted herself lucky when a position in Brooklyn Heights offered a brief measure of stability and of respite from the selection and assessment at the standout. At the end of the day, the house-keeper said to her, "You are a good worker. I have some projects that need to be completed and I could use you for a few extra days. Does that work for you?"

Dellie assented.

"Good. Then be here tomorrow. A half-hour earlier. Oh, and by the way, what is your name?"

The next day Dellie pulled her coat tight as the wind bit her. With the small sum she had earned so far at daywork and at small jobs of piecework, she had purchased a coat from a winter clothing sale sponsored by the Lodge. It would do for now, but it was thin and worn in places that the cold was clever at finding. She stepped from the trolley as a church bell somewhere rang seven o'clock. Just a few blocks more — up Willow; past Cranberry, Pineapple, Orange; up to Hicks, and then over to Grace Court. At least at this job, Mrs. Austin, the housekeeper, a tall thin woman with a pair of glasses on her nose, was capable of a smile.

As she approached, the front door of the townhouse swung open. A man in the doorway, wearing a shabby robe and slippers, took the newspaper from a manservants. Behind him a chandelier glowed yellow, its light reflected in a marble floor, laid out in an intricate pattern of black and white. The man's eyes caught hers. Dellie looked away.

The next day, he watched her from a window as she dumped coal dust into an outside bin. When she carried brush and bucket upstairs to clean the bath, she caught him, his face reflected in a mirror, eyes on her — Chandler's look. Later she glimpsed him in a hallway talking to the housekeeper.

At her break, she warmed the soup left for her in the kitchen. As she poured it into a bowl, a heated conversation played through the wall. It was Mrs. Austin and another woman whose voice she didn't recognize.

"He wants to make her a member of the staff, he says."

"Well, you know what that means. And then Miss Sabine will be in a state. And we will have to live with that…"

"True, but more so, I am not willing to be his procurer. I spoke to my priest and he says it is as much of a sin for me as it is for Mr. Harris. And besides, Dellie is a decent girl."

Dellie's spoon clattered to the floor.

The housekeeper pulled her aside at the end of the day.

"The family has requested that you continue coming. They would like to make this arrangement permanent."

"Ma'am?"

"Dellie. Certain members of the family..." She looked over the top of her glasses, directly into Dellie's eyes. She deliberately shook her head from side to side.

Dellie's shoulders sagged. She would return to the standout tomorrow. She accepted her payment for the day and headed home to Lillian's flat on Bergen Street.

CHAPTER SIX

A New York Version

Winter 1911

*T*he argument was heated and neither side saw compromise. Between the "pass the rice" and "a bit more tea" of the Sunday meal in Winnie's small kitchen, a debate raged.

"Think of the number *alone*! Imagine they were able to get thousands upon thousands to stand away from their jobs, their *livelihoods*! That is a powerful thing!" Clemmie jabbed the table for emphasis. "This is the headline in each and every paper and the talk all about the docks."

Egbert, son of the Lodgemaster, was there to pick up some Lodge papers from Clemmie. "The owners of *Knickerbocker* must be in a panic. Think of all that work piling up." He shook his head. "Imagine back home if the workers said they are not going to cut the cane, are not planning to weed, will not hoe."

Dellie clamped her mouth shut. Egbert surely had some opinions. He continued, "This is what some say will happen one day back in Barbados. The people will join together and rise up. Stop working and demand their rights."

The room fell silent.

Dellie focused on her food. Egbert was such a pompous know-it-all. The only person she knew who was capable of strutting while seated. With his airs, she sometimes found it hard to remember that he was only sixteen years old.

"Can't happen," she said. "The whole place would starve. House, field, Great Ones. Colored, black, white. All tied together, whether they see it or not. All eating rice from the same pot."

Lillian spoke up, "That is, if the *field* doesn't work. Suppose the *House* doesn't work."

A round of laughter erupted.

"And the Great Ones have to empty their own chamber pots," Winnie said between bites. She could barely complete the sentence for her laughter.

Lillian gasped. "Winnie! Such talk at the dinner table."

A loud suck-teeth sound interrupted her and silenced them all.

"Forget about what is never going to happen. This thing is happening here." Now Dellie's finger jabbed the table. She pulled a crumpled flier from her pocket and spread it out. "Someone stuffed this into my hand up by the trolley stop near the spot where the dayworkers stand. It says *Knickerbocker Clothing Company* is looking for workers."

Egbert put his fork down. "But you would have to cross the picket line. You would be what they call a scab."

Dellie ignored the comment.

Coleridge wiped his mouth with a napkin. "Isn't it something how they *see* the colored people now? Why are they reaching out to the Negro people all of a sudden?"

Egbert shot in. "Because they want to use us."

"'Tis true, you know. Can't see us before, or only give us what the white won't do, and now they turn to us?" Coleridge's voice was flat. "The colored need to stay away. We don't need them. In fact, there was a meeting at the Baptist Church over in Greenpoint where the strike leaders begged the Negro people not to work. It was in the paper. And a Negro woman wrote a piece in the *Brooklyn Eagle* about the same thing."

Dellie leaned forward. "And did the strike leaders say they have got a job for the Negro woman instead? One that does not involve her hand in a wash bucket?" Her arm swept toward the door. "Has someone knocked and offered me something? It could be the opportunity for the colored woman, the Negro woman." She tapped her chest. "For this colored woman, this Negro woman. Whatever the difference is between the two. 'Tis sure my eyes can't see it. Show them what we can do in this country. To show them we can do any kind of work." She tapped her chest. "And *this* colored woman sitting here is tired of scrubbing floor for a few raw-mouth pennies each week and standing out early-early so the matron can look me over before she point to me as worthy to mop up for her. Check my hands to see if they are clean enough to hold a soggy sponge."

Egbert laid his hands on the table and leaned forward. "And if you believe this is an opportunity for colored women, then you are living within sight of both goat heaven *and* kiddie kingdom. If they treat white women so, you really think they got better planned for anyone else?"

Lillian's eyes pleaded concern. "Besides, Dellie, you are going to cross the picket line? It is the principle. And they say the conditions are poor."

Dellie's face hardened as she looked at Egbert, then Lillian. "So were the conditions at home. So is the condition of me on my knees, hands in a bucket. And..." She cut herself off. They didn't need to hear about the man at Grace Court. She flattened her hands on the table. "I spent hours learning to sew by hand and on the machine. I have a skill that I came here to use, and I am standing out each day to do the work that Cal and M'Ma, and even Henry, struggled to give us the chance to avoid. Don't forget what we left. I don't want my life to be a sea of endless days with my hand in the wash bucket. Don't forget home."

"That's right, Ruth Adele. Don't forget and walk right back into it." Her older sister looked at her without flinching.

Each one crossed her arms over her chests.

Dellie chupsed again, louder this time. "What are they going to show me that I have not seen already?"

———

In the early hours, Dellie found her way across the bridge to Manhattan. The conductor pointed her in the general direction, past lines of dingy, lurking buildings and alleys choked with bins piled high with all manner of garments and fabrics. Already the streets were crowded with people pushing and shoving along the narrow cobblestone ways. Newsboys, faces grubby with smeared ink, mingled with streetwalkers making their way home or drunks sleeping off the night's libations. Street sweepers pushed their brooms in a futile attempt to maintain some semblance of cleanliness.

Ringed around food carts, workers jostled for bread and coffee. A few crammed hot rolls in their mouths, jaws working, crumbs flying. Dellie grimaced. She had seen that kind of belly–to–your–back hunger before, back home, in people tossed from the land, the chattel house that was their home, a pile of boards by the road. Here, too?

She looked anywhere but at them to avoid adding to their shame.

Horse carts cluttered the street as they collected or dispensed goods. She tried, but failed to pick out individual sounds over humming motors, shouting hucksters, and the rumble of wheels on cobblestone. The smell of urine, rotten food, horse droppings, and human sweat mingled together and filled her nostrils.

Bile rose into her throat. She forced it down.

Finally, she caught sight of her street. Adams Place. She knew the building was near the corner. Hunter must be the next one; it was the cross street and she was to use that entrance.

The building loomed like its neighboring structures, distinguished only by the sign painted on the massive façade: *Knickerbocker Clothing Company*. Her mind searched for something else to cling to. Suddenly she was at a clear, green spot near the crest of Free Hill back home. As children, she and her sisters had made the small meadow at the top one of their own secret spots. The only baobab that grew on the island offered its shade as shelter. They'd watch the mist dissipate from the St. George Valley and, if they were lucky, catch a double rainbow after a sudden shower.

A voice, half growl, erupted from beside her. A man pushing a bin overflowing with bolts of fabric glowered. "You're in the way. Move. If you're one of the *schwartzen* that they are bringing in" — he thrust his thumb to the right-- "that's the door."

Just then, a young woman was thrown from the building onto the filthy cobblestones. A man bellowed, his face almost against hers, "See what happens if you bring that garbage in here!"

He tore up a sheaf of papers, showered her with the shreddings, and disappeared back into the gloom of the building.

Dellie's mouth was a grim line. A huddle of women pushed by her and into the building. Shoving away Lillian's warning, she headed to the doorway into which they had disappeared. A rangy, sleepy-eyed man, breath sharp with liquor, opened a creaking metal door.

"Here to work?"

A surge of women, accompanied by a phalanx of burly men, pushed forward. Unable to move either left or right, she was swept along. The movement of the crowd, now a single body, a single entity, stopped. A man with a chewed pencil and a clipboard appeared. "Name!"

She gave it.

"Stitcher," was his response.

"Actually I am skilled in…"

"Stitcher! You start as body stitcher." The voice was a command. "Where's your thread?"

Dellie looked confused. "I…"

"You're supposed to bring your own. Stupid cow."

Dellie's eyes widened.

"Well, we'll provide the thread for today, but it will come out of your pay. What are you standing there for? Find a place. Over there. Ninth floor."

They were herded into an elevator. Dellie gasped and struggled for balance as it jerked upward. Neither she, nor any of the other women crammed in had ever ridden in such a conveyance. The door opened and they stepped into a room bordered by large windows on all sides.

It should have been light and airy, but it was not.

Dellie's chest tightened. Hanging in the air was a cloud of dust thrown off by bolts of fabric being thrown, cut, and stitched. Her mouth, nostrils, and eyes were wicked of any moisture. She stifled a cough and moved ahead.

A short man with a measuring tape about his neck gave instructions. "Take a seat at a machine. Sew from the pile next to your chair on the right. When you finish your job on the piece, put it in the basket at the center of the table. Clear? Anybody speak English?"

Rows and rows of tables, stacks of fabric, lines of women, a few men, many colored, many not, all bowed over, feeding fabric into an army of machines.

Except for the hum of the machines, the room was silent.

Dellie took a seat and began stitching together the pile of crisp white pieces of fabric before her into a shirtwaist—the smart women's blouse that was all the rage.

From time to time she looked up.

Women, young like her, filled the room. The clothes they wore had been washed and pressed dozens, if not hundreds, of times. A few of the women were older, with creases on their brows, the parts in their hair revealing scalps stained black from an overzealous dye job hastily made to stave off the label "too old." Others were much younger, children really, faces thin, pinched, pale.

A small office stood in the corner of the massive room. Every so often the door opened, and a small man clad in shirt sleeves, black suspenders, and self-importance emerged. She caught a glimpse of his workspace. It consisted of two wooden chairs, a small sofa, and a credenza. A screened window opened half-way, a breeze from outside stirring the papers piled high on a massive desk.

On the sewing floor, a man with a long switch behind his back strode up and down the rows, barking orders for faster work. He stopped by a machine, lay his crop upon it, and cut a garment from the spindle. He pulled the woman manning it up by her arm and bellowed at her — pointing out the crookedness of a seam.

"See this!" He thrust his finger at the white fabric. "The stitches are supposed to be a straight line."

The woman trembled. "Please sir, I will be more careful. Don't fire me. Don't let me go. Please. I promise to be more careful. I do."

He pushed her back into her seat and slammed his crop on top of the pile of fabric. She winced. "Make sure you are. There are plenty of people to take your place!"

The room grew hotter as the sun arced through the sky. There was no break to use the toilet or get a cool drink of water. The woman next to Dellie squirmed in her seat, a red stain widening at the back of her skirt. Dellie watched a woman across from her press her arms against her breasts in a useless effort to stem the milk that leaked from them, her eyes willing the floor manager to not see her hands away from the machine.

The air did not move. The windows could not be opened for fear of getting the grime of the city on the crisp, fashionable, white shirts.

———

The sound had droned on for several hours, nagging the edge of Dellie's awareness. It was impossible to make it out clearly over the dirge of the machines. Only at the lunch break did it emerge clearly.

Chanting.

The whispered news telegraphed among the women jammed shoulder to shoulderin the lunchroom.

"It is the strikers."

"They are outside protesting. I heard that Bertha Hamill herself was to be here today."

Bertha Hamill. Dellie had seen her name in the paper. She had been at each of the union rallies.

A small woman hopped onto the broad windowsill and kneeled for a better view. "Come see, they are right below us now!"

Dellie and a group of other women rushed to her side.

Voices, louder, clearer, shouted in unison proclaiming their demands. Suddenly the floor manager broke in, arms flailing wildly. "Put your food down. Now. Just drop it!" He and his lieutenants hustled the workers back to the farm of machines.

"Back to work! Every one at a machine! Now."

Dellie looked down at the pieces of fabric and then at the dozens of shirtwaists heaped into a train of bins.

A shudder ran through her. She was back in Barbados, in Eva's house, the old seamstress carefully considering her work.

"Dellie, you and Winnie have real gifts with the needle. You do more than follow the pattern and keep the stitch tight and straight. I see you change the pattern not just to fit, but to suit each woman and your fancy work with the thread is like a painting." The scene in her head shifted again and she was looking down at the cane fields, watching workers stooped over, weeding, hoeing. Row after row in endless labor, the product of which would sweeten someone else's drink, the profit of which would increase someone else's wealth.

She choked back tears. Suddenly, her leg cramped from the constant pressure of her foot on the machine's peddle. She stood up and took a step back away from the bench to bend and stretch the muscle in her leg.

The floor manager was before her in a flash, slamming his switch hard on the table. She flinched. His face, distorted and red, loomed over hers. "Sit down! There is no time for a break!"

"But, sir, I do have a stitch in my leg."

"It is not the stitch in your god-damn leg that I am concerned about." He grabbed a fistful of fabric. "It is the stitches here that matter!"

The workers to either side of her station kept their heads down and continued sewing. Dellie pulled herself up, the fear a ball in her stomach. She called to the women who had gone before her. *Be with me, Cal.* She asked for strength. *Be with me, Jesus.* She smoothed her skirt and her own shirtwaist, now sodden with sweat.

"I am leaving."

He bent until his face was level with hers. Operators lifted their feet from the pedals. The room fell silent.

"No one leaves till the shift is over!" His mouth sprayed spittle. His face was nearly against Dellie's and purple with anger. She gripped the back of the chair for strength.

"Excuse me, sir, but I am leaving."

Two other women from tables across the room also stood. The floor manager flung Dellie's chair to the side.

Come, Jesus.

The shop owner appeared in the doorway of his office, drawn by the silence of the machines and the clatter of the metal chair on the floor. All heads turned.

"Let them go. Just let them go." His hands gestured downward in a patting motion. "They're probably rabble-rousers from the outside. Union infiltrators. Likely some kind of socialists, anarchists maybe, or communists. Get them out of here."

He pointed to the other two women. "Boys! Them, too!" He jutted his chin out at two rough-looking young men hanging at the edges of the floor. "Make sure they don't take anything. See them out. All the way out." He set his mouth and shook his head.

The boys shoved them across the work floor to the door. The thugs paused long enough to allow them to take their coats and bags from the hooks by the elevator. Then one by one, the grimy boys pushed them against the wall in full view of others.

A tall boy, hair slick with grease snatched Dellie's bag from her hand. The breath ceased moving in her as he tore into it. She shuddered as his sausage-grease-and-potato hands touched her things — a handkerchief from M'Ma, Cal's lock of hair, a cow-eye nut that the little boy had given to her, the bit of blue sea glass, the letter from Pendril. Once he finished with his invasion the three boys forced the women into the elevator. Then the biggest of the boys drew his arm back and struck Dellie, full force, in the face.

She stumbled. The two women grabbed her as she fell.

He laughed.

When they reached the ground level, he pushed them outside.

For a second, the women were dazzled by the brightness of the cobblestone alley. Without a word, they made their way to the main street, through the gauntlet of deliverymen, Dellie stumbling along as the other two women held her up.

As they approached the sidewalk jeers and curses from the strikers assaulted them.

"Scab!"

"Lackey!"

"Traitor!" Someone kicked at her legs. Dellie hit the ground hard, the wind knocked out of her.

"No! Stop!" A woman stepped forward arms raised. At the sound of her voice, a foot, ready to strike again, stopped mid-air.

"These women are leaving! Are you crazy! We're not thugs like the bosses!"

Dellie tried to focus on the whirl of faces and bodies around her. Her right eye was swelling shut, but she could make out the shape of a young woman.

The figure bent over her, stretching out an arm to help her to her feet.

A sudden flash of light made Dellie wince. The woman turned and shouted.

"Can't you photographers control yourselves?" She turned her head back and whispered to Dellie, "I am sorry."

She helped Dellie steady herself. The firm pressure of her hand on Dellie's back encouraged her to breathe. She sucked in air in brief jerks. Dellie followed the woman a step away from the crowd.

"I am Bertha Hamill," she said. "And you?"

"Dellie Standard."

"Well, Dellie Standard, you left. Or got thrown out. I guess you see now why we strike." Bertha took Dellie's hand in hers and raised them both in a gesture of power and solidarity. The photographer snapped, and snapped, and snapped.

CHAPTER SEVEN

Own Way

*T*he picture was on the front page of three newspapers. Caption: *Unionist Bertha Hamill and an unknown target of factory thugs.*

Dellie smoothed the paper and stared at the photograph. There she was, front page. She held her face in her hands for a moment then read on. The paper mentioned the unions involved in the action: *the local 25, The Women's' Trade Union, the International Ladies Garment Workers Union.* It described Bertha Hamill as an activist, noting that she lived in Manhattan and was an immigrant from the Russian Ukraine. The articles also described the society women—Anna Morgan and Alva Smith Vanderbilt Belmont—who supported the strikers. It went on to describe the bosses, who owned three such factories. Dellie's head jolted up from the page. How many women's lives were in that trap? The paper did not mention Dellie or the other women cast onto the street like dogs. Lillian and Winnie took turns reading the coverage aloud to each other, adding comments meant to be lessons for Dellie.

"What were these Great Ones there for?" Winnie sucked her teeth in derision and pointed at a photograph gracing page two. She called Lillian's name, but trained her eyes on Dellie. "This one, with the fur about her shoulder. How much does she pay the woman who cooks and cleans for her? Who washes her garments after her monthlies? What are the conditions for the workers in her house?"

Lillian's head bobbed up and down. "Whenever I see that many last names upon one person, I know they're trouble." Lillian's eyes were on Dellie. "Winnie, *you* know anybody with sense stays away when trouble is brewing."

"Of course, and it doesn't take much sense..."

Dellie stood, upsetting Winnie's teacup, and stormed from the room.

Dellie's story raced from ear to ear. Everyone in the Bajan community and Brooklyn neighborhood had something to say as they dropped by with food and well wishes that night.

Mrs. Iannacci: "We all came here for something different and found the same. That's why Ettera and me opened our own store. We live by our own rules now. We benefit from our own sweat."

A man from the trolley stop: "One day the Negro people are going to join together like those garment workers and demand change. You wait and see."

Zuleika Williams of the Lodge Sick Committee: "Remind me again why we came here?"

Dellie was grateful for the end of Lillian's editorializing and for the cool packet of herbs and ice that her sister placed against her eye. She remained curtained off in her room all the next day. Now contrite, Lillian checked on her almost hourly. She enticed her with tea and cocoa or one of the dishes prepared by the women from the sick committees of the Lodge and of St. Philip's Church.

"Dellie," her words were gentle. "Dellie, try some coconut bread from Estelle. She made it special."

The answer was curt. "Leave me, sister."

On the second day, Lillian was more insistent.

"Dellie."

Dellie didn't respond, and kept her eyes closed.

"Dellie! That Hamill woman is here to see you. She brought some food and some papers on the union for you to read."

"Tell her I appreciate the visit, but I am unavailable."

Later, Lillian called to her again. "Dellie, it's Anelle, Reverend Fletcher's wife from St. Philip's. She says she wants to read some of the Psalms with you."

"Just tell her I am unavailable, but I am grateful for her concern."

"*Dellie.*" She could hear the horror in her sister's voice. "Dellie, she is the *priest's* wife."

"I am unavailable. Can't you leave a body alone?"

When Lillian left, Dellie lit the kerosene lamp. She pulled her handbag from its place atop the makeshift dresser. The clasp opened easily and she overturned the bag, spreading the contents on her bed. The glass piece caught the light of the lamp and she picked it up, its blue translucence still calling the color of the Barbados Sea. She touched the cow-eye nut, the smooth brown of its surface, soothing. She reached inside the bag, her fingers remembering the small pouch that held the lock of Cal's hair. She pulled it out and held the handkerchief that she had tied around the dark swirl of chestnut locks so long ago. She lifted it to her nose, the almond smell filling her spirit, pulling her back. She longed to feel Cal's arms cradling her.

Steps silent, she made her way to the roof of Mrs. Cumberbatch's brownstone and stepped into the chill night. The whole of the borough, down to the bridges and up past the park, spread before her. It was the gloaming, and as the full moon gained its advantage, a breeze, chill and silent picked up. She felt the cold on her bare feet, bare hands, on the straight part in her hair and on her exposed neck.

Dellie closed her eyes and felt herself float up, up, up. She was back on the street among the strikers. She walked through the sea of faces, of those who had manned the picket line. Eyes looked through her as she strolled across the factory floor. Her eyes caught those of a young girl, as a man emerged from the manager's office and wrapped the small figure in yards and yards of fabric that transformed itself into the girl's burial cloth. The scene shifted and she was back in Barbados. She stood in Eva's sewing room and watched herself sewing a gown for one of the young women of the Great House. She walked past herself, sitting, and stood by the stack of fine fabric on the table — silk, voile, linen the weight of tissue. Back again in the factory, she sat before a sewing machine, her hands affixed to and part of the equipment. She pulled and pulled, struggling to release them, but they were held fast — she and the machine fused as one.

As the moon made its nightly circuit, Dellie crafted her plan. By morning, she knew what she would do. No more waiting to be accepted or to be summoned, she would craft her own way. She brought the proposition to Winnie at first light. Together they worked out the idea, worked the figures and laid out the time table.

The clear, end-of-day shafts of light lay boldly across her sister's table as Dellie stepped into the kitchen. Lillian looked up and her face fell. While the swelling was down, Dellie's eye and cheek still wore their badge of unnatural yellows, purples, and greens. She had made no attempt to hide it.

Dellie cradled her hands around the cup of tea that Lillian set before her until her heart released her voice to speak. She spread her fingers wide on the smooth oilcloth.

"These are the hands I have got to rely on. I talked to Winnie earlier today. We are both going to save to buy a machine. We'll take in basic sewing from the small shops and fancy work from the big ones. I will have to find a family to work for, one with children to be cared for, and a mother who needs help though, since that will not be enough to live on. No more daywork. No more standing out like stock each day like some goat or cow being examined by the speculator back home, checking for an investment. No more working in one of those factories. I will try it for one year."

"Dellie, part of the reason we came here was to stay out of some Great House. Sister, you walked that road already. Coleridge and I..."

Dellie silenced her sister. "I came here to make my own way. If it doesn't work out, I'm going back."

Lillian gasped. "Going back! Dellie, you can't."

"That is right, going back. I didn't leave one hell to jump into another. At least at home, I understand the boundaries. Here, I haven't seen one yet. These people here are without limit."

Dellie listened to her sister's silence.

CHAPTER EIGHT

Some Time Together

*A*lthough she saw him sometimes with the neighborhood men since the day he stopped by with newspapers and magazines for Coleridge, Owen Gibson had never done more than tip his hat in her direction and, as good manners required, smile when they passed each other on the street. Today, he actually spoke: "Miss Standard…"

Dellie jumped. A gas lighter came by and lifted his flame to the globe. It cast a pool of golden light about them as the glimmering blue dusk crept across the city.

Dellie smiled.

"I see you have a newspaper there. I take it you have been following news of the strike." His voice was deep and silky, words colored by a languorous accent hinted of trees and open fields. Thick, long lashes set off an intense gaze.

Dellie's smile wavered, but she nodded. "I read about it every day."

"I've been following it, too. Not too many of our people have had an interest. They feel it doesn't have anything to do with them. But I believe that what is happening with the garment workers will affect us all. Sooner or later."

Our people. Dellie's brow furrowed. It was rare that anyone, either American Negro or West Indian acknowledged any commonality and used "us" or "we" when referring to the two groups.

"Hmmm. I see that the Great Ones are the same here and back home. But back home, nothing like that happens. The place is so small that the Great Ones can control the lot of things. Control who can work, where they can work, who can get an education and for how long. My mother knew that and tried to tell me. She made me promise to come here. She believed that leaving would make the difference. But I am not sure that is enough of a change. I do think here, though, people have different expectations. Will try to make their way. They are not going to put up with such foolishness."

She looked at him. "From anybody."

"That's God's honest. Miss Standard, I would like to talk to you about these matters some more. Perhaps one day we can spend some time together?"

———

"You are going with *whom*?"

"Owen, I said. Are you hard of hearing?"

"But he ..."

"Yes, Lillian, that's right. He is taking me on a walk."

A warm breeze took the edge off the end-of-winter damp. The pair wandered through the warren of streets in Brooklyn Heights that served as a prelude to the vista of Manhattan. The window boxes sat dormant, waiting to color up with geraniums as soon as warmth gained the advantage. Occasionally, a spear of green strained through the loosening soil. They turned a corner, and Owen led her to the loading dock of an old building on the shore, not far from where Clemmie and Coleridge worked. Dellie caught her breath as she viewed the river and the sky.

"I worked here when I first came to the North. I unloaded tobacco from ships coming from the South and elsewhere. I'll never forget the view from this spot."

The blue-gray of the East River glistened in the midday sun as if someone had cast jewels on a swath of iridescent satin. If she listened closely enough she could hear the cracking and pinging from islands of ice melting as they drifted downstream. Straight across,

Manhattan rose — acres of trees, their light trunks blushing green with the hint of late-winter warmth sat against the oil gray of the tenement and factory districts. To her right, a bridge arced over the water. To her left, another bridge framed the port where she had entered. The sheen of the open ocean lay beyond.

She rested both arms across the railing. "I came here, thinking I knew what to expect. And I see now I couldn't even imagine it." She turned to Owen. "I think of my father and my brothers and sisters back home. They don't even have the words to conjure this place. Henry is always writing about the land back home, and he doesn't know a place like this exists. Beautiful and terrible. It's like home that way. Paradise and hell. And yet..."

"But, Dellie, there isn't any place you can just see or read about, or even just visit and understand. No more than your home or mine. You're right, though. To me, sometimes when your family describes Barbados, it sounds like paradise."

She looked at him, surprised that he actually remembered the name of the island. Didn't call it Bermuda or Bahamas, or worse, "that place you come from."

His voice called her back. "And you're right, other times it sounds like someplace else. Like someplace I know."

She ignored the subtle chide at her choice of the word "hell." Owen continued, his eyes now on a scene somewhere else. "Sounds the same as North Carolina."

"Owen." She touched his arm to pull him back. "The Lodge gives us lessons in citizenship. It tells us how the government here works. It takes you to the bank so your money will be safe. It helps you with your plan. But I do tell you, the Lodge folks have never seen the things I saw in those six hours at Knickerbocker. Row upon row of people, their lives tied to a *machine* and a man yelling, 'Faster! Straighter!' It was just home in a different dress. I still have dreams about it."

"Home in a shirtwaist," he said, his voice filled with irony. "But the Unionists will rally the people and there will be changes."

"The conditions and pay are important, yes. But that was not the worst of what I saw that day. Not even the shop hooligans with their hands all over us and our things, or my blackened eye."

She looked at the dark rookery of tenements across the river and thought of the lives of the people she knew and of the ones she had seen in the shop. Every person there concerned with family, and

111

each someone's mother, sister, brother, father, uncle, son, daughter moved by a hope and a plan.

"The worst was not being *seen*. Not being a person. The worst was seeing my photograph in the paper with the woman who claimed to help me." Dellie looked away from Owen. "I saw her face, the look in her eye. I was not a person to her. I was just some *thing*, someone to make a point through all the newspapers. The shop saw me as a pair of hands for their use. She saw me and my black eye for her use. Nothing more. The same for all of those women lined up at the machines as if they, too, were part of the machinery."

Owen's finger tilted at the air. "But once the unions and the movement take hold, things will change. I can see it already beginning on the rails. We see ourselves as brotherhood. One man, Freddy Edmunds, talks all the time about coming together to improve the conditions we railmen work under."

He leaned toward her, arms waving to make his points about life on the rail line — the chance to see some of the country against the long hours, the humiliation of being called "George," after George Pullman, the owner of the company, and not by his own name as clearly written on his name tag. He talked about "spotters" placed on the trains by Mr. Pullman to keep porters in line and to report any organizing activity.

Owen's eyes set on her, and his voice took on a cadence like that of the priest back home at St. George, on the days when he was filled with his words. Though she was the single being in his audience, Owen sounded like he was addressing a crowd, his eyes wide, seeing something else altogether.

CHAPTER NINE

With Delivery

*T*he day was unexpectedly warm and Coleridge placed a chair in the small patch of grass that posed as a front yard. Dellie waved from down the street, picking up her pace as he gestured toward her. Coleridge spoke first.

"Dellie-girl, a letter came today from Pendril! I just started reading it. Listen."

Dellie was rooted to the spot. There had only been a scattering of letters, and with the arrival of each one she waited and hoped to hear some mention of her name. "How is Dellie? Have you seen Dellie? Will you give my regards to Dellie?" But she never did.

My dear cousin Coleridge,

I know that it has been a while since you have heard from me, but please know that I think of you often. I remember when we were boys and killing time down at the docks. It seems we were always in trouble with someone back then, the schoolmaster, the dock master, your father, my Auntie. Remember the time we found that pack of drawings of naked women and your father cuffed us and confiscated the pictures?

Dellie chupsed. Clemmie reddened. "I suppose I should have skipped that part."

Or when we stuffed ourselves on candy from the bits of change we made from delivering papers here and there for the dock foreman? Remember when we used to fashion small boats and set them to sail, imagining where they landed? Well, there are days when I wish you could be with me, man, to see what I see. This world of God's is truly something.

Dellie pictured Pendril, pen in hand in some crude room in an exotic port. When he wrote and when she read his letters again after Coleridge had finished, she could hear his voice, hear him say the words he had written. The letters, where she was not mentioned, was all that was left of him. All the remains of what they had been together. The words, written to someone else, would have to be enough.

———

Dellie laughed as Winnie overturned her bag on the table, scattering a ream of paper—pages torn from women's magazines and catalogs. "I have been looking into sewing machines and pricing them. I spoke to the owner of the shop where I work, and she gave me some ideas of what to look for."

They spent the next hour sorting through by style, model, and brand.

"Winnie, these are all too dear. Even with a loan from the Lodge, we'd be bent with age before we laid down a stitch."

"And so? You have an idea?"

"I have seen a shop off of Atlantic Avenue that is chock full of second-hand goods. We should look there.

The host of goods for sale nearly obscured the gold lettering in the window—*Sacklow and Sons*. Save for that, it was impossible to tell where the street ended and the shop began. After making their way through a maze of wardrobes, old dry sinks, and musty wing-back chairs, Dellie and Winnie found the door. Inside, mismatched stacks of china plates teetered next to piles of books. Spoons of all sizes overflowed from a pasteboard box. A rack of hats adorned with drooping feathers stood like a sentry before a line of never-to-be-worn-again men's formal wear. It appeared as if chaos itself had taken up residence. In the filtered light and swirling dust, a jowly, red-faced man with a crown of white hair sat at a desk, his face creased as he worked rows and columns in a ledger. Dellie pulled a kerchief from her handbag to muffle a sneeze. The man looked up.

"Good morning?" he said, a question at the end of his voice and in his eyes. He squinted. "I have never seen red hair on..." He caught himself. "On someone...ah, on someone..." His face flushed a deeper crimson.

Dellie kept her gaze steady. "Yes, often people are surprised to see red hair on someone in need of a sewing machine." She hoped that his embarrassment might help drive down the price.

"A sewing machine! Well, ladies, I just got some fine ones in."

Winnie hissed in Dellie's ear, "How did you find this place? It came to you in a nightmare?"

"Just mind that your sleeves don't topple something that we will have to pay for. Let's see what he has to offer."

They wended their way behind the proprietor further into the shop. "They are back here, next to the fishing gear."

"Of course, where else would they be?"

Dellie ignored Winnie's muttering.

"Here they are, ladies. Do you have something in mind?"

Winnie pulled a sheet of paper from her purse. "This is what we are looking for. Something on a stand, with this type of choke, a vibrating shuttle, and this sort of feed..."

Two machines met their criteria. "One moment, ladies." He called out in a language neither woman understood and a young woman about Maude's age appeared, curly, black hair piled on top of her head. With a flourish, the proprietor extracted a rag from one of his pockets and handed it to her. The woman took it and brushed several decades of dust from the machines. At a gesture from the man, she demonstrated the trestle, the feeder, and the storage drawers on each machine. Their eyes fell on the same one, an established brand. Legs sturdy, no wobbling. A bit of machine oil and some polish and it would be perfect. The proprietor caught the look between them. The silent young woman then smiled at Lillian and Dellie before disappearing again into the darkness.

"I can give you this for seven dollars."

"With its rickety legs!" said Lillian.

"The brand is old. Other makers have come along," Dellie added. "More modern. We were thinking four dollars."

"Now, ladies." He dragged the syllables out.

"Come, Winifred. I know of another shop." She pulled Winnie's sleeve and turned toward the door.

"I'd be willing to come down a bit. Six-fifty."

"Come, Winnie. We don't have time to waste with people who are not serious."

"Six."

"Five"

"Five-fifty."

"With delivery?"

The man paused. Dellie turned to go.

"Fine. With delivery."

"I think we can have a deal. Now let's consider a payment plan. We are prepared to put a dollar down."

"A payment plan?" The proprietor's voice was incredulous.

This time Winnie turned toward the door.

The storeowner sighed. "Come, ladies. Come to my desk. Let's work out a payment card and I'll give you a receipt. If you come and I am not here, you make your payment to my niece Pauline." He gestured toward the shadows.

The transaction completed, the two women headed toward the light, the likely direction of the door. On the edge of a shelf, Dellie glimpsed a slim book, binding frayed — *The British Mercantile Marine* by Edward Blackmore. She pulled it down and opened it. It was a detailed description of British shipping and commerce, the education of the Mercantile Officer, duty and discipline in the Mercantile Navy, as well as routes and ports.

She thought of the letter nested deep in her handbag and found the proprietor's niece. "How much is this?"

Pauline raised her right hand, fingers apart.

"Five cents?"

Dellie rummaged in her handbag and pulled out a coin.

"I'll take it."

CHAPTER TEN

Mrs. Cumberbatch's Proposal

Winnie promised that something long term with a family would come up soon to save her from the standout. They had found a machine like they planned, hadn't they? Each day Dellie went over her figures. The daywork she was back to doing brought in something, but she still had expenses. She needed something to give to Lillian and Coleridge, money for home, and her part of the payment on the machine.

But Winnie turned out to be right. Clemmie came home one night after cricket, with news. "Dellie, my friend Hal...he is in the Lodge, the one who thinks he knows how to play cricket...he heard about some work. His wife's friend is leaving her job because she is moving to New York."

Dellie looked confused. "I thought we *were* in New York."

He came to her rescue. "You know, the *City*, gal, across the bridge. She works for an Irish lady. Lace-curtain kind. Mrs. Fettes. Says she is good to work for. So with her girl leaving, Mrs. Fettes will need someone to help her clean, cook, and take care of her children. They are Catholic, though, so they have got that strangeness, you know, the Pope, and only fish on Friday. But that is not any of your mind. The trolley runs right near her place. The pay is decent. She needs the help for sure, with a new baby on the way." And so it was arranged.

The house on Clinton Avenue stood across town from the Holders on the west slope of Clinton Hill. At the hill's crest were the fine mansions — homes that the rich City people, the Pratts and others, had built for their children. On the south east slope were their carriage houses with servant quarters above. The west slope and its brownstones were becoming the favored neighborhood of the up-and-coming children and grandchildren of the first wave of immigrants from Ireland.

Dellie checked the address on her paper and that on the plaque hanging from the gaslight in the front yard. This was the right place. Roses still weeks from bloom crawled over the wrought-iron pole in the yard; ivy wound through the grates covering the windows at street level. Dellie climbed down the steps to the door. She didn't have the chance to knock. The door flew open, revealing a pregnant woman with two children swirling about her skirt.

"See, I told you I saw her!" said the taller girl.

"I saw her first," said the younger one. "Can she play with us now, Mummy?"

Mrs. Fettes smiled and laughed. "These are my two children. I hope they don't frighten you away! You must be Dellie. Come in."

Mr. Kevin and Mrs. Grace Fettes had just bought the house a few years ago. He was a druggist who ran a small pharmacy on DeKalb Avenue, one of the main thoroughfares of Brooklyn. A hard-working man, he left early in the morning and returned late at night. Three days a week, he came home for lunch with his family. There, every day, was also Mrs. Fiona Watson, Mrs. Fettes' mother. A sturdy woman with striking white hair and an enormous bosom, she took the trolley mid-morning to spend the day with her only daughter. The only surviving child of Irish immigrants who had arrived on the Coffin Ships, she possessed both a determination that informed every movement and a manner that reminded Dellie of her own grandmother. She, too, had M'Ma's sharp eyes, and the gentle hands that loved to pet her grandchildren. Just like M'Ma, she found every excuse to touch them — from brushing Margery's hair to wiping Molly's ever-running nose.

The Fettes house teemed with activity and Dellie fell into the daily rhythm. Clear the breakfast dishes and sweep the kitchen floor. Dust and straighten the upstairs. Play with the children while Mrs. Fettes rested. Prepare lunch for the family. Go shopping with Mrs. Watson. Tuesdays wash, and Thursdays supervise the coal delivery. And in between, play with the two girls who followed her about and found her every move fascinating.

"Dellie, I can help you! I can spread the jam!"

"Dellie, tell us the story about the monkey again!"

"Dellie, draw me a picture of Clive the Parrot. Draw it right here!"

"Let's play 'the Man in the Cane'! I'll be the man. You run away. See my fangs!"

Grace Fettes smiled as she handed Dellie the smooth white envelope at week's end. Dellie's hand trembled a bit as she put it in her handbag. She had been counting and recounting this money in her mind. Some for Coleridge and Lillian, some for trolley fare, she also needed new stockings and a new pair of shoes to replace the ones broken down by the New York cobblestones. And she'd put some with Lillian's to send home to help with the children and towards with Maude's passage.

"Thank you, Mrs. Fettes. You don't know what this means." Mrs. Watson stepped in to prepare a cup of tea. "Yes, she does know. And so do I."

Dellie was the first to arrive home. Winnie knocked a moment later. They counted the money in the envelope.

"If I give this much to you toward the machine and this to Lillian and Coleridge, then I can..." A sharp rap at the door interrupted their calculations. Winnie rose.

Mrs. Cumberbatch stood on the other side of the door, her face fixed as if assaulted by a bad smell. From one of the smaller villages in St. George Parish back home, Florence Cumberbatch and her husband had been one of the first to leave for New York. She and her husband owned the building and lived on the first floor. Several young women rented rooms from her on the second and third floors. Mrs. Cumberbatch reveled in her role as property owner. There were many questions among the Brooklyn Bajan community about how the Cumberbatch family had amassed so quickly the resources to purchase a home in the borough. While Mr. Cumberbatch and their son were generally regarded as harmless dupes, almost every bit of speculation on the part of the community involved some unethical, criminal, or outright malevolent action on the part of Mrs. Cumberbatch.

"Where is Mr. Green?" she asked Winnie coolly.

"Not back yet, Ma'am."

"You are Winifred Holder, aren't you?"

"Yes, Ma'am."

"You are not residing in here now are you? The Greens seem to have some sort of guesthouse going."

Winnie's eyes widened. "No, Mrs. Cumberbatch. I live not far from here with my husband."

"Oh, I see. Well, you tell Mr. Green the rent due tomorrow. I expect it by six o'clock." She glared over Winnie's shoulder at Dellie. "And, girlie, since you *are* living here, then this is a *three*-person place. Tell him we got to talk." She turned and headed to man her station at the top of the stoop.

Winnie drummed her fingers on the table. "Needs to talk. That can't be good. She is up to something."

Dellie cradled her head in her hands. "Lord, how is a body supposed to get ahead here?" She pulled a scrap of paper from her handbag then foraged for a pencil among Lillian's jars.

The two were still at the table working when Lillian arrived. "What are you ladies up to?" she said as she put the kettle on for tea.

Dellie and Winnie looked at each other. Dellie answered, an edge of panic in her voice. "Mrs. Cumberbatch was down here earlier looking for the rent. I think she is going to raise it, because I am here. Said my being here makes it a three-person place."

Lillian sucked her teeth. "Do not let her mark off a place for herself in your mind. She is always looking for a way to line her pockets. Last month it was something else." She turned around. "Let Coleridge take care of it. You want milk in your tea? A biscuit with some butter?"

———

Coleridge's loud steps reverberated through the flat long before the door opened.

"Well, I talked to *Mr.* Cumberbatch, or maybe I should say to Herself's husband. He is now serving as the go-between, like Mr. Gladstone did for the Queen. He went on and on about the troubles of being the landlord and how much things cost in this country and such. He reminded us, this is not home. In case we forget. Well and all, he named a proposition for a new arrangement. Mrs. Cumberbatch is going to raise the rent here, or let Dellie rent one of the rooms up by Enid, on the second floor, when that tenant moves out next week. Then, and hear this, she claimed she lost money when my cousin was here for a few weeks way back in the spring. Remember? Before Dellie came? Him using more water. I told Mr. Cumberbatch that my cousin is in the habit of washing only one side of his face each day, so he couldn't have used too much."

His laugh rang out at his joke, but the concern in his eyes was evident. Dellie and Lillian looked at each other, then away.

Dellie chewed on a pencil as she ran sets of figures through her own mind.

She touched her sister's hand, and pulled from her pocket the paper with the figures. "I am going to give you all something toward the rent. You are both too good to me. This will make it easier. It is to help out. I will take the place upstairs. I came here to try to make my own way. And with the Fettes money and the sewing I can."

Lillian looked at her softly, "Dellie, you are the one who is too good. We are not taking your money. We all have to be together for each other." She turned to Coleridge. "That battle-ax upstairs doesn't think anyone has got a life and plans but herself." She shook her head from side to side.

Coleridge chupsed. "You'd better be careful what you say there, darling. She is going to be around a long time, you know. Heaven don't want her, and the devil won't take her, yuh know nuh."

He threw his head back again. Lillian swatted him with her dishtowel. Dellie looked down. Another reason why she needed a place of her own.

She pulled her coat from the hook by the door. "It is light out. I am going over to Winnie's before it gets dark. We have matters to discuss about our sewing business." She turned to Lillian and Clemmie. "I'll be back when the lamplighter comes round."

Dellie buttoned her coat and stepped onto the sidewalk. She glanced up at Mrs. Cumberbatch at her post in the parlor window. At least it wasn't high summer and she would be spared the land-lady's nightly declamation from her chair on top of the stoop:

"Think! The white people needed all this space! Two families and four singles can live where there was one before. How much space can a body need! A front parlor, back parlor, a study, a bedroom for each, a dressing room. Foolishness. Can only be in one room at a time I say. All these rents." At this point in the soliloquy her chest always puffed out and her back straightened. "I save to buy more house!" The whole neighborhood was glad for the still chill evenings that abbreviated her finance lessons.

————

Mrs. Cumberbatch stood in the middle of the room when Lillian helped Dellie move her small collection of things in. A short, wide woman trussed into her clothes by whalebone and cotton, she filled the room with her arrogance. Back home, she had served in one of the Great Houses. Her people were still there. There she had learned well how to treat those she considered beneath her: just as she had been treated. She turned to Dellie.

"Listen here, Dellie Standard. The rent is due at six on Friday. I serve the evening meal downstairs at six thirty weekdays, seven on Saturday and Sunday. You are on your own for your other food. There is to be no food in the room. I am not planning to be catering to rats. And no guests. I can't have people I do not know round about my house. You understand?"

Dellie nodded. "But Mrs. Cumberbatch, I will be taking my meals with my sister."

The woman turned to Lillian. "And you. I expect you to keep your younger sister close to the rules. According to the government, you and husband, Mr. Coleridge Green, are responsible for her."

"Close to the rules? But Dellie has not..."

Mrs. Cumberbatch cut her off. "That's right. Close to the rules I say. Not associating with rabble-rousers, with unionists. Or consorting with trouble-making American Negroes!"

Dellie suppressed a chupse and turned her eyes toward her new quarters. A small dresser, a chair, a mattress on the floor with a rough, gray blanket folded at the foot.

"And, girlie, don't you be turning up your nose at the blanket. It's for when you are sleeping, not for wearing to a ball at the Great House. Besides, this room is plenty warm. I don't want to see you opening the window against the heat. The outside air is for God to take care of, not me."

"Yes, ma'am. It is fine. I'm fine. I'm sure."

"You are right, it is fine. It a Great House compared to what you up-country girls are used to! Remember now, the rent. Friday at six o'clock."

Mrs. Cumberbatch left the room. The two sisters shook their heads.

"Sister, finish getting settled. Then come down to eat. I am going to prepare some dinner. I finally got my hand on some decent snapper."

Dellie shoved Mrs. Cumberbatch's manner to the back of her mind and began to place her few things on the dresser. Her thoughts drifted. She stood at the gate to the tenants' compound at Taborvilla, back home.

Cal's words replayed in her head. "You got to make your own plan." But there was something about Mrs. Cumberbatch and her questions that Dellie didn't like. It sounded as if she might have another plan altogether.

CHAPTER ELEVEN

Not Every Story

D ellie fussed as Lillian and Winnie worked on her hem. "Be still, Dellie, let me try this pin right here..."

In just a little while, the Annual Gala of the Lodge of the Sons and Daughters of Barbados of Brooklyn, New York and Barbados, West Indies would commence in the hall of St. Philip's Church.

Lillian's kitchen and front room had been full all day with women preparing fish cakes, coconut bread, macaroni pie, and other treats for the accompanying feast. Coleridge had come in but left quickly. "I will leave you women to yourselves. Just remember to only wash the forks, the cost of washing the knives will surely cut into Mrs. Cumberbatch's legacy."

With the pots and pans put away, the kitchen and front room became the salon where the domestics and needle workers of the tiny West Indian community transformed themselves into the women that they were. Hair was brushed smooth, curled with the hot iron, and pinned up. The soft rustle of tissue paper rippled through the room, as lace collars and cuffs were unfolded for pressing. Shoes were buffed to a high shine and corsets tied to a breathtaking firmness.

Like its congregation, the church basement had been transformed. Paper streamers made from old magazines adorned the
walls and ceilings. Fine glassware borrowed from the church graced
the long table of food. The refreshment committee directed guests
to the best morsels. The food critics made their notes: "Anna's cod-
fish is always too salty. I told her last time to wash it *four* times after
she flakes it. Hard headed. Humphh..."

"Clymene's coconut bread is still the finest. It is the same recipe
as her mother uses at home, that touch of nutmeg...."

The room was a swirl of people: men in their good dark suits,
saved for week after week, and women in fine dresses, their arms
bright with silver bangles that were "too noisy, too much of a distraction" for their employers. The chatter rose and fell. A quartet of
colored men played dance music.

Dellie, her face flushed in excitement, moved among the groups of
people. She drifted toward a small cluster of women on the other side of
the room. There was news going around that a man from Workman's
had been turned away at immigration. Pearl had the news.

"That's right. Poor Graham Philips was sent back. My aunt
told me what happened in a letter. When they examined him in
New York, they said he had a limp and packed him right back off!
Seems that he twisted it running for the skiff to take him aboard at
Bridgetown."

Heads shook in sympathy.

"Well, he plans to sail and try to enter again in a few months.
But it means filing again and redoing all the paperwork."

"Well, maybe he'll be early for a change and walk, not run, next
time."

Lillian and Coleridge were in a deep conversation with Anelle
Fletcher, the reverend's wife. Dellie could hear a bit of it. It involved
Henry and the news in his last letter. Lillian's tone was serious: "He
said that they were all called to do weeding at Taborvilla. I know
he must have nearly worked himself into a stroke being asked to do
such work."

Anelle answered, "All the leaving to New York, Panama, and all
around means a reshuffling of the work. I had a letter last month
from my people over in St. John's, and it is the same there."

Coleridge's voice was rough. "Lillian, tell her how Mr. Chandler
threatened to cast the woman, Louise, off the land when she groused

at him about being tasked for weeding! She has been serving in the House for years and has never set foot in the field! What is he thinking?"

Coleridge caught Dellie's eye and nodded, inviting her closer. Dellie took a few steps and settled nearer.

Charles Walcott, the Lodgemaster, joined them. "It is not what he thinks, it is what he *knows*. He knows Great House still rules. And he knows that if your Louise wants a roof over her head, she'll do what he says — weed cane, or boil eggs, scrub sheets, or dance a jig."

Dellie moved away. She didn't need to be reminded of that reality in the midst of light and music and swirling dresses.

From somewhere to her right, Dellie picked up a snatch of conversation. "My sister's husband's nephew's boy, you remember, Lane he is called..." Dellie turned toward a bevy of women. Lane. They must be talking about Pendril's friend. "Well, she heard from Lane that he is heading out of port in Morocco going toward Malta. He said that there are all manner of men from all over God's world on the boat. People from Wales, Scotland, one man from Hong Kong, and someone from Malaysia, wherever that is..."

"God's world? Sounds more like His Majesty's Empire."

"I thought those were the same thing!" A laugh rippled through the group.

"Well and all, at least he has his friend that he went off with. What is his name? You know, he's a part of the Green family."

Dellie's heart skipped a beat. She stepped into the conversation. "Do you mean Pendril?"

"Yes that's it! Is he someone you know?"

"My sister is married to Coleridge Green. He is Pendril's cousin."

"Oh, you are Lillian's sister? Come join us. What is your name?"

"It is Dellie Standard."

"Ah! I remember when she was planning for your arrival! I am Winston Albright. As I was saying, so they are off sailing through and about the Mediterranean Sea. It sounds like they are in a different port each week." He paused to take a sip of punch. "He sounds like a different man out from under back home. The letters he writes are tantalizing my sister's child. Tales of what he has seen, the things he has done. Mark my words, my nephew will be the next to take to sea from off the Rock."

Hours later, the soiree over, Dellie stood in Lillian's bathroom. The black-and-white tiles were cool on her feet. She let her shift fall to the floor and studied her nakedness in a spotted mirror. She regarded the curve of the muscle in her leg, examined the swell of her breasts and the line of her collarbone. She drew closer to her reflection — eyes examining themselves, considering the rise of her cheeks, the width of her nose, the field of freckles across the smooth skin. She looked the same as when she boarded the transport in Bridgetown. But was she? Lane was a different man now. From the letters he wrote to Coleridge, she could tell Pendril was. Did it matter anyway? It was too late for any of that.

"I know you must have nothing on your walls, saving every bit as you do. Here, this will cheer you."

Mrs. Fettes had given Dellie a calendar from the drug store. Back in her room at Mrs. Cumberbatch's, she leaned on her elbows considering it.

The calendar was printed with stylish women sipping different flavored sodas each month. Dellie had already marked a date in June. It would be her turn then to send money home. She propped the calendar on the dresser and turned to Lillian. "What do you think of it here?"

"Very nice. And Mrs. Fettes is a very generous woman. Listen, you have anything more to say before I seal this envelope for home?"

A sharp knock startled them both. Mrs. Cumberbatch opened the door.

"Here is your bill." She held a piece of paper out in Dellie's direction.

"My bill? I am sure I paid you your rent on Friday. Remember, I got it to you just at six."

"This here is for your food. For the quarter."

"My food? But you know I take my meals with my sister. I also haven't been in the place a quarter yet. And besides, meals are included. Enid and the others pay the same as I and they don't..."

Mrs. Cumberbatch didn't wait for her to complete the sentence. "I provide you with a clean room with heat and linen and food, and you have got the nerve to complain." She chupsed, a long drawn out suck of her teeth. "You up-country girls are all the same. All of you looking for a handout. I am running a business here, not an almshouse."

"I take my meals with Lillian, you know..." Dellie's voice was even.

She was cut off once again.

"Were you two raised in a barn talking back to your elder and your better? I am the one who owns the house. I am the one who makes the rules. That is the bill. Pay it. You think I don't know about you gal...There are *laws* here, you know. This is not some backwater. Laws about consorting with *agitators*. With *anarchists*. With people trying to turn others against the established order. You know someone named Bertha Hamill? I've seen your photograph in the papers. Maybe the authorities would want to know who the *unknown* person is. Pay up, girl. I will give you till next Friday, or you will find yourself walking up the hill from Workman's again. And you listen, too, Lillian Green. Don't think the authorities wouldn't want to know about people like you, mouth still full of saltwater, colluding with those who foment strife."

Mrs. Cumberbatch slammed the door behind her.

The bill and Dellie's money were within seventy-five cents of each other. Lillian sat heavily on the bed, head in her hands. No money for home. No money to put toward the sewing machine. Dellie stood looking out of the window at the street scene below. Winnie had said once: *"This ain't home. Not every story comes with a ready-made sad ending."*

Now Dellie wasn't so sure.

On her next day off she rose early and pulled on her best hat. She laced her shoes tightly, shoved her keys and purse into her handbag, and caught an early trolley. She needed to get across town before the Lodgemaster left for his job at the post office. She rounded the corner just as he made his way down the front stairs of his brownstone. She paused for a moment. Should she run to catch up with him, or call out his name down the street? She settled on a combination of walking and running. She could hear Cal and M'Ma's words: 'There is nothing in this world that would require a lady to run.'

She came up behind him, breathless.

"Mr. Walcott, Mr. Walcott." She touched his arm.

He turned around, surprised.

"Miss Standard?"

"Yes, sir. Sir, I am sorry to catch you like this, but I have a problem."

"A problem? Come, child, walk with me. You can tell me while I wait for the trolley. I am early, so you needn't rush the telling."

Dellie steeled herself and began. The plan that she and her sisters had made. Lillian and Coleridge housing her. Her work. Finally Mrs. Cumberbatch and the threat she had made to them.

He listened, eyes changing with the various parts of the story, but his face calm. She watched his jaw tighten, ever so slightly, at the part about Mrs. Cumberbatch. A trolley lumbered down the street toward them.

"I see. Thank you for telling me this, Miss Standard."

He turned and made his way toward the cluster of people waiting to board and to begin their day's business, his jaw working.

Later that day Dellie approached her sister's flat, and saw silhouetted through Lillian's curtains both Bert and his father, the Lodgemaster. They were deep in conversation with her sister and brother-in-law around the kitchen table. She burst into Lillian's flat, startling everyone.

"Is everyone alright? Did something happen?"

Egbert was the first to recover and gestured to her to sit down. "Dellie, you told my father what Mrs. Cumberbatch said to you."

"Miss Standard, I am sorry I was so abrupt when we spoke at the trolley stop. Sometimes, though, it is best that I not speak when I am angry. And situations like the one with Mrs. Cumberbatch evoke that response in me."

Dellie froze, not moving an inch. Was it a mistake in drawing the Lodgemaster into this? Was she a rabble-rouser in his eyes, her face splayed across the paper bringing disgrace to the West Indian community? She ran her fingers through her hair.

He continued, "I have some business with Mrs. Cumberbatch coming up. Do you mind if I speak to her about this? When I meet with her, I'd like you to be there, too."

Dellie's stomach tightened. She looked at Lillian, who nodded ever so slightly in reassurance.

———

In the last weeks of her third pregnancy, Mrs. Fettes was tired much of the time. That gave Dellie more of a chance to care for the Fettes children — the joy of her day. Molly was always on the move. Funny, though, that with all that energy, the only way to tame her was with paper and pencil.

"I drew a picture of Clive, the pet parrot. See, he is green just like you said? Draw me Sam the Donkey next to him. Make him eating a carrot. I mean, *please* draw me a picture of Sam the Donkey."

"I drew a house with a verandah. Do you like it? What is a verandah?"

It was as if she could be tired out only by the adventures she loved to draw on paper. Marjory was inquisitive and still full of questions about Barbados and anything else that crossed her mind. "Tell me again about the man on stilts! About the tuk band!"

As much as the children were her joy, the dusting was Dellie's nemesis. It was mind-numbing, but both Mrs. Fettes and her mother were particular about it. Mrs. Fettes kept a regiment of fine glass bottles and jars in an arrangement on top of her dressing table. Each one had to be moved and dusted, so that the light could catch the cut glass, then be replaced, just so, on the newly polished wood. Dellie finished the backboard of the bed, and then moved toward the dressing table. She picked up one of the jars of cream. The top was loose. The jar shattered as it hit the floor.

As she bent to clean up the mess, the smell of flowers carried her back. It was a cool early morning, and she was in Cal's shed, helping her mother pull petals off flowers to scent the cream she had just prepared. She heard that soft voice as if her mother was in the room. *See child, you must pick the flowers in the morning just after the dew has evaporated. You must get up early-early for that.* Dellie spoke out loud. "Oh, Cal, I does miss yuh…"

Mrs. Watson's voice pulled her back to the present.

"Dellie, what is it?

"Oh!" she startled. "I broke the…"

The old woman's voice was soft. "I can see that child, but *what is it*? You're standing there staring, muttering…"

Dellie's story spilled out. Cal's death, her journey, her worries about money, the day at the garment factory, the photo in the paper, Mrs. Cumberbatch. The obeah woman's voice rang in her head. *Hey gal! You are not so high and mighty now! Are you?*

Mrs. Watson sat down on the bed. Dellie straightened and gathered herself together. What had she just done? Telling her personal business to her employer. Her entire body began to quiver.

Mrs. Watson sighed. "Come downstairs, child. This time I'll make the cocoa."

The two older women sat with her in the kitchen. Grace Fettes spoke first. "This is something Kevin and I, along with my mother, have been speaking about. I was going to raise it with you, but was hesitant because I know how close you are to your own family." She paused. "But with the new baby coming, I could use someone to live in. There is a room on the second floor, you know. It is near the children and they might not give you much privacy. But...I was wondering what I would do. See, Dellie. This door opened for both of us to go through. Will you think about it? Living in would cut your expenses and help me. You can still see your friends when you are off."

———

The meeting that the Lodgemaster had asked Dellie to attend was held in Mrs. Cumberbatch's front parlor. His voice was deep and matter of fact. "And so, since Miss Standard here will be going to live at her employer's, you needn't concern yourself with her status, or her activities while she was seeking decent work." His manner was patient and reasonable. "Besides, you don't want to draw the authorities here, checking you for overcapacity or serving meals without proper license..."

Mrs. Cumberbatch replied, "No, uh, I don't, I am, I mean to say I am just trying to make ends meet. And provide decent lodging for folks from home." Dellie sat perfectly still, hands folded in her lap, eyes moving between Mr. Walcott and Mrs. Cumberbatch.

"Yes, and we appreciate that, and that is why the Lodge helped you to buy this house. To help you to be helpful to other West Indians. It would be a shame if next time you needed a loan to expand your property holdings...and I heard you were looking at another property around the corner...it would be a shame if people felt you had not been helpful."

CHAPTER TWELVE

All of It

March, 1911

Dellie had the day off and sat in Lillian's kitchen. "Sister, do you think that the daffodils we planted will start to poke through soon?"

"Hah! I had forgotten all about them. I—"

"How could you forget about daffodils of all things, after the headmaster pounded that poem into our heads? They spoke in unison, laughter punctuating the lines. "I will now present you with a recitation of *I Wandered Lonely as a Cloud,* by William Wordsworth.

I wandered lonely as a cloud
That floats on high o'er vales and hills,
When all at once I saw a crowd,
A host, of golden daffodils;"

"Ladies, please" Coleridge called from the other room. "I am trying to rest and you are giving me nightmares."

Dellie's laughter degenerated to a snort. "Remember the headmaster adjusting his glasses and saying how proud we should be, to be subjects of the King, all and that?" Her voice dropped in imitation of his, "when we recite Wordsworth for His Majesty's birthday we are in solidarity with school children forming one voice all over the mother-land and the empire reciting in it London, Hampstead, Malaysia, India, Hong Kong, Canada, Rhodesia, Burma, Kenya..."

"When is his birthday by the way? We musn't miss it this year. I will send him greetings from..." Lillian was interrupted by someone pounding on the door.

"Coleridge! Coleridge! It's Owen. Open up, man!"

Dellie raced to the door. Owen barged past her, laying two special edition newspapers on the table. The room went silent.

He grasped the back of a chair as Coleridge emerged from the bedroom. Owen croaked the words. "Fire at the Triangle factory in New York," he said, pointing to the papers. The rest leaned in gasping. The headlines blared the news: *Factory Fire! Many Feared Dead!*

He read the words over the photograph. "Over one hundred feared dead, bodies to be taken to Charities Pier for identification."

Coleridge picked up the thread. "Many jumped to their deaths to avoid burning or asphyxiation."

The others sat. Hands worked, eyes widened looking at Dellie. It could have been her. Her voice was husky: "All those women, some just girls. I can see their faces. All the same look." Her hands flew up in a gesture of futility. "For a few bitter pennies." She turned and went outside.

———

Later, alone, Dellie picked up the papers still scattered on the table and brought them to the space that Lillian still made available to her on her days off. The small kerosene lamp illuminated the words. Locked doors had blocked women only inches from safety. The owners had been concerned about workers leaving without permission—or slipping goods outside. Women had jumped, bodies aflame, from the banks of ninth-floor windows to be crushed on the streets below. One hundred and forty-six souls gone in a three-minute inferno.

The papers published little about the dead, just categories: immigrants, women, Italy, Russia, poor. There was no word of the hopes and desperation in which the poor, immigrant, Italian, and Russian women were shrouded.

———

The heavy air promised rain as Dellie made her way through the thicket of carts on Atlantic Avenue. She stopped mid-stride. The sign in the window of *Sacklow and Sons* read in English: "Closed to honor the passing of Pauline Thall in the Triangle Fire."

"Dear God, not that sweet girl." Below ran more words in Hebrew.

Over the next few days, the story came out.

"Her aunt identified the body. She recognized her. Easily, thank God," said Mrs Iannicci as she crossed herself. "She'd come from the Ukraine. That's all they let Jews do there. Sew."

From Mirski, the ice man: "I was just talking to her last week. At the Post Office. She was mailing an envelope home. Her English was getting better."

From Casey, the lamplighter: "She came all this way. Three years ago. For what? This was the job that was supposed to make a difference. It was supposed to let her make her way."

Pauline had traveled south, out of the Pale of Settlement where the Russians allowed the Jews to reside, through Krakow, Lublin, Budapest, on to Trieste. She took a twelve-day voyage to get away from the cry *Bei Zhidov* — "beat the Jews." Then she landed in *goldene Medina*, the Golden Land, America, New York. The trip had cost her family half a year's earnings.

Her uncle had been the first to come. Then he sent for his wife, then for Pauline. She was to send money back home each month to keep the rest of the family alive. They were to save for her sisters' passage, then her mother's and grandmother's, then her father's, then... only her uncle and aunt would send those envelopes now. And with them the news that Pauline was no more. While she walked toward the store that Pauline and her aunt and uncle ran, Dellie thought about the story that she was able to piece together. The details were different, but the story the same as hers, the same as everybody in the neighborhood. And so, though she and Dellie had never exchanged more than a thank you and a smile, she was compelled to pay her respects.

Dellie stepped through a door that had been left ajar and ascended the steps to the second floor. The light inside was dim. The small quarters were full of people sitting on the floor or on overturned crates.

She didn't know Pauline's people's names, or their rituals or how their living honored their dead. She would be quick and not intrude. From her handbag, Dellie removed two black roses sewn from satin ribbon. One she placed on a table by the door, next to a pitcher of water and a bowl. The other she fixed to her handbag before slipping out. She didn't know it, but the rose on her handbag would be her *Kaddish*.

———

Dellie found a private glade not far from the northern entrance of Fort Greene Park. Of course she shared it with others whom she did not know, whose schedules or routines happened to coincide with hers. A gray-haired man appeared regularly. He and a small boy trained their binoculars on a nest of birds, watching them over the weeks building a nest, sitting on eggs, feeding the craning mouths of fledglings, and most recently teaching them to fly. An elderly woman, for whom Dellie served as an unknown companion, dozed in the quiet. Dellie always sat in the same spot on the same bench, staring ahead, over the dandelions that had just begun to bud and past the clusters of violets hiding in the grass. Her eyes were focused on some place inside.

Then one day Lillian was in the shade of a tree when Dellie arrived.

Dellie walked over. "Lillian? How did you find my spot?"

"Last week I followed you. Sit, Dellie. You barely talk now."

Dellie obeyed, but looked forward and crossed her legs and arms. "You know why. A little more saving and I will have enough for my passage back. What kind of place is this? It could have been me, I could have been one of those girls. It could have been you looking for some way to recognize me laid out on Charities Pier."

"But it wasn't you. And God must have a reason for that." Lillian put her hand on Dellie's. "I know. But, please, hear me, Dellie. *This* place is our home now. All of it. Just like Barbados. The beautiful and the ugly. All of it."

The tears coursed down Dellie's cheeks.

Lillian wrapped her arms around her.

"Please, Dellie. Don't leave me here."

Dellie broke away.

Lillian laid her hand across her abdomen. "The future of the family is here."

Dellie's eyebrows shot up. Lillian nodded.

"Yes, I think so. In January. A baby by the new year."

Dellie was silent for moment. "My heart is full for you." She swallowed to steady her voice and laid her hand on Lillian's belly. "This is where *your* life is, the life that you and Coleridge have made. The one inside you, and the one you live together. I am not sure what is here for me."

Lillian settled onto the wooden bench and reached for her handbag. "We got a letter from Maudie today." She pulled a folded piece of paper from an envelope. "Listen."

I will be coming soon. While I was studying and readying myself for more school, fortunately M'Ma was putting away the money that you sent for my passage. She even urged me to fill out the papers, saying it was just a back-up in case I was not called. Well, the "in case" has come to pass. The word came that I will not be attending Queen's College. Lillian, I am working with the cousin of the former neighbor of your Lodgemaster to book the passage. Expect me within three months' time.

Everything else is going on the same here. Palley did win a pin for his recitation on the War of Spanish Succession. The Headmaster pulled him aside to say he would begin preparing him for a chance at Harrison's College. It does seem that all the man does is prepare, never accomplish. Dellie, I saw your friend Rita. She is now up at the House full-time, doing much of the work that had been Cal's. M'Ma will not let me anywhere near the Great House, so with no school for me, I am making batch upon batch of Cal's creams and infusions. I have sold some and so am hoping to bring in some extra money to accelerate my passage and to have some dollars in hand when I arrive. Sisters, I cannot wait to see your faces again. I cannot wait to leave here. I am ready to start my new life in New York.

Lillian made a broad gesture with her arm.

"You promised me. And I don't need to remind you that you promised Cal."

Dellie turned her face away.

Lillian shook the papers in her hand. "Do you hear something in this letter that tells you your future is changed back there? At *Taborvilla*? What have you forgotten, Dellie?"

Dellie covered her face with her hands and bent over.

"We promised each other that we would change things and change the family and its prospects. That promise is here. You promised Maude too. Being here is not easy for me either. But

136

this is about more than just us. You know that. Dellie, please. Cal always said it stops here. It stops now. We must be the end of it. We must be the start of a different future for this family. Whatever it means for us."

Dellie stood, nodded ever so slightly, and headed down the path and out of the park.

CHAPTER THIRTEEN

Oh Maudie!

Summer, 1911

*T*he sun played on the water, and the harbor wind whipped the ribbons on their hats as they watched the long awaited reunions at the Immigration Station.

"Lillian, I have a few extra pennies. Let's stop on the way back so that Maude can taste ice cream."

"That's an idea! I still remember your face when Clemmie did tell you to close your eyes, and put a spoonful in your mouth."

"I think she will favor chocolate, though I have had none better than the peach we tasted last year."

A smile brightened Lillian's face. "Ah, here come some arrivals." The women made their way forward as a group of West Indians made their way through. Lillian called to a woman struggling with a thrashing child, "Excuse me, were you on the *Denis*?"

"Yes, the *Denis*!"

"Thank you, Miss! Oh, and welcome! Blessings on your child! Good day!"

Dellie cupped her hands around her cheeks in excitement. "So Maudie should be coming through soon!"

After an hour with no Maude, they began pacing, brows ruched with worry.

Dellie approached a man in uniform. "Excuse me, sir; we have been waiting for my sister. Coming from Barbados."

"Barbados. She would have been on the *Denis* then. Docked hours ago. How old is she?"

"Fifteen."

"Well, they wouldn't be considering her a minor, so that shouldn't delay her. Wait a little longer." They waited and the hours dragged on.

Lillian paced a tight circle. "Do you think something went awry at home?"

"Maybe she is having trouble with the questions." Dellie twisted the handkerchief in her hand.

"It couldn't be her papers. I was clear what she had to have."

An hour later their speculations changed to trembling silence. Dellie stepped up to a wrought iron grate. She tilted her head to meet the man's eyes. "Sir, we are here waiting for my sister. She was to be on the *Denis*."

He flipped through a stack of papers without looking up. "The *Denis*? It came in hours ago. She was probably detained."

Dellie sucked in her breath and turned to Lillian. "You heard that!" she whispered. "Detained!" Searching for another answer, they approached three uniformed men in succession, one next to a turnstile, one attending a marble counter, one perusing forms. It was the same from each one of them. "She was probably detained."

Dellie and Lillian both knew what that meant. Some problem with either Maude's health or her papers. The word came the next day in a dispatch. *Disease*.

Lillian rocked back and forth in her kitchen chair, hands clasped behind her back.

The tension made Dellie's voice thick. "Disease? What could possibly be wrong? Lillian, if she is sent back, I fear she will never make it over here. You know how hard-headed she is. I can hear her saying, 'If this man's country does not want me, then I will go elsewhere.'"

"'Tis true, but M'Ma will press her. And how long will it take us to gather the funds again?" Lillian leaned forward, rubbing her eyes with the heels of her hands.

Dellie sighed. "Aye, me. Pass me my handbag. I must have a cup of tea." She rummaged through it pulling out her purse and extracted a few coins to activate the gas. "You are right. That would take us time and delay the others coming."

"I am more concerned that Maude get here as soon as possible. I worry what can happen while we are waiting." Dellie's mouth formed a tight line.

"And Maude with her untamed tongue. Especially now that she is turned from Queen's College, she will say something and draw retribution from the House."

Lillian peered through the curtains and churned her fingers through her hair. "I wonder what is taking Coleridge so long this evening? He should be home by now."

The women drifted to silence as they waited for the kettle's whistle.

———

From her position at the top of the stoop, Mrs. Cumberbatch's voice echoed and reverberated across, up and down the street. "What do I see here? Who is that with you, Mr. Coleridge Green? Another one of the Standard clan fleeing the Rock?"

Dellie and Lillian flew outside. "Maudie! Maudie!"

Maude's carpetbag fell to the ground as Dellie and Lillian's arms encircled her.

Dellie was the first to find her voice. "But how? We got word that you had been detained!"

Coleridge gestured toward the door and guided his wife and her sisters. "Let's step inside to discuss family business."

Dellie shot a look at Mrs. Cumberbatch and caught her brother-in-law's eye. He shook his head to silence her. Once inside, he hung his hat on a peg. "Lillian, another dispatch came this morning after you left, and so I headed over to immigration as soon as I got off work. One of the papers was smudged and parts were hard to read. They were ready to release Maudie from quarantine, but needed a male relative to pick her up because they couldn't confirm the age. Lucky your papers with her information were all in one place here. I should have left you a note before I left. I am sorry."

Dellie interrupted. "But, Maudie, what happened?"

Maude covered her face with her hands. "I am so ashamed. You know how much I love sorrel even though it punishes me by making my skin break out. Well, I drank some at the farewell gathering. I just took a little, knowing that it would be the last time. Just a little taste on my tongue. I broke out in an itchy rash on the ship. Another woman tried to cure it with a cream she had among her things. That just made it worse."

Dellie shook her head.

Lillian chupsed. "Maudie, why, when you know..."

Maude interrupted. "Sister, do you want to hear the story, or you want to offer me for interrogation?" She rolled her eyes. "So when I arrived they marked my papers and placed me in the contagious ward. They were sure it was measles and placed me in a huge room lined with beds full of people covered in all manner of skin ailments. It is a wonder I did not catch something there. I begged the authorities and tried to make them understand it was my own foolishness and not a disease. Well, the rash cleared as I told them it would, and since I had no fever or other symptoms, doctor cleared me to leave."

Dellie reached across the table and squeezed her sister's hand. "I am so glad to lay my eyes upon you, Maudie. Lillian and I were worried that if you didn't come now, you would never come. Never leave home."

"Dellie, our mother is dead. Queen's College is closed to me. There is nothing for me on Bim. This is my home now."

CHAPTER FOURTEEN

Breadfruit? Here?

Brooklyn, Fall 1911

*T*he letter was addressed to Dellie. She stood, one hand on the gate leading downstairs to Lillian's flat, one hand holding the thin paper.

My dear daughters,

I am taking pen in hand and writing to you in the hopes that this letter will find you both well. The children are all well here. I continue to hope for the day when you will return and we can begin looking for a nice piece of ground.

Thank you for the three dollars that you sent. It covered the cost of new pants for the boys' school uniforms. Your grandmother could not take the old ones down any more. It also bought pencils and notebooks for them all. Palley and Byron do send their love.

Your grandmother is speculating on holes. She has picked out some of Emmeline's and is planning to sell the sweet potatoes from their yield to some of the fancy clubs on the south coast. Everyone knows that what grows on the Hope is the sweetest.

*I am very concerned about your sister May. Your poor mother would
be horrified to know that I caught her climbing a tree and peering into the
obeah woman's yard.*

*Dellie, I understand that you and Winnie have purchased a sewing
machine. I heard this from a letter that Mrs. Cumberbatch sent to her
people. If you wrote more frequently, I would not have to hear the news
from those with long tongues. I also have heard that you are associating
with rabble-rousers and American Negroes. First the coolie-man, no matter that he is a Green, and now this. Stick to your kind.*

Dellie crumpled the letter in her hand and threw it into the trash
can at the bottom of Mrs. Cumberbatch's stoop.

Maude's arrival was like an elixir to Dellie. She took her to the bank
to help her open an account, oriented her to the trolley, explained
how to insert coins into the gas meter to release enough for cooking.
She explained about coal deliveries, ice deliveries, the mail service,
the notion of keeping animals as pets (*you mean in the house?*), about
stores for baked goods, for vegetables, for meat, for fish, the many
clothes she would need for winter — boots, stockings, gloves, scarf,
hat. She told her where to find the parks when she was starved for
green, and the directions to the streets that led to the river when she
was starved for the sea...

With her in tow, Dellie set out, determined to know Brooklyn
better. To know it beyond the blocks bordered by Court Street,
Nevins Street, Atlantic Avenue, and Baltic Street. Whenever possible they set out around and about the borough together. It was
the cusp of the seasons and the summer's heat had retreated. Even
the sky had been a clear blue these past weeks without the hazy
heat. They walked and walked, turning this way — an interesting
house capturing their interest or at the sound of a radio or gramophone drifting through a window. Together with Maude, each step
Dellie took on the pavement made for her a firmer bonding with
this new life. They took to walking all up and down the borough,
using the storage company clock tower, by far the tallest structure in
the City of Brooklyn, as their fixed point. Sometimes it was just the
two of them who walked. Other times Winnie or one of the women

from the Church or the Lodge accompanied them. Lillian came less frequently as she grew heavier with her pregnancy. Together they explored neighborhoods, different business districts, even the factory and port areas.

It was on one of those walks, out Fifth Street, past the eastern edge of Green-Wood cemetery in one of the less developed areas near Gowanus Bay, that they observed something special. Maude spotted it first. She stopped and squinted and pointed ahead.

"Dellie, Dellie, look there."

"What?"

"Look at that tree there, in the yard by the gray house. Look, it's a *breadfruit* tree."

Dellie tutted. "Little sister, you surely are seeing things."

"Come, let's get closer."

And there it was: tall, broad, shiny leaves each shaped like a tea tray, heavy with ripe, green fruit. It stood at the center of a garden flourishing with all manner of fruit and vegetables, tomatoes, squash, broccoli, melons—growing with no regard for what was in season and what wasn't. The women stood in amazement.

"What place is this?" asked Dellie. "How can a breadfruit live in this place, survive the weather? It is full grown. At least twenty years by the trunk, maybe more." She gestured toward the ground. "Look at all that fruit going to waste." She shook her head. "Too bad it is on the other side of the fence. If we were home, I would jump the fence quick-quick and take one. It is surely a sin, good food rotting like that on the ground."

"Dellie, if you were home there would be three trees like it in your own yard!"

Dellie snorted. "I can taste how Cal used to boil it up and mash it with butter, salt, and a tiny bit of sugar to add to the flavor."

"Remember how Mina, the East Indian woman, cooked it up with onion, tomato and curry? I think maybe she also put a bit of coconut in it..."

Suddenly a man, thick yellow hair sticking up in spiky crests, came down the steps of the gray frame house. He eyed the women suspiciously.

"What can I do for you ladies? You admiring my garden?"

"Your tree actually, sir. We didn't think any like it grew around here."

144

"That's because they don't. It's the only one I've ever seen like it. And why it has to be in *my* yard is anyone's mystery." He considered it in disgust.

"But the fruit, sir. The fruit is good for eating," Maude noted.

He laughed derisively. "Not in this house, it ain't. I'd cut it down if my wife would let me."

The women looked at him in shock. From a first-floor window, a woman with matching hair, sharp face, and beaked nose called out.

"Walter, what is it?"

"Nothing, Jane. These ladies are just admiring your tree. They say the fruit is good for eating."

"That's right, *my* tree," the woman responded while considering her curved fingernails. "And don't you think about cutting it down. The blossoms are beautiful." She pointed to the tall spikes of flowers. "Betcha never saw a tree that blooms and bears at the same time! Betcha never saw a garden in Brooklyn that was green all the time! No one knows why! Not even the folks at the Botanical Gardens."

"Here we go," said Walter, looking at the sky. "If you like it so much, then *you* pick up the fruit and sweep up the spent flowers!" he charged her. "I could spend my life tending that tree. Giant green things constantly falling from it and rotting in the yard. I could use that space to grow something useful. Something *you* could cook." He looked up at his wife in the window. Again he considered the sky. "But then that would sorely limit us," he muttered.

"Walter, what is it? What did you say?"

Dellie jumped into the conversation. "Suppose we take some?"

"Take it." Walter replied. "Take it all. Take as much as you want."

"Well, we can only carry a few."

"Then come back and take more," said the woman. "Anytime. Bring your friends. It seems to drop fruit constantly. One even hit poor Walter on the head. I think that's why he hates it so." She laughed.

Somehow Dellie and Maude managed to carry four each in two slings that the woman, Jane, fashioned from old dishtowels. They left her with three recipes to use on her abundance of breadfruit.

The leftovers of some salt cod, some over-ripe tomatoes, a bit of flour, and a little of this and a little of that from various jars and cans filled a great cast-iron pot. Winnie contributed an assortment of vegetables from the overabundance that was always in her kitchen. The makings of a breadfruit stew boiled gently on the rear burner of Winnie's stove.

They huddled in anticipation. Egbert appeared with part of a jug of rum punch he claimed was left over from a meeting of the Men's Guild of the Lodge. Clemmie immediately burst out, "I have never seen any rum anything left over from a Lodge meeting!"

Coleridge hushed him. "It is one of the benefits of the Lodgemaster. He gets to set aside some leftovers for himself before the meetings begin."

Despite his attempt at discretion, the room filled with laughter.

A knock at the door. It was Owen joining the party. "I heard that you all have got something special on the stove. I brought some string beans. Can you use them?"

Dellie waved him in. "Dump them right in."

They stuffed themselves on less than half of the cauldron. Clement grinned. "The Americans have got the Fourth of July. I declare this day a holiday for West Indians in honor of the breadfruit!"

Owen raised a glass. "And the great state of North Carolina offers salutations." The rum had joined the party.

Dellie's eyes narrowed. "Shhh... is that someone knocking upon the door?"

It was Mrs. Wilkins, the upstairs neighbor from St. James parish on the east coast of Barbados. She peered in, hesitant, as Winnie held open the door.

"I am sorry to disturb you, but am I dreaming or do I smell *breadfruit*?"

Mrs. Wilkins was just the first knock. Soon Coleridge and Egbert were passing bowls of stew out of the window. ("I can't believe we haven't run out of dishes.") Clemmie and Winnie were passing cups of stew hand-over-hand down the front steps as the word of fresh breadfruit stew spread through their corner of Brooklyn. Dellie stood by the stove, ladling servings from the pot. A voice called up, Clemmie or Egbert's, she couldn't tell above the din.

"We have not run out yet?"

"Not yet!"

"How much did you say you cooked? Seems like every duppy and his dog is pouring out onto the street and lining up."

Soon a line around the block swarmed with people — girls played clapping games, boys rough-housed, old people commented on how the throngs reminded them of times back home. Mr. Kelsey, the piano teacher from two doors down, the Iannaccis from the grocery store and their brood, and Calvin from across the street (whose occupation went unmentioned by most) stood, mouths ready for the feast. The taste reminded each of something from back home: the top note of a village specialty from the mountains of Sicily; an aftertaste from a recipe made only for christenings back in North Carolina; the undertone of a dish from County Cork; the texture of something made by someone's aunt back in Calabria; the smell of something made only for Easter back in the mountains of Greece.

Dellie watched as Egbert Walcott moved in Maude's direction. He stopped at the table and ladled out two cups of some thrown-together punch. "Someone sitting here?"

"No," said Maude as she moved to accommodate him.

"Punch? I brought you some."

Dellie caught the exchange and moved closer. She heard a tinkling laughter punctuating some story that required the Lodgemaster's son and her sister to lean in close to each other. She furrowed her brow and shook her head. She recognized that laughter, its timbre. Well, how long could it last? Maude was just fifteen. Dellie glanced around the room and was back home to a day with a sapphire sky, a tuk band, and Lillian dressed in white. Once again she felt the rough grass on her bare toes and saw an emerald-and-lapis colored bird use its long, curved beak to sip from a flower. She felt soft petals falling around her shoulders, and remembered the breeze that nudged them from a star-apple tree.

Dellie leaned out of the rear window, handing out cups laden with the stew to the group now gathered in the back yard, the clear moonlight silhouetting them against the dark. As she stood up, her ears picked up a few notes, then the melody she knew from home, the one that Herbert, the Bridgetown fiddler. played. Her eyes roved to a figure silhouetted on a fire escape. It was Mr. Sacklow from the second-hand store. He nodded, smiling, never missing a note as his hands flirted with bow and strings.

CHAPTER FIFTEEN

A Real Foreigner

O wen came to Dellie with a proposition. "Join me on a trip to Prospect Park. Some of the men from the Line are getting together for a day out there." He picked a stray thread from his sleeve. "A committee is heading out early with food and to set up an area for some ball playing."

Dellie looked at him, eyebrows up in surprise. Though he was often at either Lillian's or Winnie's house talking with the men, he had never invited her into his world.

"You won't have to bring anything. Besides, I want you meet my good friend Reddick and his wife. He just brought her up from New Orleans. She doesn't know anyone around here."

"New Orleans?"

"Oh, yes, New Orleans, down in the South. She might as well be from another country though. She's got a strange way of talking and eats all kinds of things nobody around here ever heard of. Like someone else I know."

Dellie chupsed and laughed. "All right. I will accompany you, Mr. Gibson."

The steady *shush, shush, shush* of the treadle of the sewing machine provided the backdrop to the conversation as Dellie ran up some seams for the regalia in one of the other lodges. "Winnie, if you don't mind I will stay over here at your house on Wednesday when I am off from Mrs. Fettes. I would like to stay up late to get ahead on some sewing. Then I will leave early on Thursday. I have some plans for Sunday."

"Some plans?"

"Yes, I am going to Prospect Park with Owen. Some of his people from the rail line are throwing some sort of thing."

From somewhere Maude entered the room. "Did I hear you say you are doing something with Owen? Isn't he that foreign man? The one with the job on the train?"

Dellie held her voice steady. "I will remind you of the same thing your sister Lillian reminded me of when I first arrived. *We* are the foreigners."

Maude's chupse bounded from the windows and recoiled across the room.

"I beg your pardon, *little* sister, are you Henry now, passing judgment on others?"

Winnie stood up from the table, making a fuss of clearing dishes.

"What is that about?" Dellie glared at her friend's back.

Winnie turned up the water and let it pound into the sink.

Dellie rose and stood next to her, back against the counter. She looked at Winnie, eyes intent. "I said, 'What is that about?'"

Winnie didn't look at her. "You are a grown woman and can do what you want. It just seems to me that with all the men at the Lodge. Well..." She kept her attention on the dishes in the sink. "He is...you know..."

"I know what? That he is what? That he is too dark for your liking or that he is too foreign?"

"Don't put words in my mouth, Dellie Standard! You know just what I mean. These American Negroes may look just like us, but they are not like us!"

"That is right. The slave boat carried them here. Not to the rock in the water it took our people to."

Winnie turned. "Dellie, these people don't want us around. Just the other day, a boy threw a stone at me and called me a monkey chaser."

"Ah, Winnie, how many times will you tell that same story? Beside, you and I both know they are not all like that. Owen is a true friend to Clemmie and Coleridge. I am sure his friends are decent. Their work travelling all about and abroad does take them among all manner of people."

"Believe what you want."

Maude leaned two hands on the sink. "Dellie! Keeping company with an American Negro!" She shook her head. "Can you imagine what people will say?"

Dellie turned, the anger spilling out—"Maude, don't bring 'people' into this. And what people might they be? People like my own sister? I do not care what 'people' might think. This is my life, sister. Not anybody else's. Not yours."

The patchwork of colors quivering in the breeze along the alley of trees in Prospect Park drew Dellie's breath away. She remembered her first autumn in the city and struggling to find words to describe the change of the leaves in a letter home. Finally she had given up and enclosed a small handful instead so that they wouldn't think she had gone mad. Now in the morning sun, the trees glowed red, orange, yellow as if lit from within by autumn itself.

She tugged Owen's sleeve. "Slow down a bit." She stopped walking and gazed around her. "The trees. If you look at that rise over there." She pointed. "If you look at that rise over there it looks like fine needlepoint. Like someone did lay out the plan of colors."

"Yes, it is very nice. And I bet they did. This is a planned park. Come." He turned and took several steps then looked back for her. "Come, Dellie, we've got to be someplace."

She stood rooted to the spot—the trees swaying to show off their finery, the conversation of song between a bird and its mate. She looked at the expanse of grass. How long had it been since her feet had been free and not armored against the cobblestone or concrete of the streets? She pushed the reminder that would have come from Cal aside, slipped off her shoes and hose, while Owen forged along ahead.

The group of railmen, their wives, girlfriends, and children had claimed a flat open area.

"Owen, man! Glad you could come." A short stocky man reached out and clapped him on the back. "And who is this with you?"

"This here is my friend, Dellie. Dellie, this is Arthur. He's a waiter on the Line."

She reached for his outstretched hand. "I am pleased to meet…" She stopped as surprise wiped off his smile. *Her accent.* Clearly he hadn't expected that.

He caught himself. "Ah, yes. I am pleased to meet you." His eyes rested on the shoes in her hands and then on her bare feet. He turned and walked away. Dellie felt her face grow hot. She had just confirmed every stereotype of West Indians.

Owen turned to her. "Dellie, let me finish introducing you around to the fellas, and then I have to side up for the game. You're going to get to see your first baseball game today. I'll go over the rules once more with you before we begin."

The names were a blur—she would never remember them and most were names she never heard back home—Leon, Roscoe, Silas. She drifted toward a group of women opening and setting out baskets of food on cloths spread on the ground. She could make out a few of the words from one clutch of women.

It didn't take long for her to decipher what they were discussing.

"Calling themselves 'West Indians' like they're not Negroes. Like they are some kind of better."

"And yet they come over and will work for anything. How is a person supposed to bargain when someone is ready to undercut you? The place is thick with them now. You hear that sing-song accent wherever you go. A decent person can't find work."

Dellie's shoulders tightened.

"But, Lila, I didn't know you were standing out for daywork."

Dellie watched a glance slide from woman to woman.

"Me, ah noooo. Uh-uh. Not with the tips Jeffrey makes. But I hear enough from the neighbors."

Two women caught each other's eyes over the speaker's head.

A woman with a reedy voice spoke. "Anyway, I was saying, I heard that he finally brought his wife up from Louisiana. Some Creole woman, Catholic too, she's the one over there. That woman." The trio turned toward their target.

"Humpf. That long hair swinging in a braid, like she's a girl, not a grown, married woman."

"I heard she had to high-tail it out of there. Some mess with a minister. Couldn't even stick with one of her own kind. By-passed the chanting priests and went for a sanctified minister."

"A minister!"

"Yes, indeed. A *minister*. A married one, I hear. Uh huh. Nearly ruined the name of the whole family. Least that is what I hear."

"Well, you know what they say about them bayou bitches."

"I sure do. I plan on keeping an eye on my husband. Before she puts some *mojo* on him." They shook their heads in disgust. Dellie followed their gaze to a woman, standing by herself, long hair in a braid down one shoulder, barefoot and holding her shoes. Dellie headed toward her.

"I see you like the feel of your feet in the grass!"

The woman looked at her and smiled.

"Oh yes, I do. As soon as I saw this grass laid out here, I just had to take my shoes off. I am Aurelia. And you?"

Surprised by the melody in the woman's speech, it was Dellie's turn to stand with her mouth open. She recovered quickly. "I am Dellie Standard. Excuse me, but are you from one of the islands?"

The woman laughed and touched Dellie's arm. "You are too funny! No, but I might as well be a foreigner. Oh, I didn't mean that like it sounded. I mean. It's just that those biddies over there..." She turned her chin to the cluster of women. "Those women over there seem to have proclaimed themselves the gatekeepers of acceptability. I am from New Orleans and so to them a foreigner. To them unacceptable."

"Ah, you must be Jonathan Reddick's wife! I am a friend of Owen Gibson. He wanted us to meet."

"I see. I am pleased to meet you!" Aurelia offered her hand and her eyes crinkled with her smile. "Well, that is my husband over there, swinging the bat. Where are you from, Dellie?"

"I am from Barbados, in the West Indies."

"Ah, a real foreigner!" Aurelia doubled over at her own joke. "Come, Dellie Standard. I'll explain to you about baseball while we watch the game." She reached her hand out. Dellie grabbed it and let her pull her toward a checkered cloth laid out on the grass with a clear view of the makeshift ball field.

It was a glittering day weeks later, and Brooklyn was washed clean after three days straight of rain. "Maudie, come with me to make a delivery. It is to my friend, Aurelia."

"Aurelia? I do not remember her from the Lodge."

Dellie turned. "She is not from the Lodge. She is married to one of Owen's friends."

"So she is an American Negro? "

"Yes, Maude, she is, is that a problem?"

"Did I say it was? I was just curious. What do you have to deliver?"

Dellie picked up a dress with smocking on the bodice and lifted it for Maude to see.

"Ah, Dellie! It is beautiful."

"Winnie and I made three of them. Each one is a little different. They are for the little girls at Aurelia's church that can't afford a holiday dress. Winnie and I are hoping that this will also open up some new business. Their Women's Guild is paying for these, but we are hoping that people will be impressed by the workmanship and bring us more orders." Dellie turned to the coat rack. "Here." She tossed her sister a hat. "Let's go."

A flick of the lace curtains signaled that Dellie's knocking had finally been heard above the scratchy strains of a ragtime piece playing on a gramophone. Aurelia opened the door and pulled the two in.

"Quick! This is the best part!" She twirled and swung a shawl that was substituting for a partner before sinking into a soft, stuffed chair as the phonograph wound down. She threw back her head and laughed.

"Dellie, your friend must think I am mad!"

Dellie laughed and kissed Aurelia on the cheek. "This 'friend' is my sister!"

Aurelia hopped up and reached her arms out to Maude. "Yes, you two are surely sisters! " She gestured to her own cheekbones and nose. "Dellie has been talking about you. Maudie, yes?" She didn't wait for a response, but chatted on. "She has been planning all kinds of adventures. A trip to Prospect Park, to the Botanical Gardens, she even mentioned…" She turned to Dellie. "Should I tell her?"

Dellie nodded, her eyes on Maude whose face was a study in shock. "Maybe even to Luna Park!" Aurelia slapped her thigh for emphasis.

Dellie looked at Maude and struggled to suppress a laugh.

"So let's see the dresses."

The brown butcher paper fluttered away as Dellie snipped the twine.

Aurelia gasped. "Oh, Dellie, they are just precious. The women from the Guild will be so pleased." She lowered her voice and looked at Dellie. "And that will mean more business for you, I'm sure." She stood up and headed toward her kitchen. "Let me pay you before I forget."

Maude stood and walked around the room scrutinizing photographs, lace antimacassars, stuffed pillows. Dellie watched her sister, shaking her head slowly from side to side. Maudie had a lot of Henry in her.

As Maude approached the gramophone, Aurelia stuck her head out of the kitchen.

"Would you ladies like something to drink? And, Maudie, would you like to hear some music? Dellie, you remember how to do it. Right?"

Dellie slid a phonograph record from its sleeve. "Maudie, this is called ragtime. Owen has been teaching me about it. This and other kinds of American music. The musicians on this recording are named Sissel and Blake."

Maude grunted as she turned away. Dellie turned the crank, releasing the notes into the room. Her eyes followed Maude as her sister grasped the back of a chair to check herself from moving in time to the music.

The clink of glassware announced Aurelia's return.

"Maude, would you help me with this please?" Aurelia gestured with her chin, hands balancing a tray. "Just put the glasses on the table. I can manage the pitcher. I hope you two ladies like sorrel!"

Maude's eyebrows shot up. "You have heard of sorrel? You found some around here? You drink it? Your people drink it?"

Aurelia snorted. "My people?" She looked at Maude quizzically. "We sure do. Well, at least those of us from New Orleans do."

Maude eyed Aurelia with new respect.

She reached for a glass. "Just a little sip for me though. Just enough for a little taste on my tongue."

CHAPTER SIXTEEN

Lord Nelson's Tale

S he felt like a peeping Tom or a sneak thief, but that discomfort was not enough to stop her. She swore to herself each time that it would be her last, but whenever she found herself alone in Lillian and Coleridge's flat, the temptation was too great. They kept letters in an old biscuit tin, lid rusting at the edges, on the kitchen shelf beneath a sack of sugar.

With the baby coming, Lillian and Coleridge had vacated Mrs. Cumberbatch's and found a larger flat. Dellie paid careful attention when they unpacked to where that tin landed in the new place. She glanced up and could see its edge next to a small sack of flour.

As she slid a milk crate over, she thought of Pendril's last letter to Coleridge. Her brother-in-law's voice came clearly though the door, and she had paused, listening through the thin wood, her handle on the knob. *"And at every port we dock, Lane must find a tree on which to carve his initials."* She'd slid her hand away carefully to avoid the click of the latch, and checked her breathing. *"Well, the place was nothing but bare rock, like it had not seen water since the receding of the Flood. You know how determined Lane is and while all the rest of we comrades were carousing in the district by the dock, here I am trailing ..."*

Today the tin was cool in her hands. She ran her fingers over the bas-relief image of a man pushing a woman seated in a swing suspended from a tree branch. The letters, some from M'Ma, some with May or Byron's childlike script, some from Coleridge's people, were stacked neatly inside. She glanced at the clock. Plenty of time before Lillian arrived. She placed the stack of envelopes in her lap, flipped through them — the task both slaking and stoking her longing. Nothing new with an extravagant stamp in the right corner and so she contented herself with re-reading those already becoming worn from her touch. She imagined Pendril writing by lamplight, or sitting, shaded from the sun, pen in hand, with his back against a tree. She slipped her fingers in one envelope, spilling the thin papers onto her lap. She barely needed to glance at the words, committed as they were to her memory.

She didn't hear the key in the door or the crack of linoleum. "Dellie?"

She looked up; her face grew hot with the redness of shame. Her sister's eyes wandered over the stack of envelopes with their distinctive script and fantastic stamps. Questions and answers crossed Lillian's face.

Dellie folded the papers and put them back into their envelopes, into the tin, stood on the crate, and reached toward the shelf. As she stepped down, Lillian put the kettle on for tea as she did everyday. Neither spoke a word.

———

"I want it to be something special, something New York style. This will be the last one before he has a father's responsibilities." Lillian had made that announcement, and so for weeks the women had been planning a grand event for Coleridge's birthday.

Dry brown leaves ran like mice along the sidewalk as the sisters made their way along the edge of Fort Greene Park.

"If you can get home early enough from Dr. Fielding, you and Winnie could prepare a pot of stewed chicken. Winnie has a good recipe with all manner of spices that she has amassed from Mrs. Iannacci. It is quick and would be a nice surprise. I am sure that she wouldn't mind sharing the recipe. Or the spices. She has sacks of them all about her kitchen." She turned to her sister. "What do you think of that? Maudie and I can bake the cake and bring it later. That way you and Coleridge can have a nice private supper before the guests arrive."

"That sounds like a good plan, Dellie."

Maude added, "We can make it fancy with raisins, rum, and a special frosting."

"Ah, that will work. Stewed chicken is a favorite of his. But I am still wondering about a special gift. It can't be too expensive, but I want it to be something he will always remember."

Maude spoke up. "I finally found some Bay Rum in a small shop off Flatbush Avenue. You know Mrs. Cumberbatch always arranges for one of the men coming over to bring some. Then she sells it for whatever dear price she can capture. I won't buy it from her."

Dellie's brow furrowed as she turned to Maude. "What do you need man's cologne for?"

"I was looking for some for Egbert."

"For Egbert? Don't you think that is a little personal for an unmarried woman to be giving to a man?"

"No, I don't, but I do think it is not your business, Dellie Standard."

"I beg your pardon, little sister. Have you no concern for your rep..."

"My reputation? I am not the one dawdling around with a foreign man who travels all around and abroad like some vagabond. And no sign of marriage! People are already wondering, Sister. Wondering and talking."

"Oh really, and what people might those be? People named Maude Standard?"

"I am only telling you what I hear at the Lodge."

Lillian tugged Maude's sleeve. "Bay Rum would be nice and I am glad someone finally found a place that sells it around here. But I am looking for something more distinctive. Something special."

———

Dellie and Lillian mingled with the other Lodge members in the basement of St. Philip's Church. A group was huddled around one of the new members who had news from the Lodge in Bridgetown. "You know they pride themselves on being well run, the officers above reproach, not like the people from that big island." The speaker paused for effect. "Well and all, seems like the treasurer was skimming from the top, lining his own pockets. He was planning to make it to Demarara, but never made it past the Molehead.

A group of the members found him and did thrash him. Now he is a guest of the Crown at Glendairy. Goes to show you..."

Suddenly Lillian turned to Dellie, voice low. "Listen. Listen to what Rudy Atherley is saying. Behind you. Listen."

"Lillian, didn't Cal teach you it is rude to open your ears like that to someone else's conversation? Didn't she tell you that one day you will hear something you shouldn't and it will get you into trouble?"

"Dellie, hush your mouth and listen for a change!"

Dellie strained her ears to Rudy's thin voice. "And with the landlord's new rule concerning pets, we have got to find a home for Lord Nelson."

"Dellie, *that* will be my gift for Coleridge!"

Dellie turned to her sister, her eyebrows bundled.

Lord Nelson was renowned throughout the Lodge membership and beyond. The red macaw was its owner's, Rudy Atherley's constant source of stories and conversation. Dellie had a clear picture of the two together. The red, yellow, green, and blue bird perched on his shoulder, its flamboyant tail midway down its owner's back — and Rudy with lanky legs and long feet, homemade printer's cap fashioned from a knotted handkerchief askew on his head. Many wondered if Rudy was right in the head. Now Dellie wondered the same thing about her sister. Perhaps this was just some folly of late pregnancy.

Lillian moved toward Rudy. "Oh, excuse me for listening to your conversation, but Mr. Atherley, did I hear you say that you are looking for a home for your bird?"

Rudy flashed a smile. "Yes. I am. Excuse me, but are you Coleridge's wife?"

"Yes."

"I have seen him play cricket. He is fine on the pitch."

Lillian cleared her throat. "Yes, he is. But you were saying about the bird. I might be interested."

Dellie jumped in. "Ah, I think that such a big decision is something we should give careful consideration. I mean, Rudy, you are so attached. And a bird as wondrous as Lord Nelson is a tremendous..."

Lillian cleared her throat. "I have already weighed those considerations and made my decision."

Lillian solidified the deal with a handshake, completely oblivious to the stunned faces around her. Rudy would bring Lord

Nelson, the two-year-old macaw, over on Saturday afternoon before Coleridge's surprise party. The unexpected Indian summer warm spell would make things perfect for the delivery.

Dellie was silent for much of the walk back to Lillian's flat while her sister chattered on about the words, songs, tricks she would teach the bird.

"I have heard that Lord Nelson is a quick learner. He can pick up anything he hears! Dellie, do you remember Henry's parrot, Clive? How full of mischief he was? How much Henry enjoyed him?"

Dellie couldn't hold her tongue any longer. "Lillian, Clive lived outside, not in a four-room flat in the middle of Brooklyn. And mischief is not enough description of Clive's behavior. You remember what he could do? Stealing good food, fouling everything near his station, biting people at will? You have a child coming! What are you thinking?"

Lillian's look silenced her.

———

There was a flurry of activity in the Greens' kitchen on the day of the party. Lillian relayed to Dellie her plans for the evening—a special dinner for her and Coleridge after his return from cricket and then a walk through the park at sunset. While they were out, Dellie and Maude would sneak in with the cake and assemble the guests, everyone shouting, "Surprise!" when the two returned. That was what Americans did.

A knock interrupted the work.

Lillian opened the door to find Rudy with Lord Nelson perched haughtily on his right shoulder. The bird's heavy beak curved like the nose of a centurion or a Bajan planter. Lustrous red feathers transformed into yellow along his breast and into blue and green along his tail.

Dellie caught her breath.

Rudy laughed, a nervous edge to the sound as he stepped through the doorway into Lillian's kitchen. He placed some bundles on the table.

"Here is his food, seeds mostly, in this bag. I buy it at the feed store at the foot of Atlantic Avenue. In this bag is the bowl that I use for his water." He turned to Lillian. "You should change it twice a day. He doesn't like it too hot, so when summer does reach, I do keep a small jar in the icebox. And this..." He tapped a perch that stood about five feet from the ground. "This is his perch, he will not tolerate a cage."

Dellie looked at her sister's face. Growing alarm made it pale as the reality of Coleridge's gift finally dawned on Lillian. Rudy rose from his seat and pulled a carefully folded foil packet from his vest pocket. He handed several pieces of cut up apple to Lillian. "Here, Mrs. Green, you feed him. Then he will be your friend forever."

Lillian smiled, picked up a piece of apple, and offered it to the bird.

His beak clamped down on her finger.

"Oouuch," she cried.

"Uhh..." Rudy muttered something indiscernible to anyone. "Perhaps he'll do better with Miss Standard."

Dellie reached toward the bird, fruit held at the end of her fingertips.

Lord Nelson lunged, screaming.

"Mrs. Green, he must just need time to settle into his new home. Is there a quiet room I can put him in?"

Dellie gasped as Lillian gestured to the spare room that she used on her day off.

"Better yet, put him in our bedroom. That will surprise Coleridge when he gets back. Let's do that now."

Rudy bent his knees and gestured Lord Nelson toward his shoulder. The bird accommodated him, and Rudy carried the perch to the middle of the bedroom and positioned him opposite the mirror. He shook his head with satisfaction. "That should settle him down. He does like to see his own image."

The two women watched from the doorway as the bird climbed from Rudy Atherley's shoulder onto the perch. Rudy bent toward Lord Nelson's face.

"Well, Nelson, my man, this is goodbye. Enjoy your new people." He ran his hand softly down the length of the bird's back.

As soon as Rudy closed the Greens' bedroom door, Lord Nelson began to scream. Dellie watched the last of the color drain from her sister's face.

———

As the gaslights were lit, Dellie and Maude returned with the cake. Owen followed a few steps behind with two flavors of ice cream. Maude turned her head sharply as Dellie put the key in the door. "Dellie, do you hear that?"

A raw voice declaimed, *"A cloud, a host of shining daffodils."*

"Who is inside? Who would be reciting Wordsworth?"

Dellie's shoulders sagged. "It is Lord Nelson."

"You mean Rudy Atherley's parrot?" Maude's eyes widened as the pieces fell into place. "You mean that is the great surprise gift our sister got for her husband?"

Dellie nodded. As the key entered the door and clicked, the bird began his screaming.

Owen cleared the top step. "Good heavens! What is that din?"

Maude turned to him. "Our sister brought home a parrot. Lord Nelson. Rudy Atherley's bird."

"Rudy Atherley? You mean that crazy man?"

Dellie swung the door opened and the three froze in the entryway. Before them on Lillian's table were two overturned bowls of chicken stew. On the floor were scattered flowers and foliage. Water leaked from a cracked vase.

A flash of red feathers caught Dellie's eyes.

"Down!" Owen commanded. He hit the ground, the bird diving toward his head.

He stood and spun around. "Dellie, Maude!" He pulled them toward the door to the outside hallway. They reached the safety of the stoop gasping for breath.

Dellie spoke first. "I guess the party is cancelled."

———

As Dellie rounded the corner toward Lillian's on Wednesday morning for her twice-weekly break at her sister's from service at the Fetteses, she could hear Lord Nelson's gravelly voice belting out "God Save the King." Outside stood Lillian, purse in hand.

"Dellie just put your things down in the vestibule. I need you to come with me. We are going to pay a visit to the Atherley's place."

The Atherleys lived a short trolley ride away on the second floor of a small apartment building. A woman sitting and looking out of a first floor window, elbows resting on a graying pillow, called to Lillian and Dellie as they mounted the steps.

"Looking for someone?"

"Mrs. Atherley," replied Lillian.

"Oh, she's up there. Doesn't have to come tearing out at the first of dawn, baby all bundled up to escape that infernal bird no more." She took a pull on the cigarette between her fingers and gestured toward the door.

They rapped the flaking knocker on the door several times. The nameplate under the knocker was clearly marked. The women could hear movement inside and a child snuffling. They knocked, again, louder this time. Suddenly, the snuffling muted and a window shade flickered ever so slightly.

"Dorothea, Dorothea." Lillian paused for a reply. None came.

Dellie ventured, "Dorothea, we know you are in there. We can hear the baby fussing."

A moment later the door opened slowly, not enough to admit the visitors, but enough to reveal part of a face. The woman's voice was low, barely a whisper. "You are here about the bird. I know. I am sorry. Truly. But I couldn't stand it anymore. And then the landlady said the bird had to go. I can't believe that Rudy gave it to people we know."

Dellie's fists clamped tight with anger. "Then why didn't you say something to Lillian?"

Dorothea's shoulders shrugged weakly. "I convinced my mind that it would work out. That he would behave for you. But I see now that it is just for Rudy that he acts civilized. I am so sorry. I must get back to the baby. Goodbye."

She closed the door.

———

Saturday, when Dellie knocked, Lillian pulled her into the apartment.

"Dellie," she said, hysterical, her eyes ringed with dark circles. "Dellie, thank God."

"Lillian! When was the last time you changed your clothes or ran a comb through your hair?"

"Shh, shh...Dellie, keep your voice down!" Her eyes ranged across the apartment.

Dellie lowered her voice. "I am sorry. Is Coleridge sleeping?"

"No! Well, I don't know. He went over to Clemmie's to get some rest. My things are in the bedroom. Coleridge can only get in to snatch a few things at a time. We have been sleeping in the spare room that you use on your days off. Lord Nelson has commandeered our room." Lillian sat heavily on the sofa, steadying herself to counter the weight of her stomach. She covered her face with her hands. "Sister. Dellie, please. You must help me. Please. You were right. The bird is plaguing us."

Dellie reached out to steady her sister's hand that quaked with exhaustion.

"Oh God, Dellie. It is dreadful. During the day the bird makes a sound just like a baby crying. One of the neighbors called in the authorities to investigate, thinking that I had the baby and was leaving it to cry. Then, that's not all..."

Her face went livid with embarrassment. "You know how it can repeat any word, mimic any sound. *Even the sounds of married people.* Well, I know more about the Atherleys' private life than I need to. Coleridge has been trying to give the bird away, but Lord Nelson is notorious. It seems like everyone on the face of the earth knew but us. But me."

Dellie gestured toward the window. "Why don't you just let it out?"

"Dellie! It couldn't live in this city! That would be like murder. It is a living thing. It speaks, no matter how rude it is. And it has a name."

Dellie plotted a number of means to resolve the problem, but all involved Lord Nelson's demise, and Lillian would have none of it. Finally they came up with a solution. So, while Lord Nelson perched in Lillian and Coleridge's bedroom, alternating between crying like an infant, saluting the King, imitating the throes of passion, and swearing with words to make a sailor blush—the women worked in the kitchen.

"You say the bird does favor raisins?" said Dellie, reaching for a box.

"That is right," replied Lillian as she clutched her arms around her body and rocked back and forth on the edge of a kitchen chair.

"And where does Coleridge keep his rum?"

"There." Lillian pointed. "Next to the sugar."

Dellie volunteered to face Lord Nelson's wrath. She stepped to Lillian's bedroom door and slowly turned the knob. Lord Nelson's screeching stopped. Dellie locked eyes with Lillian for a moment, took a deep breath and stepped through the door.

Lord Nelson stood on his perch, shoulders hunched and wings standing out along his back like a coattail. He turned as Dellie stepped in. Without taking her eyes off of him, she crept forward and poured the rum-soaked raisins into his dish. She backed away, feeling behind her for the doorknob.

The women waited until they heard the heavy "thunk" of the intoxicated bird falling to the floor. Dellie worked quickly, gathering the bird in a pillow case, taking care of its beak and claws. Lillian found an old crate and lay Lord Nelson in it, his tail trailing over the edge. The bird captured, they slipped out of the building as night fell. "First we will go past Aurelia and Jonathan's flat. She knows the streets well. She can come and help me find the garden where we picked the breadfruit. I am going to release Lord Nelson there. He can live in the trees. Lillian, you go as far as her house then go back home and get some sleep. I will take care of this."

"Ah, sister!" Lillian clung to her. And clung to her.

Dellie squirmed to free herself. "Lillian, Soul, you must release me now. Come. We have to get going before Lord Nelson wakes."

———

"I think we can take a trolley out that way," Aurelia suggested.

"But I am afraid that if the bird wakes, we'll draw the police."

"That is true." Aurelia thought for a moment. "Dellie, wait here." She rapped on a neighbor's window and chatted quickly with the boy who answered. She waved to Dellie. "He will let us use his wagon for a nickel. Come, put the box in here."

They walked down Fifth Avenue alongside the Green-Wood Cemetery, and then through the Gowanus neighborhood.

"Dellie, we have got to hurry. He is beginning to stir."

Ahead, the thick green of the plot lay in contrast to the burnished leaves of the trees surrounding it. The women quickened their pace, struggling to keep the bird in check. A voice calling caught their attention. It was the man, Walter, keeper of the breadfruit-tree garden, perched on the steps of his house.

He gestured to Dellie. "Miss, Miss, ain't you the one I gave some of the big green fruit to once?"

"Yes, sir."

"Well, what have you got there? In the box. Something alive?" He looked at the package rattling in Aurelia's hands with interest.

Dellie stepped to the bottom of the porch stairs. "A bird. We thought he would be happier here in the outdoors. We knew that your garden is always green."

The man cocked his head. "What kind of bird?"

"Parrot."

The man's face exploded into a grin and he called to his wife. "Jane! Come quick! See this! A parrot!"

The woman swooped down the stairs and tore the top off of the box. She picked the bird up and cradled him in her arms. Fully awake now, Lord Nelson fluttered his wings, flew in a circle around them and lighted on Walter's shoulder. The man, the woman, and the bird cuddled, caressed, and kissed. Dellie and Aurelia looked at each other and then at the scene in stunned silence.

Suddenly, Lord Nelson spread his wings and, in a glorious display of color, flew to the branch of a macadamia nut tree covered both in flower and fruit.

"He's beautiful," Walter muttered as he watched the bird preening himself. "Does he have a name?"

"He is called Lord Nelson."

"Lord Nelson," sighed Jane. "We have always wanted a parrot! Can we keep him? We have just the place for him. A room just off the porch! There is a mirror in there where he can look at his handsome self! And when he wants to, he can fly among the trees!" She turned to Aurelia and Dellie. "Please, take some breadfruit. Fill your wagon."

Dellie smiled, "I think we will. We haven't celebrated my brother-in-law's birthday properly yet. And maybe Lillian will settle for a bottle of bay rum for his gift."

CHAPTER SEVENTEEN

Lillian's Tale

Brooklyn, Winter 1912

Dellie hummed to herself, hitting the highs and lows with ease as she set out four cups and saucers, a plate of warm gingerbread, and a dish of applesauce on the fresh oilcloth covering Winnie's kitchen table. Outside, light, fine snowflakes began to stick, muffling the sounds of the Brooklyn streets.

Dellie sighed. She moved to the window over the kitchen sink and parted the curtains. Such a pretty sight. Who would think that something so different from the green lushness of home could so tantalize? Day crept toward evening, the January sky a deep glowing blue against the yellow gaslights along Warren Street. She could smell the cold air and somehow sense the snow collecting in it.

She put her hands against the glass, and felt the cold burning against her fingertips, then turned to the stove giving the pot of rich, dark liquid a stir. The women would gather soon, as they did at the end of each workday, for a steaming drink of thick cocoa before heading home. Maudie was halfway up the street. Through the window, Dellie watched her bend against the quickening wind. Lillian, too, would be arriving any minute now. From the other room, the whirr of the sewing machine accompanied Winnie as she sang to herself.

Dellie turned to add more milk to the pot. Winnie came into the kitchen and stationed herself near the window. "I see Lillian just turned the corner. The way she is walking... Hmm..." She flicked the curtain aside. The snow is starting to come down now. Hard, too. Dellie, another cup, I hear Maudie on the steps."

Moments later, they heard the whoosh of the front door closing against the gathering wind. Lillian's heavy tread thudded against the steps, signaling her arrival before the ring of the doorbell. Dellie pulled open the door to the vestibule, letting in a cold blast and a few stray flakes of snow.

Dellie helped her sister remove her heavy black wool coat, shaking the snow off before hanging it on the wooden coat rack. Lillian stamped her feet on the rough fiber doormat, making her protruding belly jiggle. She rubbed her stomach to calm her passenger.

"The baby has been jumping about all day."

"Well," said Dellie with a smile. "I guess this American child can't wait to get here. In a rush like everyone else in this man's country. Come. Maudie and Winnie are in the kitchen."

"Wait. Let me take my shoes off. I don't want to track up the floor."

"Don't worry about that. We'll get those wet shoes off in the kitchen and rub your feet with alcohol. You know the snow does collect all the germs in the air. Winnie. Get the alcohol for Lillian's feet!" she called to the kitchen.

Lillian sat on one of the wooden kitchen chairs, taking care not to lose her balance. She placed her hands on both sides of her back and stretched. "My back has been tight all day..."

Winnie and Dellie passed a look between them.

Dellie, armed with a bottle of rubbing alcohol, sat down and lifted her sister's feet onto her lap. Maude sighed as she watched her sister unlace Lillian's ankle-high leather shoes.

"Lillian, your feet are all swollen!" Maude said. "Let Dellie rub them good and give you some relief..."

"How long are you going to keep trudging over to the Colored Home?" Dellie wondered aloud. "How long is Dr. Fielding going to let you in the building?"

"You know the work I am doing is not too taxing on the body. Helping with the books and chatting with the residents. I can manage it. Oh, by the way. I saw your Mrs. Fettes the other day at the bank. Is she having another baby?"

"She hasn't said anything to me. I don't think so."

Winnie chimed in. "I am not so sure about that. I saw her, too, at the dress shop the other day. No woman that tiny has a bosom that big unless she is carrying. There is going be another one in that house by summer for sure!"

Dellie shook her head. "I do hope for Mr. Fettes' sake it is a boy! He was complaining the other day that keeping a house of three girls and a wife is driving him to the poorhouse. He claimed it is cheaper to outfit the army. That he never has a penny to his name, paying for all the clothes women must wear. Stockings, a slip, a camisole, a corset, drawers. Said he is taking the whole family and moving to the Pacific jungle to live among the people there, each person in his family naked as the day they were born. I thought Mrs. Fettes was going to faint hearing him talk so."

Winnie cleared her throat and the women turned toward her. "Speaking of babies." Her voice dropped to a whisper. "I have one coming too. At last." Her eyes filled. The women cried out and rushed her with hugs. Dellie pulled her close and whispered in her ear. "Ah, friend. I know how long you have waited. How long you have been praying for this." Tears of happiness fell.

"Well, you can have some of these loose dresses and blouses." Lillian looked at Winnie and tugged at her top. "I have had enough of them. I feel like I have been carrying forever."

Maudie cut another square of gingerbread. "The applesauce does go well with this. Please, pass it."

"And I'll have one more cup of cocoa, please, Winnie. Actually make that a half," Lillian said. "Dellie, your hands upon my feet do feel good."

"That may be so, but I don't see how you are going to get your boots back on..." sighed Dellie.

"Ah, this cocoa is good. Takes the chill off better than tea, I think."

"I sprinkled a little cinnamon in it. That adds a little taste of heat, you know. And a different kind of sweetness." She rummaged through her handbag as she moved to the kitchen counter. "Listen, while we are all here, I got a letter from May!"

"What!" Maude laughed. "She does deign to take pen in hand and remember she has relations here?" Dellie swatted her sister's hand.

"My heart is always full about May." Dellie shifted in her seat, shoulders sagging. "We all had Cal to raise us up and care for us. May was only eight, yuh know? And always wild. Even M'Ma had trouble with her. Still does."

The women pulled closer to the table. Dellie began to read:

I hope this letter finds you each as well as it leaves me. M'Ma and I spend each day thinking about the new American baby that you are carrying, Lillian. Know that our prayers are with you when your time comes. Nothing unusual is going on here. I will be taking my exams this spring as you know and the headmaster has given extra work. Mrs. Chandler has started asking me to make extra creams and tinctures from Cal's recipes. I think she is planning to sell some to her friends. The Great House and the rest of us along with it continue to suffer with the low price of sugar.

With the money you sent, we were able to buy Sam the Donkey from Emmeline. We are hoping that he will help cart ground provisions for sale. I can see why Emmeline treated him the way she did though. He does not seem to understand the meaning of work and acts more like a dog – following people about, begging for food – than a donkey.

Browne is still tending the garden. It flourishes madly, however, under her care. Some say she gets the fertilizer from the droppings of the obeah woman's frizzled chickens and that it is worked with some obeah. The clematis blooms have attained the size of charger plates, the perfume from the freesia buds could choke a body, the morning glory is like a jungle mat and daily it breaks from its confines to twist about the feet of those few who venture too close. If Henry or Josh did not constantly beat them back, the wild roots would under-mine the foundations of the Great House. Mrs. Chandler has refused their requests to plow it under. She believes that the blue ribbons and accolades from the Windward Islands Horticultural Society for her extraordinary achievements set her apart. Please write as soon as the baby comes. M'Ma cannot wait to brag about her American great-grandchild.

Dellie cradled her face in her hands and leaned on the table. "May does weigh on me. You see how there is not one word about her making plans to come. And now this going on and on about the garden. It is beyond me...it is close to madness."

"Just like my sister." Winnie ran her finger around the rim of her cup. "She won't come, either, no matter how much Clemmie and I beg her. You can't worry about it, though. They both will come when they are ready."

"And what is going to make them ready?" Lillian shook her head and looked at the ceiling. "They must be expecting an engraved invitation from President Woodrow Wilson himself." Lillian sucked her teeth and changed the subject. "Winnie, how is your sewing going? There is a Lodge ball coming up and on top of that you have got all those hats to sew for the investiture."

"I am making progress. The hats are sewn. It is the embroidering of the fish that is the trouble." She gestured toward Maude. "Since you are keeping company with Egbert, please tell his father they need to adopt a new symbol that is easier to sew than a flying fish — a square, or better, just a line. Or tell these Bajans to stay out of Brooklyn — go to London, England!"

"Still, Winnie, that sewing machine was the best investment you and Dellie could have made! You two are your own business women!"

"'Tis true for sure. I was going to ask you, Dellie. We got an offer for more work. You enjoy the fancy embroidery more than I do, and I don't want to have to turn business away. Mrs. Charles, you know her, the Trinidadian woman, approached me about sewing the regalia for their lodge. I told her I would get back to her. But if you are willing to take that on as your own work, I will tell her yes. Anymore fine sewing is going to make me blind."

A smile passed between the two women.

"Maudie, how is your work going?" Lillian asked as she shifted position to accommodate her back once again.

"With Mrs. Frost, you mean? All I can say is the name does suit her. She pays well, though. And her children are not much trouble."

"Oh, listen!" said Winnie with a mischievous glint in her eyes. "Have you heard Mrs. Cumberbatch's son Roger is getting married!" She paused for effect. "I hear he is marrying a *foreigner*!"

The gasp was uniform save for Dellie.

"Yes, for sure! A foreigner. An *American Negro*!"

Dellie looked away, her jaw tight so they would not see her annoyance.

"And on top of it, her family is from the *Bronx* of all places!" This time, Dellie gasped.

Winnie folded her hands on the table and let the magnitude of the news sink in. The room fell silent. "I hear Her Majesty fainted dead away."

Dellie broke the silence with a loud laugh. The other women followed.

Winnie cradled a cup of cocoa in her hands, enjoying the warmth that crept up her fingers. "I heard the girl's mother and father aren't happy either. They say she is going to throw her future away marrying a foreigner, a monkey chaser just off the boat."

The women fell silent again. Dellie sucked her teeth.

"Foolishness," she declared. The music from the bangles circling her arm hung in the air. "Like colored aren't colored here or somewhere else. Some white here are colored, too. I butt up against all manner of people all mashed together on the trolley, all working for a few slim pennies. Colored from here, colored from abroad, white from here, white from abroad. When is someone going to realize the Great Ones rule here too?"

"That is for sure," added Lillian. "You see in the *Eagle* the picture of Mr. J. P. Morgan's new house in the city? It puts the Chandler's Great House to shame." She took a sip of cocoa. "So when is the Cumberbatch wedding?"

Maude picked up a napkin. "I hear it is going to be in the spring. You know, by the time the warm weather does reach, maybe the mothers will be speaking enough to plan the party. I think both sets of parents will see reason when they know how much property the other family has. The two will merge and own half of Brooklyn. They will be like the Negro Morgans and Vanderbilts."

Laughter rang through the room.

"Well, ladies," Lillian said with a glance around the table, "I'm going home. My back is aching like I have been weeding cane all day. Winnie, help me with my shoes, please."

"Soul, there is no way these shoes are going on those feet!" Dellie exclaimed. "Winnie, have you got some old shoes of Clemmie's?"

Winnie searched the back of her closet and found a pair.

She sidled up to Dellie.

"I can't believe she doesn't realize it, but she is in labor. And is ..." her voice trailed off. Dellie looked up sharply from the sink where she was cleaning up, a shard of fear burning her face. Her voice dropped so only Winnie could hear.

"Oh, Winnie, ...Her hips are so narrow and her belly so big..."

Winnie touched her arm in reassurance. "Don't worry, she will be alright. She's fine-boned, but she's strong. She has filled out with this child. It hasn't sapped her strength like some. Don't worry. Remember, I used to go with your mother and grandmother too, sometimes, when they were tending. And Lillian herself sees how Doctor Fielding does. Plus, he has seen her a few times. He regards her like his own family. If we need him, he'll come."

That assurance calmed Dellie a bit, as did the thought of Lillian's own skill.

Winnie's voice took on a commanding tone, and Dellie looked at her in surprise. "Wait up, Soul. Dellie and I are going to walk with you. You are not used to those shoes and the snow is coming down furiously now. Maudie, you stay here and clean up. Then leave a note for Clemmie, and walk over to Lillian's house." Her tone left no room for questions.

Lillian looked from face to face and then shrugged.

The women, bundled and stooped against the wind, lumbered down the street as the snow swirled and drifted around them.

They met Coleridge up the street as he stepped off the cross-town trolley.

"You three are a sight!" He stopped abruptly. "Mrs. Green! What are those things on your feet? The newest fashion?"

Winnie broke in. "We are walking your wife home. Trying to make sure she doesn't slip. She is wearing Clemmie's old shoes."

"Well, thank you, ladies, you can head home out of the snow. I..."

Winifred cut in again. "It is all right. We'll walk you to your house and warm up before heading back."

Coleridge began to protest, pointing to Winnie's place. "But you are less than..."

Her look silenced him. The figures bent into the wintry breath of the wind. They helped Lillian up the eleven steps to her front door, her face now grim with pain and effort. Her water broke in the vestibule. The women banished Coleridge to Winnie and Clemmie's house, with the order to send Maude over right away.

They barely got Lillian over the threshold of her bedroom before pain gripped her like a tight belt across her back and belly. Dellie mumbled a prayer. The next hours would be long.

Toward morning, Dellie looked out the window. The sky began to lighten and take on a winter glow. She could see the morning star through the topmost branches of the bare maple across the street. They continued to take turns walking Lillian through her contractions, and now, close to daybreak, it was more dragging than walking.

"That's right, Lillian. Lean on our arms. We'll help you." Winnie's soothing voice covered the constant moans. Suddenly, Lillian's breathing became ragged.

"I have to push," she half panted, half screamed. She gulped air as the women guided her to her bed.

"Dellie and Maude, support her legs!" Winnie commanded. "That's right. That's right, Lillian. Good girl, again push, push hard, as hard as you can! That's it! I see the head. Just one more time. Dellie, Maudie—hold her tight. Now Lillian, now girl, push!"

A perfect baby girl slipped into Winnie's hands. The women's faces glowed with joy. Their first American child had been born.

The clean, warm towels and clothes lay ready. Dellie dipped a cloth in a small basin of warm water sweetened with rosemary and squeezed it over the child's limbs and wisps of hair on her head. Maude wiped the baby's eyes gently with a cloth, and watched them flutter open.

Dellie bent closely and whispered in the child's ear, "Welcome, little one. Welcome to the family."

Winnie laid her hand on the small chest in blessing. She quickly slipped on a pair of boots to protect her feet from the snow, then took the basin outside to pour the wash water at the foot of the small tree growing in Lillian's backyard.

Dellie swaddled the baby in a tiny blanket. "You are beautiful, little sister," she sighed to the squirming bundle in her arms. The bright eyes, wide open, surveyed the room. Dellie patted her dry. The baby's smooth skin was the color of warm caramel. Her task completed, she carried the baby to her mother. "Here…"

Still shaky, Lillian reached her arms out. She said a prayer as she cradled the small life in her arms. The women paused and joined in. Lillian offered her a breast and ran her hand over the child's arms, legs, chest, and face in wonder.

"I have a child, a child," she said, "I am someone's mother."

"Lillian." Dellie pulled a small glass bottle from deep in her pocket and remembered the day she pulled away from home. Byron and Palley had pressed a small brown bottle into her hand. "Take this" said Palley. "It is seawater so you don't forget us." Byron had chimed in. "It is from Worthing."

"Sister, I brought the seawater that the boys gave me," said Dellie, her voice low. "I put some in a small bottle that Mrs. Watson gave me." She held it for Lillian to see. Its facets caught the light from the sun cresting over the roofs of Brooklyn and cast rainbows across the room. "It will remind these new ones," she reached toward the baby, "of home. So they won't forget who they are and where their people come from."

She waited for her sister's assent. Lillian looked out the window, her eyes focused on a distant place. Dellie saw the old conflict surface and play across her sister's face.

Dellie took a step closer.

She looked into the baby's face, her eyes now closed, long thick lashes resting on the rise of her cheeks. Dellie spoke, holding her sister's hand. "It is all a part of life. The terrible and the beautiful. Like home. Terrible and beautiful. Like you told me. Take it, make it your own. Like you have done here. Like we all will have to."

Lillian shifted position in her bed and smoothed the coverings, making the rainbows dance across her and the sleeping child. Maude and Winnie appeared in the doorway, both spent from the night's ordeal.

Lillian opened her hand. "Let me take the water, Dellie." The light, sun, shadow, rainbow created a pattern like lace on the figures of the women and baby. Dellie removed the glass stopper and watched as her sister touched the cool seawater to the baby's forehead. "Millicent, that is your name little girl. Millicent Augusta."

The other women, Winnie and Maude each touched the child in blessing.

Dellie's voice was thick with feeling. "Maude, go down the street, please, and tell Coleridge he is a father. That he has got a daughter. Now, Lillian, we are going to clean you up and get the child swaddled properly. I love you," she laughed, "but you are surely a mess!"

———

Six weeks later to the day, the morning dawned with the bright clear sunlight that only winter could bring. Dellie was up, sitting by the coal stove, putting a few last stitches of special embellishments on the white gown she had begun to stitch the day after the baby's birth. She had searched the streets of lower Manhattan for finely woven cotton. She purchased a length of lace from the old Irish woman around the corner, who had made it in the ancient way.

Dellie held up the garment, examining the line of stitches at the seam and the fine work around the hem. She had worked on the gown every free moment. Now she tipped her head back and sighed. She was an aunt and with Winnie's news, likely to be a god-mother soon. There would be other nieces and nephews to come. Yet for herself, what awaited her? She eyed the tin on Lillian's shelf. *Pendril. Pendril.* "Enough." She spoke aloud though no one was awake to hear her. "Enough. You made a decision. This is your life here."

The gown that lay on Dellie's lap glowed with lilies, star-apple flowers, cooing doves, flamboyant blossoms, and flourishes of curli-cues, tendrils, and swirls worked in silken white thread. As she made each stitch to finish the dress, images rose before her eyes. She saw a line of children — all colors, all sizes, boys, girls, hair long, hair short, curly, nappy, straight, black, auburn, red. Names came to her. She saw two girls sitting on steps somewhere playing jacks. She saw a young, brown-haired man climbing a mountain with a view of two oceans. She saw a man, a woman, and three children posing for a photograph. Before her were two women, mother and daughter, signing papers for a wall house over in St. James. There was a young man, traveling pack on his back, among a group of men wearing saffron robes. A girl with long, dark hair dragged a suitcase up a long flight of stairs. A young man, tall and thin, swam in an immense lake. A man who loved to play ball, showed his son how to throw and catch. She saw the family unfolding, unfolding, each generation stepping further into God's world.

Each stitch Dellie made held a prayer for the family — for its safety, for its prosperity, for the children yet to come, generations hence. All would wear this gown that she sewed on a street in Brooklyn. In New York. In America. She prayed that they would remember what she knew and that the spirits would tell them of Bim.

PART THREE
Dellie's Claim

CHAPTER ONE

That Door in Her Heart

Winter, 1914

Dellie ran her hand over the sheer onionskin sheet and lifted her pen. In her last letter, Eva had scolded her. "All the other girls from your sewing group who have gone to New York manage to write regularly. Don't tell me you forget your teacher." Dellie's eyes ranged over the Fetteses' kitchen as she gathered her thoughts.

Eva was right. Dellie hadn't written, and now so much had been packed into the more than a year since her last letter that she didn't know where to begin. The babies had started coming — one for Lillian, one for Winnie and both of them expecting again. She was sure that she had written soon after Maudie and Egbert married, and surely the news had reached her that Maudie was carrying and due in a few months. She would have to be sure to clarify that for Eva. Dellie loved her friend and teacher, but knew that she had a weakness for tale telling. She would be sure to pass it on to the other long-tongued women that Maude was due a full year after the wedding.

179

She put pen to paper and wrote quickly, doing her best not to smudge the ink in her haste. Owen was picking her up at Maude and Egbert's flat and she could picture his foot-tapping annoyance if she kept him waiting. And she hoped to prevent any extended exchange between Maude and Owen. There was no love lost between the two. Owen couldn't bear Maude's constant scrutiny. For her part, Dellie knew that her sister found little agreeable in him and finding fault was becoming habit with her. His southern drawl: "He talks so slowly you want to jump in and pull the words out." His job: "Riding round and round, all up and abroad the country like a vagabond!" And most of all his attire and concern for his appearance: "Wastes money on all that finery. He is likely to show up King Edward himself." Dellie shook her head, stamped the letter and headed for the door. *Maude. West Indians.*

As Dellie rounded the corner, she could see Maudie in the window, Winnie's little girl in her arms. Dellie waved.

Dellie pulled her jacket close against the damp as Maude fumbled with the door to the vestibule.

"Ah Dellie, come in. I am watching Cicely for a little while. She did just learn to walk you know and now she won't be still. Winnie dropped her off a little bit ago while she went to do some errands, but in that time the child has run me and herself ragged. I just put some water on for tea. Listen for it while I change her. I think she is wet. Have a cup of tea before you go? There is a chill in the air today." She shuddered to emphasize her point.

Dellie had barely gotten the cups out before the doorbell rang. She turned toward the door, but heard the light tip of Maude's shoes as she went to answer it. She glanced at the clock on the school across the street. Precisely four-fifteen. Just as Owen had said.

"Oh Owen, come in, come in. So good to see you." Dellie's mouth tightened at her sister's gift for dissembling. "Come on in and sit down. Dellie is here. She is making some tea. You'll join us?"

Dellie could see the scene reflected in Maude's glass cabinet. "I'll be there in a minute!" she called. Owen shot her a pained look that made his thoughts transparent: *"Please God, don't let it be a colored minute."* Dellie jogged the kettle in a hopeless attempt to speed its boiling.

Winnie's daughter, Cicely, gurgled her greeting, earning a quick kiss from Maude. She turned back to Owen. "Can I take your hat and coat?" Maude said with a smile. Dellie watched as Owen hesitated a moment before turning over his pearl gray felt hat, just purchased on a run to Boston, noticing some moisture from the baby's mouth on Maude's hand. He always made sure his attire was impeccable. She knew and Maudie knew too, even if she wouldn't admit it, that if a man of his complexion didn't dress like somebody, he'd be treated like nobody. Maude pulled the hat from his hand and and hung it on the coat rack.

Just as the kettle finally whistled, she heard Egbert's voice. "Hey man! How have you been?" She saw Egbert gesture toward a chair. "So man, you think DuBois means West Indians too, or is he only thinking about American Negroes in his plans?" As soon as she heard DuBois, Dellie knew this conversation would keep them occupied. "Maudie, let Egbert hold the baby and come help me a moment!" she called out. She could at least give Owen that relief.

Egbert and Owen nodded their thanks as Maude placed a tray with cups of tea in front of them. "I see the colored organizing and have been watching the Jews coming together since before that factory fire. Things are changing, man. You are right about that."

"Here." He handed a roll of newspapers fastened with a rubber band to Egbert." I picked these up on my last run. I thought you might find them interesting. A lot in there about DuBois. There is also a copy of his new magazine, the *Crisis*. The man isn't afraid to say what he thinks. What a lot of people think, in fact."

Egbert leaned toward him to make his point. "But I ask you, is there a place in this talk for West Indians? I know that is where DuBois' people were from, but he was born here, an American Negro. Is he thinking about us? That we are part of it?"

"Here Egbert. Read it yourself." Owen pointed to the paper then put his hand on his chin and looked up, his eyes serious. "This *I* know for sure. Time is here for a man with a vision and resources to make his move..." Dellie's return to the room broke his train of thought. He stood.

Dellie smiled as she turned to her sister. "Maudie, I did venture into your closet to borrow this." She buttoned a waistcoat over her light-colored shirtwaist." I think I will need something under my coat to ward off the chill. I hope you don't mind."

Dellie sat, and let Cicely climb into her lap. She picked up a copy of the *Defender* and scanned the photos of Negroes with fine cars, houses, and a society page covering the news of doctors' daughters marrying the sons of funeral parlor owners. She had just started an article about a woman named Ida B. Wells and her crusade against violence towards black people, when Owen stood, signaling his readiness to leave.

"Well, thank you Mr. and Mrs. Walcott, but Dellie and I should be on our way."

"So where are you and Dellie off to today?"

"Just over to the movie house on Flatbush, and maybe something to eat. But I don't want to miss the newsreel."

Dellie stepped toward the coat tree where Maude stood, Owen's hat already in her hand. She watched as her sister extended it toward him. As his fingers grazed the brim, she was certain he saw a glint in Maude's eye, as she fumbled the hand-off, and Owen's new hat landed, crown down on the mat by the door.

It was near dusk when they left the movie house. The fine mist that had softened the city earlier in the day was beginning to freeze, painting a thin glaze on the sidewalk, making walking treacherous. A cluster of newsboys finished their sorting and scattered, thin coats pulled close, hands red and raw from the gathering cold. A lamplighter picked his way down the street avoiding ice-slick manhole covers and grates, his work barely noticeable as the winter night gained ground against the fading shadows.

As they walked, the commercial traffic thinned along the main street. The city began to turn inward with the end of day. They bypassed Tafts Restaurant, its fine wood gleaming in the yellow interior — not gracious to Negroes — and turned the corner, settling on a small, family-owned establishment on the second floor of a building above a food importer. It was a new place. The sharp smell of fresh oilcloths rose from the tables. Gilt lettering proclaiming its name was not quite complete on the door.

Dellie and Owen had been keeping company, on and off, for years, with no progress, and that suited her fine. Oh, they shared good times — socials at his church (Concord Baptist), socials at hers (St. Philip's Episcopal), baseball games, cricket matches, and, once, an elegant dinner at the Marshall, the famed Negro hotel (in Manhattan, no less!), where Theodore Drury, the copper-colored opera singer had sat at the table next to them. She and Owen put up with speculation from friends and relations eager to see her settled down and cared for, even if he was a foreigner:

"...saw her fingering some fine white fabric the other day, maybe they've been talking marriage..."

Or: "...he tarried talking to the priest after service."

They both were silent when words from the wagging tongues of bad-minded people reached their ears with fantasies about him.

"...that's right, I hear he has got a family somewhere, a wife and two kids..."

Or, about her.

"Well you know, they say she is not partial to men."

But that's how their thing had been going for years now. Stuck in limbo. And that was fine with her. He was a good companion.

Dellie gazed out of the window, one elbow on the table, chin resting on her hand as they waited for their order. Through the steamed windows, she watched for the occasional figure passing by—a person planning each step, planting each foot just so to avoid a fall as a glaze began to form on the street.

"Dellie, I have told you before about my plan for a hotel."

Something in the tone of his voice caught her attention and she examined his face for some different meaning. "Many times, Owen. Something in Delaware, you said."

"That's right. Not too far from the rail line. Something that would cater to Negro people who are travelling. I have been keep-ing my eye out for such places. Talking to the owners when I'm out on a run. I know I could make that business work."

Dellie put her fork down. This was not just another review of the usual talk with Clemmie and Coleridge.

"I have put in for a transfer to the line's *20th Century Limited*. The run out to Chicago. It is the flag of the New York Central Line. It won't come through right away. But I am on the list. I know you've seen the write-ups about it in the papers. It's capable of travel nearly halfway across the country in sixteen hours. It is the train of all of the rich businessmen. If I get the transfer, it would be a major boost for me."

His eyes were bright, his brooding seriousness cast aside.

"I could begin to really make some plans for a piece of land down South and a hotel. Maybe buy out someone and just change the name. I'd always thought the *Blue Nile* would make a fine name." He paused. But maybe you would help me choose something?"

Dellie swallowed hard as the thought raced across her mind. "He is asking me to marry him. Why can't he leave well enough alone?"

His hand shook as he laid it atop hers. She looked up, surprised at the tenderness of the gesture.

"That is, if you would join me in this plan. If you would marry me..."

Her head buzzed like a thousand insects swarming, and his words ran together: wife, leaders in the community, something to pass on to their children, a legacy, she could continue her sewing if she wished...

Her heart pounded. He was a good man. He treated her well. He had plans and the means to achieve them. *But Pendril.* It was perfectly reasonable. *But Pendril. The small triangle of hair on his breastbone.* Yes, they made fine companions. *Pendril, the crinkling of his eyes when he smiled.* He was a good man. *But Pendril. The velvet of his skin.* He was upright, dependable. A union between the two of them made sense. *But Pendril.* She silenced the name that thumped through her head.

"Yes, Owen. I will marry you." The words were dry on her tongue.

———

Lillian was at the park with the children, leaving Dellie by herself in the flat. She double-folded and smoothed a sheet on the kitchen table. There was still some time before she would need to head across town to the Fettes house. She glanced over at the basket beneath the window. "Well, I might as well iron and fold the clothes too. Save Lillian the work.

She pushed a step stool to the counter, stood on it, and rummaged her hand about on the high shelf in search of the iron. Her hand brushed a cool metal box. She ran her hand across the top, her fingers anticipating the impression of a woman on a swing.

Dellie stood still for a moment, thoughts tumbling. She rested her hands on the counter and paused before brushing a few stray crumbs aside, then reached up and pulled the tin down.

She sat on the step stool and ran through the stacks of letters. Lillian had sorted them by sender — from M'Ma, from Henry, from Maude, from May, and from Pendril. Dellie pulled out the stack and untied the twine that bound them together. She didn't need to read them, she knew by the picture on the extravagant stamp in the corner of each from where it was mailed and what it said. She flipped through them, remembering his words and seeing what he had seen.

From Cardiff, Wales: *Despite the summers and winters I have spent in this port, I am still amazed by the light. Summers, the sun is out until well past ten o'clock, winters are dark nearly all day.*

From Morrocco: *I stood in the shadows of buildings with domes round and peaked like onions. Inside the place was ablaze with blue tiles... Their patterns would dazzle you.*

And more recently from Edinburgh: *They are changing the name of my ship from the Hun to the Pict with these rumors of war with the Germans.*

But in none of them any greeting for her, any mention of her at all.

Just days ago she had told Owen that she would be his wife. She rested her elbow on the counter, hand covering her eyes as memories played before them: Pendril's wild unruly hair, his vague scent of cocoa butter, the way he had walked with her to St. George behind the carriage bearing her mother, a moment by a lagoon, luscious blooms left on the steps of Miss Crane's shop, and a piece of blue sea glass. Despite herself, the tears flowed. "Foolish woman." She chastised herself aloud. "You came to this place. Now you must make a life."

She reached across the table and grabbed her handbag. The letter that she had taken all those years ago sat in a deep corner. She took it out read it one more time then stood, placed it with the others in Lillian's collection, and returned the tin to the shelf. Lillian would be back soon, and Dellie would have the ironing finished when she returned.

———

He conceded the church — St. Philip's Episcopal, not Concord Baptist. She conceded the decision on a wedding trip, she had no real preference for any place. Owen chose a seaside resort in Connecticut, *Dad's Hotel*, run by one of his retired Pullman brethren. It would give him a chance to talk to the inn's keep about the business. Both agreed on the date, July 26 — after the June rush that was the nature of her sewing business.

Dellie and Winnie had converted the smallest of the bedrooms in Winnie and Clemmie's new flat into a sewing room. At the beginning, the work consisted of just the regalia for the Lodge and the repairs on the vestments and altar cloths for St. Philip's Church. Clemmie had only agreed to permanently give up the space ("I was planning on using it for a boarder!") after he saw the business expand. Dellie and Winnie now took in the work for the other West Indian lodges, and their reputation for fine and fancy sewing drew in business for weddings, christenings, and other events. With that work and the job with the Fettes family, Dellie had finally had enough for her own flat, shared with one of the women from the Lodge.

Today, at Winnie's, instead of a customer standing on the little rise that offered a better angle for hemming and fitting, it was Dellie.

The room was a hive of activity as she stood for her final fitting. Her hands moved through her hair as she positioned and repositioned a comb, trying different styles and looks.

"Keep your arms at your side. You know when you move you jostle the hem. Be still!" Winnie was firm.

Dellie's arms dropped.

Maude used a brush to try to tame a length of Dellie's hair. "Have you thought about it up like this? I could put a few curls in it with the iron. You want to try it and see?"

Dellie's right hand moved instinctively to her neck and hair, followed by Maude's, armed with brush and comb.

"That's it!" exclaimed Winnie, mouth clenched around a mass of straight pins. "Everyone out. Sit in the front room till we are through. And keep an eye on those children! I don't want jelly hands all over everything!"

Dellie listened to Maude and Lillian fussing about the kitchen as they prepared lunch for the small brood of children. She smiled down at Winnie. "Well, Cal would be surprised that Maudie is someone's mother now. And that she found someone who can manage with her!"

"'Tis true, and I know Cal would be glad to see this day coming for you, Dellie. I truly believe so."

A tribe of children — Lillian's, Winnie's, and Maude's — moved as one unit toward the kitchen, some walking, some crawling. From the kitchen voices drifted in to where Dellie and Winnie worked as the sisters prepared something for the children.

"So now we are only a week away."

"It is not some doom that we are counting down to, Maude. It is your sister's wedding. You need to cleanse your bad mind and your bad mouth." Lillian's voice had an edge.

"I know, but Lillian, I'm afraid he is going to try to make her an American Negro. She already had to insist upon the church. He will make her a foreigner."

"Maudie, excuse me, but I remind you once again that *you* are the foreigner."

"Well, I don't like him. And I heard him talking to Egbert about how he is going to buy some sort of hotel in the South. He is planning on taking her away."

"Maudie, it is not your business. He makes our sister happy and offers her a good life. That is what you should concern yourself with. She has got a chance to leave house- serving and he has got a plan to make his own way. Besides he loves her, you see the way he looks at her."

"That's the other thing," said Maude. "You don't see her looking at him the same way. He isn't Pen..."

"Don't say it."

Dellie stared through the doorway at the women in the other room. She could feel the heat that she knew flamed her cheeks and neck from her effort to banish the words that she knew were true. *"He isn't Pendril."*

She stepped from the rise, pushed past Winnie, and closed the door to the fitting room.

———

The sun and clouds danced as guests ambled into the church. Dellie watched from the vestibule as her wedding began to unfold. At the altar stood Owen in a dark suit, a white rosebud gracing his lapel. He cut a striking figure. Even at this moment, a few of the women on the groom's side of the aisle tried to catch his eye.

Each assembly, the bride's and the groom's, was cautiously gracious, afraid of making some sort of faux pas that would either offend or reflect badly on themselves or their respective communities. On the left side of the Church sat the bride's family — the West

Indian contingent, new families reconfigured from the island's old clans.

Dellie peered around the corner as one of the groomsmen seated an elderly couple. The husband's losing attempt at a whisper reached her ears. "My, my but these West Indians do all look the same." Dellie turned her head, her eyes scanning the pews. He was right. They all looked strikingly similar, the same bone structure — varying only by skin color in which was reflected the mix of South Asian, white, African, or Indian in their veins. Over the course of three hundred years in a 166 square-mile space every family somehow related by blood or marriage.

Her eyes drifted to Owen's people — some friends from the contingent of émigrés from the South, others drawn from the brotherhood forged on the rails in the Pullman Cars where Owen worked. The shades of skin among them reflecting the varieties of blood — Indian, black, white, in which was reflected their history.

A few families or individuals among the West Indians who had already found prosperity (Cumberbatch, Walcott), or who had brought it with them (Sealey, Wilkerson, Pilgrim), had purchased and named pews that comprised the first five rows of the sanctuary of St. Philip's. Some now even had upholstered cushions. The back ten, where the latest of the Bajans to arrive in the city sat, were still wooden folding chairs, creaky and uncomfortable.

Today, the sanctuary was full for the grand event. Women on both sides of the aisle were fully adorned. Hats were bedecked with flowers and feathers. Lace and chiffon competed for space in the pews, the aisle, and the vestibule. The abundant and ubiquitous silver bangles from the bride's side played their music throughout the room. Seated in the first and last seat of each pew on the left was a lodge member in full regalia.

The tones from the upright piano swelled. Maude kissed her cheek. Lillian turned. "Are you ready? This is your moment, Sister." Dellie swallowed the tight ball in her throat and worked to conjure at least a sliver of the feeling she had felt on Lillian's wedding day those years ago. Those were days with Pendril when they had plans together. She turned to Lillian, the question in her eyes adding a question to her words. "Owen is a good man. He is responsible, intelligent, a good provider. This is right. *This is right.*" Lillian squeezed her hand in response.

Guided by Aurelia, the mass of children from both the groom's and bride's people drifted down the aisle in contained disorder, spreading petals of fragrant white blossoms on the cloth runner.

Blossoms cascading down. Kisses under a star-apple tree.

She arranged her face in a serene smile, inhaled, stepped down the aisle, and closed that door in her heart.

The touch of Owen's hand brought her back to the moment as they faced the priest. Father Fletcher used the most formal words from the *Book of Common Prayer* to bless their union.

"I now pronounce you man and wife."

She was married. Owen's lips touched hers.

CHAPTER TWO

Didn't Notice

"*O*wen, what should I make?" Dellie was in a state. Aurelia and her husband, Jonathan, were having guests over for one of the rounds of socials that Owen's brethren from among the Pullman Porters often hosted. This one would be Dellie's first since her marriage.

"Owen, I am talking to you. Tonight is the gathering at the Reddicks' place. What should I make?"

He looked up from his pile of papers. "I'm sure anything would be fine."

He looked down again, keeping the edges even as he clipped articles from the stack of newspapers before him for his scrapbook. He had boxes of them held carefully away from damp or mold to assure the preservation of a record for the future. He referred to them as his history books and kept them stashed in a box to the side of their bedroom closet. Those from his early days on the rail were made from random sheets of found paper, bound together with wild stitches of thick thread. As he had become more serious about his project, the clippings had been fixed into children's school notebooks. His collection chronicled the significant events covered in the *Defender* or in the white papers of the major cities that he was familiar with—New York, Chicago, St. Louis—that had affected

Negro people since he assumed his legal majority and began criss-crossing the country.

Dellie stepped over and placed a hand on his shoulder. Her choice of dish might not be important, but she needed Owen to see that this plate — cookies, peas and rice, whatever — was more than just food for the common table. She needed it to be accepted, to demonstrate that she was part of his community, of his family, not just hers.

"Owen, do you have any suggestions?"

He did not look up. "Dellie, you are a fine cook. Whatever you make will be a delight to all, I am sure." He picked up a notebook and scanned his spread of clippings about the election of a Negro to the municipal government of a town in central Florida.

The decision, therefore, was reached in Maude's kitchen. "I tasted it at the last Lodge social. Rosalie, Mrs. Cumberbatch's poor daughter-in-law, made it. Remember, she is an American. She called it pineapple upside-down cake. I'll help you make it, sister."

And so Maude's household was emptied out and fortified for the baking. Nothing — not the clamor of children (Egbert took the brood over to his uncle the Lodgemaster for a visit), not the pounding of workmen in the street, not the cry of peddlers of various wares (windows were fastened against that sound) — would be allowed to jeopardize the project at hand.

The outcome was perfect, with crunchy brown sugar circling ringlets of pineapple. A flourish of cherries preserved in brandy, donated by Mrs. Iannacci and arranged in a floral pattern marked each slice. It was beautiful.

————

The house on Putman Avenue was not the most fashionable on the block, nor was it the least. Without the lush pediments of the homes that bracketed the street corners, but instead adorned with subtle egg-and-dart engraving, it blended in with its staid neighbors in a block-long enclave of up-and-coming Negro families. The corner house had been claimed by Dr. King, one of a sprinkling of Black doctors in the borough. Next was the home of John Woodward, the undertaker. Three doors down was the property of Reuben Adkins, a Pullman brother who had told Owen about the opportunity for ownership when the notice of sale for the next house over became public. Owen had turned it down. Savings needed to be held fast for the inn.

They walked up the front steps of the limestone elevation and pressed the bell. Aurelia opened the door and pulled Owen and Dellie into the warmth of her home from the chill of the evening. Chatter and laughter bounced across the room from one cluster of people to another, all balancing plates laden with foods still new to Dellie — greens, fried chicken, corn pudding, potato salad. Owen melted into the mass of people. Dellie stood frozen on the spot until propelled into the kitchen by Aurelia.

"Dellie, I am glad you came. Now I have someone to talk to besides that murder of women in my front room!" Dellie laughed. "Help me get the rest of this food out."

"Just a minute. Let me put this down." Dellie rested the box on the table.

"What did you make?" Aurelia raised the lid. "Ah, it is beautiful, Dellie! My grandmother used to make a cake like this. Just a taste." She broke off a small piece and popped it in her mouth. "Ahhh...tastes just like home. Sometimes she would put a little whiskey in it. One time I remember she served it like that to the women from the church. Well, you can imagine them all shinnied up..."

Suddenly she was off in another time and place, her thick eyebrows pulled together. And then, just as suddenly, it passed. "Oh, and what a beautiful plate! Your dessert will be the showpiece of the table. And we'll use this fancy server to cut it with. Come. Let's set it out." She gestured toward the men. "The Baker Heater League will make fast work of this."

Aurelia found a place for it at the center of the table.

It was the usual gathering. The men congregated in one room. Jonathan had staked a place on an ottoman and was telling a tale to a young man about the mythical Daddy Joe, the first of the Pullman Porters. "Well, son, maybe you'll have the chance to run the route he did. Have you heard the tale yet of how he dealt with a band of thieves ready to make trouble out near Salt Lake?" Another group huddled around Owen as he talked about the advantages of some sort of industrial association of the brothers on the rails.

Owen stabbed two fingers into the palm of his hand. "If we all banded together, we could make progress together."

A tall man whose name she didn't know nodded, his lips tight. "That's right, but convincing a man that he is not putting his job *now* on the line for some 'maybe' in the future…"

Owen interrupted. "We as a people need to think about what we want things to be, not just what things are!"

Jonathan ended his story and broke in, "You're right, but rent is due now, food must be bought now…"

Dellie drifted toward another room, the same old talk.

Among the women, talk rambled in a different direction. Dellie stood on the edge of a conversation. Lena, the tall, thin wife of one of the Pullman waiters was speaking. "I was reading in the *Defender* of another rash of attacks on Negro men in Virginia." She shook her head. "I wish Calvin would put in for another line. Something up North."

A woman with thick glasses noted, "I'm not sure that it matters. There was some incident in Ohio a while back. All you need is a Negro in the wrong place and some sheet-loving white folks."

Aurelia moved over and joined the conversation. "Indiana, too."

Dellie stepped closer. "I saw that in one of Owen's papers. And that a woman, last name was Wells I think, was demanding change." A glance passed among several of the women. No one responded. Aurelia raised her eyebrows and looked around the group.

Dellie raised her voice ever so slightly. Perhaps they hadn't heard. "I was saying that a woman named Ida B. Wells has written to the President. She is working with others for change." The group was silent.

Aurelia looked at Dellie, and then around the circle of women. "That is right, Dellie. Ida B. doesn't stand for any foolishness. And neither do I." She snorted and pulled Dellie by the sleeve toward the punch bowl.

Dellie's face was deep red. "Aurelia. I can't believe…" She struggled to find the words.

"Don't pay that bunch of biddies any mind" Aurelia snapped. "They all must have been raised in the same barn. Let's have some punch." She ladled out a cup and handed it to Dellie.

"Hold it still." She turned her back to the crowd, reached into her dress pocket, and pulled out a small bottle. "Here, quick, before someone sees." She poured a splash of amber liquid into Dellie's cup. Dellie sucked her breath in and tried to speak. Aurelia put her fingers to her lips. "Hush now. It's just some whiskey. It will help you bear the rest of the night." She dumped the rest of it into her cup. "Me too." The glasses clinked as they touched them together. Dellie stifled a laugh.

Cup in hand, Dellie joined a circle of women. A short, plump woman was speaking, "Elizabeth, you've got that long, lush hair. Ever think of selling for Madame Walker? People would flock to you. And her creams and pomades are top shelf. On her way to being a millionaire, I hear."

Dellie stepped in to the covey and spoke. "It is top shelf, I started using it. It does make the brush and comb run through easily, but I am not comfortable selling to strangers. Are you?" Silence.

Dellie turned, her eyes drifting toward the dessert table. Two of the wives approached it, one reaching to cut a slice of the pineapple-upside down cake. The other shook her head and whispered something in her ear. Her hand fell away.

From across the room Aurelia watched the drama unfolding and stepped toward Dellie. "Listen, before I forget. Come. I want to show you something." She led her into a bedroom and lifted a patchwork quilt from the foot of the bed. Dellie had never seen anything like it. Her fingers reached out tentatively.

"Aurelia, such a pattern! The colors!"

"Isn't it something? I knew you would appreciate it. It just arrived in the mail from my Aunt Nan in Mississippi. It belonged to her mother, my grandmother. I never met her..." She ran her hand over the ridges of corduroy, the smoothness of a patch made from worn gunnysack. "My sisters and brothers played with it when we went to visit her once. We used it to make a tent over some chairs, or sometimes tunnels on the bed. She was not happy, us using it that way. Each of these patches tells a story."

Dellie looked closely. "Let me see the whole thing."

Aurelia cast the quilt across the bed in a whirl of color.

"See the pattern the patches make? My great-grandmother used to call this pattern 'Rosebud.' My Aunt Leola says they call it 'Duck Tracks' in fancy sewing books."

Dellie looked at the dancing pattern of colors—light moving against dark, one patch playing against another—and at the thousands of tiny stitches that held it to its stuffing and backing. Her hands tingled at the skill of its sewer.

"You don't see anything like that at home. Too hot for such covering and so we take the old fabric and scraps to use for cloths for the table, or clothes for the small children..."

"My grandmother Bet stitched these pieces before the Civil War—you know, Dellie, the war here that freed the Negroes. See how worn they are?"

She gestured to a set of squares and triangles near the right hand corner.

"These pieces, here and here"—she pointed with her finger— "were an old shirt that belonged to her son, Uncle Zacaria in Mississippi. See this brown patch here?" She pointed again. "It belonged to my father. Came from a pair of his old pants. Look."

Aurelia laughed as her hand ran over a square of fabric that had once been blue.

"She added a piece of my dress here. I remember that dress from when I was a little..." She didn't finish the sentence. "My aunt sent the quilt to me to keep me company. She said it will keep the family with me." She laughed and took Dellie's hand as she brushed away a tear. "I don't want to show it to the other women. They all think that since they are Porter's wives they have to give up these old things— just be up-and-coming women. But I knew you would appreciate it. I was also thinking that you and I could start making one."

"Aurelia, such a project would be a lot of work! Gathering the fabric, laying out the pattern. All those stitches..."

"I know, but down home these are also called 'friendship quilts.' Made to honor a friendship." She reached out and hugged Dellie. Both of their eyes filled.

"Because you are a true friend to me, Dellie, and I to you. I want you to always remember me. Even when you and Owen head to Delaware."

Dellie stiffened. "Come now, Aurelia. This is your party. Time to socialize."

"I will have to gird my loins for that."

———

The men were huddled in a corner craning forward in their seats as Owen read something aloud from the latest issue of the *Brooklyn*

Eagle. Jonathan Reddick and a few others bobbed their heads in agreement.

Dellie surveyed the table and the dishes nearing empty that it held. Her eyes narrowed as the Lane cake disappeared, the sweet potato pie vanished, the ambrosia, berry cobbler, and syllabub got carried off. Meanwhile, her cake presided over the table untouched. From across the room Aurelia stood up, marched across the room and cut herself an enormous wedge of the delicacy and elbowed her way next to Lena to eat it. Besides Owen, she was the only one to taste it.

———

On the walk back to the trolley, Dellie was silent. Owen took no notice of it. He spoke at length about a reported conversation between a Pullman brother and the famous Booker T. Washington.

"They met and talked about putting together a program for the progress of the Negro. That Washington, he is a man of action. Built up Tuskegee from nothing. You know Dellie?" His eyes tightened and looked ahead down the street, gesturing as if a part of another scene altogether. "He met with the President you know. Imagine that, in the White House, meeting with the President. I am telling you Dellie..."

He didn't pause from his oratory when she dumped the left-over cake and its box—her plate and all—into the first trashcan they passed. He didn't notice when she remained silent for the trolley ride home, her eyes on the modest dramas unfolding on the streets of Brooklyn. He didn't notice the woman next to him as he considered the weighty issues of the day.

CHAPTER THREE

Sweet Boy

Brooklyn, Spring 1914

*T*hey had chosen the flat because it came with the use of the yard. When it became clear that no one else in the building used it, Dellie claimed it and planned a garden. She spent the entire winter laying it out, but mid-May had come before the danger of frost disappeared. She had sketched it out on paper—it would only accommodate the barest essentials—a few vegetables, and a cluster of herbs on the small patch outside the kitchen just before the brick path began.

She kneeled down trowel in hand and thrust it into the moist earth, pulling up a clump of warm, black soil. She cupped it in both hands and raised it toward her face. Her eyes closed as she blocked out all sounds of Brooklyn and let the sharp, rich smell envelope her. "It is going to bear well." She could picture the neat rows of beans, peas, and tomatoes, canned and lining her shelves. She turned and imagined the spot a few months hence— well, maybe she could squeeze in a few hollyhocks and some sunflowers for color.

"Dellie! Dellie?" A voice calling from inside caught her attention.

"Outside, Lillian! In the yard."

Her sister stepped out from the kitchen, broad smile on her face.

"It is a glorious day!"

"'Tis true. I think I will begin to put my plants in this week. Like I showed you." She gestured to her right and then left. "Vegetables there, flowers here. Just smell this."

Lillian leaned in to draw her sister's hand closer, accidentally bumping her and spilling a bit of soil down the front of Dellie's apron. She moved instinctively to brush it away. She pulled her hand back.

"Dellie! Your bosom!"

Dellie's face was a mix of feeling—joy, self-consciousness. Her hands moved down, fingers of both hands spread caressing her belly. She smiled. "Yes. It is coming in December. I wanted to be sure before I told you."

Dellie felt her sister's warm hand on top of her own. She looked up at the patch of blue visible above the roofline of the brownstones, and uttered a silent prayer.

He arrived on a day whose warmth held in it the memory and hope of warm breezes, the perfume of flowers, and expectant green of buds. He was beautiful. Smooth head of a perfect shape, skin the color of maple syrup, and eyes with the same chesnut color as hers. He looked around, eyes moving until they came to rest on her face. She reached out and touched his cheek. He smiled, toothless. The women surrounding her laughed.

"Who has ever seen such a thing?" Maude looked at her sister with a grin. "This one been here before, for sure!" She stepped aside as Dr. Fielding took the child, laid him on a clean sheet, snipped the cord that linked him to his mother, and handed him to her to nurse. She and Owen had a time with the selection of a name. If the child had been a girl, it would have been easy—Owen's grandmother was named Caroline, like her mother. But a boy? He offered Sidney. She said no. She offered George. He shook his head and made further suggestions. Michael? Joseph? Eric? Robert? It was a letter delivered to the wrong address that settled it. Mr. Alphonso Frasier. Alphonso was out of the question. So Frasier it was. They both loved the name and loved the boy.

Dellie looked at the letter on the table, sealed and ready to be posted. While she had written M'Ma of all of her news over the years, she had never told Henry of her marriage, of her child. She knew what his reaction would be. She had plenty of other news to fill the pages of a letter without being curt—the goings on at the Lodge, at St. Philips, but she would not write of Owen, nor of Frasier. Particularly not of Frasier, nothing, not his first tooth, not his first step, not his first words, not about the bushy halo of curly, mahogany-colored hair that framed his face. She wouldn't have him dirtied by someone's scheme of color and place in life. Not even her father's.

She was confident, though, that Henry knew all about her life. The newswire from Barbados to New York and from New York to Barbados vibrated at a high whine. There were, without a doubt, countless sources of information about Dellie and her foreign husband. And yet, for his part, Henry had never mentioned his son-in-law or his grandchild. She sighed as she placed the letter in her handbag.

Her son lay sprawled, arms and legs out like an X, the position he had collapsed into after a morning of play. It was his routine, and so also hers, and today was no different. He would wake at the first notes of dawn offered by the birds setting about their day's business. His hushed rustling would wake her too, and she would watch as first, just his limbs, arms, and legs waved over the side of his cradle. Her eyes never left him as he stretched, played with his toes, tried to grab the shadows his fingers made on the wooden slats that kept him safe, and finally, sat up, eyes wide, staring at her. She was always surprised at how he watched her, sometimes dreamy, sometimes pondering, sometimes with a deep inquisitiveness, brow furrowed. It seemed as if he was considering a time in his life before birth and some difficult question that he was still puzzling. He would then break into a broad smile, pull himself to stand, reach his hands out, and say, "Mama."

Dellie looked at the ceiling, her throat tight. Four children had come after Dellie: Maude, May, Byron, and Palley. Palley. A wave of unease drifted over her. Palley, gone to Panama with no word since. According to the papers the Americans were finished with the Canal work, so where was he? Dite had taken his Panama money and gone to Canada. Byron was off on a ship somewhere, sailing with Harrison's line. The sea...her mind started along that circuit; how long had it been since she had seen Pendril? She put the thought out of her head.

———

Dellie took the long way to the Post Office to take advantage of the sun and the bright, fall leaves. She kept up a running conversation with Frasier. "Look, Baby-One, see the color of the leaves? Back home, God paints the flowers all the blazing colors; here, he paints the leaves." She reached up and picked a flaming red leaf from a maple tree. "Here, Frasier, look."

She leaned close and waved the wide leaf before his face. He smiled his wide sparse-toothed smile. She held the leaf up to the sun, silhouetting its veins and variations in color and casting a warm shadow against his skin. She tickled his cheek with its edges and fanned a small rush of air across his face. Dellie laughed at his posture, ramrod straight, and at his attitude, like some potentate being fanned by a household servant.

Mr. Buree, one of the elder statesmen of Hansen Place, chuckled and drew her attention. "Ah, Mrs. Gibson with the son and heir. How are you both, today?"

"Fine, sir, and you?"

"Never better." He reached into the stroller and rubbed a finger along the baby's cheek, eliciting a flurry of syllables with the cadence of English. Mr. Buree laughed again. "He'll be giving a speech soon, that one!"

It was that way with everyone whom they met.

"Good morning, Mrs. Gibson. How is that fine fella?"

"Dellie, how's that handsome boy?"

"Ah, here comes the next mayor!"

Around the curve in the path, Dellie could see Aurelia and her son chasing squirrels on the expanse of grass at the center of Fort Greene Park.

"Dellie!" Aurelia waved.

Her son raced up to Dellie, his hands scouring the pocket of her waistcoat for the treat he usually found there. "Here, Theo. It is not in my pocket today." She reached into a space in her handbag and pulled out a treat wrapped in a bit of waxed paper. She handed it to the boy, who took it in his fist and scooted to a bench to enjoy it.

Aurelia laughed and shook her head. "You do spoil the child, you know."

"It is just a small treat. It is my plan to spoil all these children for as long as I can. They will find out about the harshness of the world soon enough."

Aurelia chupsed.

"Hah! So since when are you sucking your teeth? You Bajan now?"

"That's you and your sisters rubbing off on me! You know Jonathan said the same thing to me when I served him peas and rice the other day!"

"Ah, is he back from a run?"

"Since Thursday. He doesn't go out again for a day or two. What about Owen?"

"He is on a run right now. He's planning on putting in a few extra days so he can exceed his savings goal for the month, for the land he has picked out in Delaware."

"Hmmm…I heard him talking to Jonathan. Hopefully the transfer to the 20th Century will come through soon. It would be nice if the two of them could work together again. Plus, the tips are so much better. He wouldn't have to put in so many extra hours."

"That's true, but the runs are longer, aren't they?"

"Yes…But the spot he has been talking about sounds ideal for his plan. And something you would like too, Dellie. Out of the city—enough space for a proper kitchen and flower garden. Plus being innkeepers, you would always have a host of people around." She looked at Dellie, her eyes twinkling with mischief. "And I know how you Bajans like to have a mob of people around."

Dellie laughed. But that was the part of Owen's dream that gave her pause. People? All right, but whose? New York was becoming her place now, but that was with her sisters and with Aurelia, who was like a sister now. Frasier provided another sort of entrance for her, but she still remained in the shadows of Owen's crowd. Who would see her in Delaware? How would it be possible to make a life for her self, in a place where she would not be seen? Her throat tightened. A sudden laugh from Frasier, at the antics of a squirrel, pulled her back to the moment.

CHAPTER FOUR

Laughing on a Fluffy Sheepskin

*T*he photographer's studio wasn't hard to find. It stood on the corner of Myrtle and Clermont Avenues. The El put patrons off only a block away. All of the colored people in Brooklyn knew him and set aside a bit each week to save for a photograph. Mr. Leonardo Cruz had been a photographer in Cuba before the collapse in sugar prices had driven him out. He had arrived and set up business years ago with props and fine clothes for those of modest means whose budgets didn't allow for lace bodices, satin sashes, starched collar stays, or finely stitched shoes. For those who could afford at least a few luxuries, he accommodated them with backdrops to complement a favorite dress, or hat, or watch. His poses were arresting, capturing not only the figure in best view, but also the character of his subject by the subtlety of a hand gesture, tilt of a head, turn of a shoulder.

It had taken some convincing. Owen had thought the whole proposition an exercise in vanity, but when he saw the proofs from Dr. Fielding's family's sitting, he was captivated. He would never say that she was right, that it was a good idea or that the pictures had come out well, but when she found him surveying the front room for a spot for a large, framed version, in a size comparable to what now hung over Dr. Fielding's substantial mantelpiece, Dellie knew that he had capitulated. Plus, the discount earned by bringing another family meant he needn't dip into his Delaware money.

The plan was simple. They were to stop by Coleridge and Lillian's place and walk over to the studio together. The day was overcast with the sun breaking through only sporadically. The plan had been for both families to join in a happy outing. Mr. Lorenzo Cruz, the photographer and proprietor of Peregrine Photography, would capture both families as a testament to the present and future. Then they would all go out for ice cream at one of the neat little shops along the thoroughfare on Myrtle Avenue. That was what it was supposed to be. But Dellie would feel lucky if there wasn't a murder in the process. She tried to reason with Owen. "You must dress the boy up like a girl, so that you don't tempt fate upon him. That is why he is wearing the little dress that Millicent used to wear."

"Dellie, that is foolishness, and you know it. This is the 20th century. You are a modern woman. This is New York." Owen didn't wait for her reply. He simply dressed their son again. They made their way to Lillian's in silence.

"I'll ring the bell and let them know we are here." Dellie pushed the bell and waited. She pushed it again and waited. She turned and caught Owen's eye as he tapped his foot on the hard pavement. He shook his head in annoyance.

"Frasier and I will wait outside. I'll walk him around the block." She waved him on. "I'm sure they are almost ready." She rapped on the glass of the front door, finally attracting the attention of a neighbor. As she opened the door leading to Lillian's front room, she said a prayer of thanks that Owen did not have to be caught up in the maelstrom that was her sister's flat.

"Sit down, Henry! Wait right there for your father to finish dressing you! I must comb your sister's hair." The tiny girl in Lillian's lap cried and wriggled beneath the comb and brush. "You now! Be still, I'll put more pomade in to make the brush glide better." Lillian groaned. "This is impossible. Dellie, see if you can find a jar of Madame's Pomade!"

"Lillian, I will comb Millicent's hair. You finish dressing yourself. We are already going to be late. Owen will have an attack of apoplexy." She sat down and tried to modulate her voice to a whisper to calm herself and the child. Two fingers swirled around in the tin and pulled out a dab of the oil. Dellie sighed and worked it through her niece's head amid gasps, tears, and gulps of breath from the child. After a moment her patience ran thin and she gave way to exasperation. "Be still!"

From another room Lillian's voice rang out, "Coleridge!" Her voice carried and bounced from the kitchen, through the parlor, to the bath, to the bedroom. "Coleridge, I asked you to dress the baby, please!"

He entered the room, church clothes on, collar in one hand, a child's lace outfit in the other. "Dress who? You don't need to shout. You are not home, calling all up and abroad like the fish monger!"

She reddened. She modulated her voice. "I said, please dress Henry."

"That's what I thought you said. But these are girl's clothes." He held them out to her for inspection and confirmation. Dellie looked at the floor.

"I know, but that is what Dorothea Atherly says he must wear so we don't tempt fate on the boy. We will trick it to thinking he is a girl." She averted her eyes to Dellie's hairdressing project. The chupse was loud enough to be heard three rooms away.

"Dorothea? Since when do you listen to her and her hoodoo right out of the bush! Seems like fate has already gotten the best of her! Have you seen her lately?"

"Coleridge, I'll do it," offered Dellie in the interest of harmony and the slim possibility of punctuality. "At least let him wear the bow. I brought one for Frasier, see?" She pulled a large satin accessory from her handbag.

———

They arrived at the shop, one child crying, one silent and sullen, one fast asleep. Officious Mr. Cruz took on the role of an aide de camp and got the full entourage into shape. "I'll start with the littlest one. They are always the easiest." He laid a white sheepskin on a table before a screen decorated with a muted design of cherubs, and gestured to Owen to place Frasier on it. Dellie handed him off carefully, not wanting to startle him awake.

"Just lay him in the middle of the throw." The photographer cleared his throat. "Ahh, is he too young to sit?"

"No," Owen snapped. "He has been sitting for months. The problem is that he is fast asleep. We were delayed..." A look from Dellie silenced him.

"For months! Perhaps then he is tired from sitting so long!" The man adjusted his lenses and laughed at his joke. No one else did.

"Well, ahhh, ahhh, perhaps we'll begin with the other family. I'll let you get the baby arranged on the fur and I'll be back." He strode to the other side of the room.

"Sir." He gestured toward Coleridge. "Sir, let's try you standing and the Madame sitting with the young one on her lap. That's right. Now you stand behind her. Put your hand on her shoulder. Let me fix the little girl's bow. It is blocking part of your face, Mrs. Green."

"He is a boy," Coleridge corrected him, his face grim. "The child is a boy."

"A boy. Oh, I see," said the photographer, his mouth a straight line.

Coleridge reddened. "No man. I don't think you do." He shot Lillian a look. When he spoke, the annoyance in his voice was palpable. "My wife..."

The photographer interrupted. "Sir, I meant nothing. I realize that some hold the belief..." He checked his commentary and refocused on the task at hand. "Perhaps you could all settle into your places as I indicated?"

Lillian shifted in the fine, tufted chair. Mr. Cruz fussed about arranging and rearranging his subjects in the hope that it would give Coleridge time to rearrange his face from a scowl.

"Mr. Green, perhaps you would do better with your wife standing. Let's put the older child here. Mrs. Green, you stand behind your husband. This little one here." He paused, afraid to utter the last instruction. He summoned the courage and looked calmly at Coleridge. "Adjust the bow a bit to the side." Coleridge, not quite resigned to his fate or the reality of the image that would be preserved for all time, moved the bow as if it were a foul thing.

The photographer exhaled a sigh of relief and surveyed the scene once more before retreating under the shawl at the rear of his camera. He readied to trip the shutter and the flash. "One, two, three — eyes on me!" As if on cue, Henry tore the bow from his hair and uttered a howl loud enough to wake the dead in Hong Kong. Dellie tucked Frasier's bow back into her purse.

It was a soft spring day when Dellie and Lillian went to pick up the finished photographs. Dellie had considered the poses she would choose. A full-length portrait of her, Owen, and Frasier; one of her holding a bouquet of flowers, leaning on a pedestal table; one of Owen sitting in a chair with her next to it; and one of the child sitting, laughing on a fluffy sheepskin. Owen had agreed to the extravagance. She had already crafted in her mind the letter she would write home and had decided who would get what pose (Henry would receive the portrait of her alone). The phrases turned in her head as they made their way through Fort Greene Park. She and Lillian saved the trolley fare today, taking advantage of the gentle weather, enjoying the trees in full blossom. The chestnuts were her favorites, with their tall cone spikes of flowers and thick, heady smell.

The phrases for her letter rose and fell in her head. She would have to be careful about tone. She wanted Henry and the people of Taborvilla, to whom he would no doubt read it, to be proud of her, but she didn't want to appear to show off. She also didn't want to tempt fate and commit her joys and struggles to paper. But that was always the debate with each letter.

She thought back to a day at her kitchen table with Lillian. She had been livid over her latest correspondence from their father and his pronouncements and now was ashamed since she learned of his health. The letter that came from May, which she and Lillian had read, brought devastating news of some attack that Henry sustained. The words were marked in Dellie's mind:

> *Henry was on the verandah, planing the edges of the screened door. You know how its sticking has been plaguing him since he had hung it years ago. I saw him totter and lose his balance, squeezing the sides of his head. He fell to his knees, then onto his back, and his water left him. He couldn't speak clearly, but I thought I heard him calling for M'Ma, P'Pa, and Cal. He had reached his hand out as if to grab someone, and then closed his eyes.*

Now, May wrote, she and M'Ma and sometimes Joe Burroughs and Josh, took care of his needs—mashing his food, feeding him, bathing him, setting him up for the day under the flamboyant tree with Clive for company. They took care of getting him prepared for bed at night. The picture was clear in Dellie's mind. Henry—her father, omnipotent, with his hopes, his plans, and his portrait—now lay unable to move unassisted, trapped in a chair overlooking the Chandler lands of Taborvilla and Coventry Hall, under a tree in perpetual and riotous bloom.

The painful irony made Dellie shudder.

———

"Ah, Mrs. Green and Mrs. Gibson. You are here for the photographs. Sit down, sit down. I prepared a set of proofs. Mrs. Gibson, these are yours. Some fine shots. You have a handsome boy. You can take a look at them. Take your time and then let me know which ones you want. Remember, the package allows you each to pick several poses."

He gestured Lillian aside. "And yours, Mrs. Green." He placed a small packet on the glass counter. "You know, you ladies can take them with you." He crossed the room and stood next to Dellie.

She looked up, detecting a touch of sympathy in his usually businesslike manner.

"You two may wish to discuss the selections with your husbands." He looked at them both mournfully. "It's a shame that women like you both, with your, ah, qualities should have to put up with such....gruffness."

Lillian looked at him with a sideways glance.

She reviewed the pictures, having thought before which one would show her little family in the best light. There it was. An image of Frasier sitting on a fur throw, looking at the camera with her and Owen seated on a divan behind him. She had already picked out a frame with silver filigree and rose enamel flourishes. It would sit on the nightstand next to their bed.

The photographer's voice interrupted her thoughts. "That is a fine choice. The same sizes and quantities as we discussed before?"

"Yes, but I would like to add a few more of the smaller to give to friends and family. And maybe." Her hand hovered over a photograph of Owen seated, gaze toward the camera. "Lillian?" Her sister turned toward her.

"What do you think? Too much extravagance?"

"It is a fine image. And how often will you have this opportunity. It is an extravagance, but a small one. Go on Dellie."

"Mr. Cruz, I'll take this one also." She handed him the photo.

"Maybe this one too." She tapped a print of the child and smiled to herself at the thought of the display that would grace her mantle.

CHAPTER FIVE

Frasier's Tale

Brooklyn, 1916

*D*ellie jumped up and ran to the door after Frasier. Somehow he knew when Owen was home from a run before his key met the lock.

Owen stepped through the door, arms full. "Dellie! Frasier! I have a surprise!" He tossed his coat.

"It must be quite a surprise," Dellie thought as she watched the garment come to rest on the floor. "Owen, what have you got there?"

"A phonograph! You've seen it in the papers and Jonathan Reddick and Aurelia have one."

"But, Owen, it is such a luxury, we can't..."

"Ah, but, Mrs. Gibson, we can! I got it to celebrate! At last I got the transfer to the *20ᵗʰ Century Line!* Hah!" He slapped his thighs, picked up Dellie, and whirled her around. "The flagship of the line! This is what we have been waiting for!"

Her face clouded. It had come to pass. Delaware was in sight.

"Dellie! Don't worry so about the cost! The phonograph is just a little pleasure. Plus we need to expose the child to music and something of the world. He is going to live in a different time! Right, my boy!" He picked up the child and swung him high.

Dellie pushed the coil of worry back. "This sweet boy...this is for his life too." She pulled her face into a smile.

Owen buffed the great bell with his sleeve and fitted it in place. He wiped a record on his pant leg, rested it on the turntable and cranked the handle with a flourish.

The music began with a creaky screech and then found its tone. Notes clear, happy, whirled and cart-wheeled through the air. The small boy did a funny little bouncing dance, dipping and bobbing to the sound, his father following his steps, his mother standing, watching, a smile on her face, head moving ever so slightly to this music still so new to her.

Frasier stopped and ran to her. He grabbed her hands. "Come, Mama!" He pulled her. "Come, Mama! Dance, just dance!"

———

A breeze flirted with the curtains and kept the midsummer heat at bay as Dellie put a few final stitches onto a girl's dress. She glanced at Owen, hunched over a set of papers at the kitchen table. She folded up her sewing and took the few steps to the icebox for a cool drink. "Owen, would you like something? I am pouring myself some cool tea."

"No, I am fine."

Dellie slid into a chair beside him. Her eyes fell on the set of folders labeled "Delaware" and bound by a length of string.

"You are working on the figures?"

"Yes, figuring my average tips. I am also thinking that if I add a couple of more runs, maybe the shorter line between here and Boston or here and Albany..."

"But, Owen, we are not wanting for anything! And you are gone so much already. You see how happy the child is when you are here!"

He lay his pen down.

"Dellie, you know that this is for all of us. Times are changing and if we are to be a part of it, we have to act now. You know I have had my eye on a piece of land with a house that could be made into an inn. My brother took a trip up from North Carolina and looked at a piece of ground. He spoke to the current owner. I want to act before someone else snatches it up. At least put some good faith money down on it. Besides, if I have my own business, I will make my own hours." He patted her hand. "Dellie, bear with me in this. It is best for all of us."

Dellie tipped her head back and looked at the ceiling. Where had she heard this tale before? She sighed and tapped her finger on the table. "Show me again on the map."

Owen pulled out a folder from among the stack before him and pulled out a paper marked with lines and notes and circles. "See, here. The town is Aberdeen." He ran his finger along a black line. "See this is where we would be. Right on the rail line, last stop before Jim Crow kicks in and Negro people would have to seek separate accommodations."

Dellie fingered the sweat running down her glass of tea. "Tell me again, Owen. How far is it?"

"It is about six hours by rail from the station in New York, a growing area. I am telling you we could be prominent people there. Leaders among the Negro people."

"But we have a good life here, Owen. My family, your Pullman brothers..."

"There is more to be had. Times are changing. I will be a part of it. Frasier will be a part of it. I can see you in one of the women's clubs, or leading the Sunday School."

"Owen, you know, except for Aurelia, the Pullman wives barely speak to me. What makes you think it would...?"

His voice took on an edge. "Because we would be property owners! Business owners. We would command respect. Beside, this is my dream for the boy." His eyes burrowed into hers.

His dream for the *boy*?

Dellie changed the subject. "When Frasier wakes, I am meeting Winnie and the children for a walk in the park. Will you come? Frasier loves to be pushed in the swing."

"I am working on this. You go on."

CHAPTER SIX

No Room for It

Late summer, 1916

*T*he breeze danced through Dellie's garden, offering perfume from a profusion of flowers at summer peak. The cool tea she passed around to the men sitting in a circle was a gift to keep the heat at bay.

Drama and tension had been building all summer. Headlines screamed in the papers, opinions strongly voiced through the static of radio broadcasts, and heated conversations rose in the market or on the trolley. Even at St. Philip's, Reverend Fletcher joined the fray in his lengthy sermon on war or rumors of war. He alone took heed of the President and remained, at least from the pulpit, "neutral in fact as well as in name."

Dellie's palm barely registered the rough wood of the lattice-work that framed the small brick patio. The gathering had been predictable lately. The group of men—Clemmie, Egbert, and Coleridge—sitting, gesticulating emphatically, slamming dominoes. They could not veer from the events unfolding in Europe and in Mexico, each sharing a fact or subtle interpretation that would shed light on the whole.

On the days when Owen was there, the conversation without fail turned to unions, the concept of the New Negro (the West Indian contingent still trying to grasp the concept of *Negro*, new or old), and the prospect of the changes at hand for colored people.

A sudden burst of children's laughter rang from the circle of shade cast by the neighbor's maple tree. As usual, Frasier was the center of attention. As the youngest, he had the equivalent of six siblings, each of whom competed for his attention and followed him about like a Sultan's entourage. This moment's game involved chains of dandelions and Queen Anne's lace fashioned into crowns, belts, and necklaces.

"Dellie, come," called a voice from inside. "I will try to teach you once again how to make gravy that is not lumpy."

"Leave her, Maude," interjected Winnie. "The lumps are the hallmark of Dellie's gravy. Wihout them, it could pass as anyone's."

They all laughed. Dellie reddened. Then she laughed, glad to be able to bring something of her husband into their world. "But remember, I usually don't have to make the gravy. Owen makes the best by far. The porters know all about that kind of thing from the cars."

"He's been traveling a lot lately," commented Winnie.

"He has been working more since he got his wish and transferred to the *20ᵗʰ Century Limited*. He gets more tips on that line." She paused, gathering both thoughts and feelings. "You know he wants to put a big payment on the land he picked out in the South." There, she had spoken the thing that had remained unsaid between them for months. His life would take her away from Brooklyn.

She dried her hands on her apron and sat in one of the kitchen chairs. "He has told me all along that this is his dream, to move down nearer to his people and own a hotel. The birth of the child has accelerated his plan. He is also working more now that we have more expenses, so that he can still put money aside."

Maude took a seat beside her at the oblong table. "Egbert showed me on the map one day. Delaware is a long way from here."

Dellie knit and unknit her fingers. "I had put the thought out of my head, thinking it would be years in the coming, if at all."

Winnie tried to be encouraging. "Who knows, Dellie? It isn't here yet. Maybe a chance will break around here. Maybe a chance will come like the one that did for the man whose place you stayed at after you and Owen married. Who knows how a plan is going to play out?"

"You know that is true, Winnie." The two women looked at each other.

"But it isn't just the thought of packing up and starting a new life again. It..." Dellie's voice dropped and grew heavy. "It is like he never stops to see this life. Like he is missing what is here now, always looking for what is to come."

There was an edge of reproach in Maude's voice. "I know no one ever thought I would say it. He's a good man, though, Dellie. He provides well for you and the child. He doesn't ever go out on a trip and not come back without some little something for you and Frasier. He provides a fine house, a yard..."

"Henry did the same for Cal. Don't be so pious with me, Maude, and make me into an ingrate. You know what I mean. God gave me the hands to provide for myself. I am talking about what is more than just giving *things*."

Maude's face was impassive at the rebuke.

"Sometimes I am lonely with Owen on his route for time on end. Here, I have you all. Who will be down in Delaware?" She paused, knitting her fingers together. "But you are right. Perhaps something, you never know how a plan will play out. I know I shouldn't say it, but I can still hope." She was silent for a moment. "I remember what Cal always said, not to pray for anything but strength to bear what comes."

Lillian opened her mouth to say something but changed her mind, focusing her attention on pulling the silk from a strainer full of corn ears. It was Winnie who broke the tension. "Dellie," her voice was soft. "You know we are with you, whatever."

Coleridge's noisy entrance, Frasier in his arms, called their attention. "Someone give me something for Frasier. All of a sudden he is hot and coughing."

Dellie gathered him into her arms and cradled him while the women returned to preparing the Sunday meal. Heat radiated from where he nestled his head into her neck. Her face knit its concern.

"I think I am going to take him to lie down a bit. It's warm out. He seems a little overheated. Some quiet will refresh him. Winnie, can you bring me some cool water from the ice box?"

Dellie pushed the bedroom door open and paused as her eyes adjusted to the dimness of the room. A breeze nudged the curtains and added coolness to the calm. She sat the child in the middle of the bed. Her voice was gentle. "I am going to wipe you with a cool rag, then we will lie down and rest."

"Drink, Mama, firsty," he said in his baby voice. A cough. Another. "Hot, Mama, hot."

He tugged at his shirt.

"Aunt Winnie is coming with a drink. Here, let's take some of these things off." Her motions stopped as her eyes fell on the sheen of sweat on his small body. Quickly she wrung out a cloth wet from the bowl and pitcher on the dresser, and dabbed cool water on his chest, neck, face, arms, and legs. She wet the cloth again and rubbed his hands to force away any germs.

"Too hard, Mama. Soft, nice," he demanded.

"Yes, soft, sweet boy."

Winnie appeared in the doorway, baby bottle full of cool water in hand. "Everything all right?" She looked at the pitcher, washbasin, and cloth.

"His skin is a little hot and he is coughing. I am going to lie down with him a bit. Can you give him the water?"

Dellie took off her dress and shoes and sat in her shift next to Winnie and the baby on the bed. She watched her small son cuddle into Winnie's arms, eyes closed, little hand turned palm out, resting on his forehead.

"Dellie. They aren't being harsh. Lillian and Maude are just afraid. Afraid you are going to leave for the South. I am, too."

Dellie looked at the floor. "So am I, Winnie. It is another world. Here I have got you all, the Lodge, the Church, and I can take the rest as I want or need. There…"

She stopped to touch the child as he pulled away from the bottle Winnie held to his lips as he again coughed.

"More than that, it is the time when he is on the road. A porter has already got a job that means travel. Why does he have to add so much to it? He is missing the child growing up. He rages about the need for the workers to organize for better pay, better conditions, better hours, then he volunteers to do more hours to save for the land in the South. This land passion, I have heard it before you know? And that doesn't include the time he spends organizing. Better conditions? For whom?"

"Oh, Dellie."

"Sometimes I feel like a widow, or worse—an outside woman. Only it isn't another woman I have to strive against. It's the job, the plan, the land, the future he has in mind. Maude is right, though, this is the life I chose." She paused and lifted her hand. "Enough though. I am going to lie down with Frasier."

The small boy nestled back into the space between her breasts and hips—a close approximation of the space and position he had held inside her for nine months. She traced her fingers along his hairline and into the mass of thick curls that crowned his head. She breathed, drawing into her own body the warm smell that was his alone. She thought about this small person, in the world such a short time, and how he had redrawn her world with himself at the center. Her fingers traced his eyebrows that punctuated his every expression. She could hear the family saying their good-byes. Soon the only sounds left were Lillian rustling in the kitchen, and Coleridge whistling a tune that sounded like it belonged to Herbert the fiddler. She fell into a light sleep.

It was his coughing that woke her. Coughing, coughing, coughing as if choking on a hastily gulped drink. Her eyes flew open. The child lay next to her. Splayed out on the bed, skin flushed, eyes bright with heat. Coughing, coughing, coughing.

Dellie drew herself upright, fully alert. Her hands ran over the child—up, down. In a single movement, she covered him in a small light blanket and bolted to the kitchen. Eyes frantic, voice shrill: "The child is burning up!"

Lillian turned from drying the last dishes from the day's feast. "Dellie, calm down. You know children always..." She cut herself off as she glanced through the door to the child shuddering and prostrate on the bed. Her voice was modulated as she spoke. "Dellie, I am going to send Vere, the Selman boy from upstairs to get Maude, and then send Coleridge to find Dr. Fielding. Listen to me." Dellie looked into her eyes.

"See if he'll drink some cool water. Then sit him in the sink and run cool water over him. He is going to cry, but keep pouring cool water over him. It is not what they would do at home, but do it. Keep it cool to take down the fever. I'll be back."

Silence and solitude clanged about her as she squeezed water over her sobbing, gagging child. Maude burst in. Together they dried the child and wrapped him a light blanket. They took turns walking, rocking him. The prayers of one woman alternated with the silent screams of the other.

Dr. Robert Fielding came and opened his black bag. He examined the child's body — chest, throat, reflexes, measured the height of his fever, plumbed the deepness of his cough. He offered little, save a small bottle of yellow liquid, thick and foul. He pulled Lillian aside to a corner of the front room and whispered, "Hospital won't make a difference. Watch the other children. Make the boy comfortable."

The angle of his shoulders, and the cast of his head as he proceeded to the door emphasized the details.

So it was up to the women. For three days, they directed their prayers. First pleading, then angry, then challenging and defiant to the god who threatened to take him.

For three days, they tried poultices on his chest — mustard, mint, rosemary to burn away or, failing that, to modify the phlegm packing his lungs. Mrs. Iannacci joined the women and tried to heal him in the Italian way, using a glass and a candle on his chest to draw the sickness out. Mrs. Greenbaum tried the way of the Jews from her shtetl back home — bay leaf, oil, black pepper. Aurelia came with a thick mentholated salve to spread on his chest.

Everyone in the neighborhood worked for, cried for, pleaded for, and prayed for the life of Dellie's little boy. Candles for him blazed at St. Philip's, in Mrs. Iannacci's St. Charles Borromeo, at Mrs. Fettes' Queen of All Saints. For three days, Dellie sat and held her child. She sang to him the only song she knew, the one that Cal had sung to each of her babies. On the first day, she made a request. "Send for Owen."

It was Egbert whom the men chose to take the trolley to the Pullman headquarters to get word to Owen. There, he wired a message forward. On the second day, Dellie asked, "Where is Owen? Any word?"

No one had a reply.

And so the women sat, huddled in the bedroom as Dellie rocked, and rocked, and rocked the child. Her eyes never left him, focusing on the strained rise and fall of his chest and the dreadful retraction of the slip of skin on his throat above the collarbone.

She willed each ragged, rasping, rattling breath for him. Suddenly her movement stopped. Her voice was calm and flat. "He's gone."

She did not cry; the tears, she knew, once begun would never end. She did not moan; if she did, she would never stop. She did not fall to the floor, as she knew she would never get up. She walked toward the bed and laid the small form down for the last time. She caressed his limbs and laid his small hands across hers, right, then left, as she had done every day of his life. She memorized the freckles, the plump of his earlobes, and the curve of his lips. She sang his lullaby. When finished, Dellie placed a light cloth over his body, covering him from face to toe. She placed him with the memories that were her heart. It wouldn't be necessary to speak his name again. Not ever. Not ever. Not ever.

Egbert carried the news to the Pullman headquarters. "Man, it's urgent. The child is gone. The funeral is tomorrow. Can't you find him?"

The man behind the desk was somber. "We've tried. He must have traded with someone and the message went astray. We'll keep trying."

"Well, whatever you can do."

———

Dellie stood like a statue in the front row of St. Philip's Church. She knelt as required, crossed herself as required, genuflected as required. She saw what happened around her, but it was as if she were watching a movie—no color, no depth. The ability to see any hue had drained from her eyes with Frasier's last breath. Everything now was flat and in shades of black, white, and gray.

She was reminded of when she and Owen had first begun keeping company; he had taken her to a silent picture show. She recalled the dramatic motions, flickering black and white images, an off-key piano. A novelty, but what had been the point?

From the corner of her eye, she saw a child fidgeting. Instinctively she moved to give a calming pat. Her hand stopped mid-air. She noticed an aching in her arms where Frasier had once lain. She remembered Cal and M'Ma once talking about tending a man who had lost an arm at the cane mill and how the arm still pained him though it was gone. The missing of it was in his body. Dr. Fielding had called it having a phantom limb. Suddenly, a thought that had been gnawing at the edges of her mind gained form.

She turned to Maude, who stood next to her. "Where is Owen?"

Maude didn't answer.

———

The message never reached him. It missed him in Buffalo, was delivered to the wrong Gibson in Lorain, and by-passed him in Chicago. The man at the desk didn't run it again or follow through, and Owen volunteered to fill in on a short trip to Boston.

It was eleven days after the funeral when Owen, dog-tired from traversing half the land, arrived back home. Dellie stood as his key slid into the door and made the familiar click. He stepped through the doorway, placed his bag on the floor. She followed his eyes and looked about at the home they had made together. Neat. Ordered. Everything remained in its place. A small bunch of cut flowers in a wide-mouth jar sat on the table. Lace antimacassars, a wedding gift from a neighbor, softened the back and edge of a sofa, and the gramophone sat on its table by the hallway. He looked around foot-by-foot, piece-by-piece. A pile of fabric lay stacked by the machine in the corner. Curtains stirred in the breath of a breeze. Perfect. No baby's shoe kicked off, one here by the kitchen table leg, the other one there, by the sewing machine. No soft blanket on the sofa waiting to be grabbed up at bedtime. No pots and spoons — the makings of a one-man band — strewn about the floor. No half-empty bottle of milk on the kitchen table. No sharp smell of nipples being sterilized. No small voice singing or asking, "But why? But why?" No slap of bare feet on the floor. No voice greeting, "Papa! Papa!"

Sunlight insufficient to add light or warmth to the room highlighted the dust motes suspended in the air. Dellie registered his puzzlement at the stillness. She knew that nothing in her look signaled a change. Same as usual — dark skirt, white blouse, bangles, red hair upswept.

"Dellie?"

She looked at him and asked a four-word question, her voice clear, low, and empty. "Owen, where were you?" She didn't wait for an answer but spoke the news. Son, dead, buried, eleven days ago. She heard the tone in her voice. Prosecuting attorney, judge, jury. And it didn't matter. She watched her husband sink to his knees.

———

What had been their love, their marriage, their life together now stood between them. It had become something dangerous, something capable of wounding. They both knew it and were afraid of it and so it remained cordoned off, unopened inside each of them and between them. It sat there, like a toxic plant that sucked the oxygen from the air and emitted a vapor in its place, colorless, odorless, thick, palpable, and unwholesome. They went through the motions. When Owen was not out on a run, they took their meals together, table set with flowers, each utensil in its place. They went for walks and commented on the plants pushing through the soil or on an unexpected snowstorm. They made love, their bodies moving and responding as expected.

And then one day, Owen touched it. He spoke of the future. He spoke of a plan.

"Dellie." He put his hand on her shoulder to get her attention. "Dellie, Reddick is gathering some of the Pullman Brothers from our line up at Dad's Inn in Connecticut in a few weeks. I was thinking that we could go and ... well, I mean maybe a change of place for a while would do us good."

"It hasn't been a year yet since..." She looked out of the window, eyes on a group of children occupied with a game of potsie. "Besides, Winnie and I are coming up on a busy time with the sewing."

She felt him looking at her. Pity? Was that it? Did he regard her as pitiful? Or maybe it was annoyance? Resignation, or resentment, whatever it was, she had no room for it.

"Dellie, go with me down to my people in Carolina. We can see the land I've been putting money on in Delaware. I am nearly ready to put down good faith money. Land we've been talking about. Planning on." She saw that he regretted the sentence as soon as he uttered it.

"Who has been talking? Who has been planning?"

"Dellie. We are still alive. But this is no way to live. Can't you see a future?"

She looked at him, face impassive, then turned to watch the children and their game. Why did he touch the dangerous thing, the unspeakable thing? Why did he speak about the future? How could he talk about that empty space and still draw breath?

"Dellie?"

—

Finally, his packing was done. Dellie watched as he placed his schedule on the mirror of their dresser as he always did, as if nothing was amiss or different. He came to the window where she was sitting and kissed her gently on the forehead, then on the mouth as usual.

"Dellie, I am heading out." She noticed the box of history books pulled from the corner of their closet under his arm. "Dellie, I..."

She touched her fingers to his lips and shook her head. She didn't need to hear the words. She didn't need or have room for an explanation. She knew he wouldn't be back. She squeezed his arm as was her way when he was hitting the rails.

He turned, picked up his bag and went out, closing the door behind him without a sound. As he always did. She sighed and turned back to the window and watched the staccato, grainy, black-and-white film that was her life, continue to flicker past.

CHAPTER SEVEN

Is it Too Late?

Brooklyn, 1918

*T*he house on Columbia Heights was the finest on the block and so were its occupants. He was a physician in his prime; she, a blueblood, a bluestocking from an old Connecticut family. Their children were two boys, ages seven and four, a girl nearing three, and a girl, one. It was the situation Dellie needed: live-in, care for the children. There were also dayworkers on staff—a cook and her husband, who served as a driver.

Dellie brought little with her—the gramophone went to Maude and Egbert; her dishes, kitchen utensils, and bed linens to Winnie; Aurelia took a pile of unfinished squares from the quilt they had begun; the credenza went to Lillian. Lillian also took away, when Dellie left them behind, the photographs from Peregrine Studios in their lush frames-including the one of a small boy seated on a fur throw. The rest of Dellie's life had been sold or given away, save for her sewing machine.

The Frosts allowed her to continue her sewing business with Winnie. Mrs. Frost liked both the frugality of a sewing nursemaid and seeing Dellie's fancy work on her children's clothes and her household linens. She assumed her new worker, sister to her old one and so deft with the needle and adroit at adapting patterns to make them distinctive, was color blind. Or if not that, perhaps she was expressing some strange West Indian trait. Those were the only reasons she could think of for the odd color combinations that Dellie chose for embroidered accents or when dressing the children. Mrs. Frost gave up any attempt to educate her and learned to lay out the children's clothes or to choose the thread colors before sending Dellie off to do her work. It never occurred to her that her new servant, wonderful with the children, talented with the thread, so reserved, didn't just fail to distinguish between green and red, but couldn't see color at all.

Maude had put in a word to her former employer. Mrs. Fettes affirmed it, so opening the opportunity for Dellie. Mrs. Fettes and Mrs. Frost had met each other years ago. Their husbands, as pharmacist and doctor, knew each other professionally. "A fine family," Mrs. Fettes said. "And no one works harder than these West Indians, you know..." She had gone on, the way Mrs. Frost had noticed the Irish were wont to do, something about the woman now being alone and having experienced a "great loss." She nodded to be polite, but she didn't need to even begin to know the details of her help's personal life. She had gotten the key information. She was clean, reliable, and of decent morals. She didn't care to know how or hear speculations about why the ability to see color had suddenly drained from Dellie's eyes on the day of the child's funeral. She had no desire to know about the source of her need for order, neatness, regular lines, schedules, and predictability.

And so Dellie stepped into the situation. The room she occupied on the third floor had in it just what she needed: a bed with a white chenille spread, a dresser with a crocheted runner left by the room's previous occupant, a table suitable for writing, and a chair. A small closet was only partly filled—several uniforms, light gray with white collar and cuffs, a dark skirt and a white shirtwaist, and two dresses, one loose and comfortable and one fancy, for church.

It had been three years since the death of the child and one year since Owen's departure. Many commented on how well she was doing.

"She is handling things well, don't you think? Always so composed," noted one of the Lodge women to Maude.

"She's an example to others of bearing the tests the Lord gives us," commented Reverend Fletcher one Sunday to Lillian.

"A pillar of strength," Winnie overheard at the bakery.

Those who knew her saw something different, and were troubled. They watched her rest her eyes on the clock, and knew that she was counting in two directions, ticking off the time left for her to bear life and also counting the seconds, the minutes, the months since that terrible day when Frasier had left the world.

Since that day when the color had drained from her eyes and the past filled up the present and the future, she had ceased planning, ceased the recklessness of hoping (that was a type of planning wasn't it?), and had begun merely regulating her life. The Frosts' lives kept hers on a schedule. Off on Wednesdays, so time for sewing and weekly dinner at the home of Lillian, Maude, or Winnie. Off on Sundays, so time for church. From time to time, Aurelia would invite her to do something, and they would walk through the park or chat over tea. The other days were spent attending to the schedule dictated by the needs of the Frost children—breakfast, a walk to the park for play, back for a snack, and stories and quiet play or a nap, lunch, then out again for a walk through the winding paths of the park and back for dinner, time with parents, and then the children to bed.

That left only the hours after dark. During those hours, after every other light on Columbia Heights had been extinguished, hers continued to cast a muted glow as she rehearsed and dissected the period leading to the loss of the child. Where had she been slack? What had she not seen or not done? The weather had been warm, not even a sign of chill in the air. Should she have covered him better at night? There was the day he had splashed his feet in a puddle. Had she not dried them properly? How many choices had she made during that time? Should she have turned left, not right, when she took him for his walk? Had the germ that took him been lurking in that direction? Should she have insisted on his wearing the bow at the photographer's session to trick fate as Dorothea had told them? Had she been smug in her letters home? Which choice had she made? Which one could have offered a different outcome so that a small boy who loved to dance would still have his life and be in the world?

She feared that she had caused it. Had it been the talk that day in her kitchen about something preventing a move to Delaware? Had her wish taken him? Her need for her own way? Cal all over again? Her breath stopped when her mind moved down that track.

She wrote letters home to Eva and others with no mention of the details of her current situation. May, the last of her sisters, would be coming at last. A letter from her told of Henry's passing. May had returned from a day at the Great House to discover him slumped to the side in an impossible position, eyes glassy, a thread of spittle from his mouth to his top button, lips working to no avail.

Not knowing what to do, unable to find M'Ma, she had run and picked her way across the obeah woman's yard. She had found the ancient woman, the one whom everyone considered mad, in the middle of her piece of ground with a round, flat basket in hand, broadcasting feed for the frizzled chickens pecking around her legs. She brought the old woman up the hill. Just after the moon rose, in the house that he had built so long ago for Cal, Henry had stopped breathing. In the end it was the old woman, M'Ma, Josh, and Cuffee who helped her meet Henry's final needs. Everyone else had left the Chandler's piece of land called the Hope. Everyone except the too sick, the too old, and those in short pants, along with those waiting in some limbo of their own devising for what might or might not be.

Henry had never stepped off of the 14 by 21 mile piece of rock in the sea. Only ventured from the Hope a few times. But perhaps that was a blessing, Dellie mused. It was the proceeds from the house that buried him — the one he had built those years ago for himself, as head carpenter, and for his wife, the niece of the mistress. Dellie had heard that the Parris boy, married now to one of Cal's cousins, had made an offer to buy it. He had looked it over — sound wood, sound joints — made in the way for which Henry was known. It wasn't much now, but with some paint and new jalousies it would be fine until a more permanent structure, a wall house, could be constructed. The Parris boy had come back from abroad with his pockets filled with Panama money and spoken to old Mr. Chandler's lawyer about a piece of land at a good price. He dismantled it and packed it up. Henry's house with the rose-colored verandah would stand now on a piece of land bought by someone else, with money pulled from a ditch in Panama.

According to her letter, May would be bringing few things with her when she came. There would be some money from the sale of the house after the burial, so the last sister emphasized that they were not to worry about her coming empty-handed. She would come bringing with her a small copy of the massive photo portrait of Henry and their mother's comb-and-brush set.

Dellie read and re-read the letter that May had sent. It described the end of something, the closing of something that she should care about. That was what the words said, and what her mind understood. She stared into the mirror that hung over the dresser in her room on Columbia Heights, and wondered at what manner of woman could read such words, and feel nothing.

———

She sewed for the Lodge, for the Frosts, but still she had time to fill. She needed a project, something to fill the hours by herself in her room. And so she began sewing handkerchiefs.

The work was agreeable to her. Stacks of squares cut from smooth, white fabric, fine, small stitches, rolled hems, and fabulous embroidery — white on white, threads removed to create shading, a heavier stitch here, a twist there. She sewed things that she had seen, and things from the short list of places to which she allowed her mind to wander, mortally conscious of where and what she must avoid in her brain. The stacks of squares filled her dresser, the top shelf of her closet, spilled from boxes underneath her bed. Some she gave to Mrs. Frost, who was enchanted with the designs of palm trees, flying fish skimming over waves, monkeys, and parrots, and passed them on to the ladies of her circle at board meetings, garden parties, and fund-raisers for significant causes in lands faraway. And that was Dellie's life.

———

One Wednesday afternoon Lillian handed her the packet of letters.

"They arrived day before yesterday in a package addressed to Coleridge. They were in this brown paper tied together with a string. Coleridge read a letter that came for him in the same bundle. Then he sat for a long time with these upon his lap. Finally, he stood up, and brought them to me, saying they are for you."

Dellie reached out a trembling hand. There were thirty, at least. Some were in envelopes worn around the edges. Some were made from intricately folded light blue paper trimmed with stripes. Some were marked with smudged fingerprints embossed onto the paper.

Some were written on thin, white onionskin, their sheerness reveal-ing words crafted in a swirling hand with dark ink.

The stamps also drew her eye. She remembered the concept of color and knew that these were bright. Unlike the utilitarian squares sold at the Post Office on Jay Street, these were bold and imaginative, their lines curling into outlandish shapes and shame-less designs.

"They're from...?"

Lillian nodded.

Her voice was even and calm. "But why?"

"He wrote to Coleridge that he was leaving the sea with the end of the Great War. Coming to New York. He needs to know if it is too late. He said he had written from each port over the years but didn't mail the letters. He said that this stack had filled the bottom corner of his sea bag. According to the letter for Coleridge, he is here in Brooklyn at this address." She tapped at the corner of the wrap-ping paper.

Dellie flattened her palms on the smooth table, the oilcloth cool against the hot rush of feeling jolting through her body. She recov-ered, pressing and folding recollections of another life on a small island back into their set places in her mind.

Her sister's hands lay on top of hers. The sensation registered at the edge of Dellie's brain.

"Dellie, he left it to Coleridge to decide whether or not to give you the letters. All of them are there." Lillian paused. "I can take them back."

Dellie's eyes remained on the small stack of papers filled with words tied to a long dashed set of hopes drawn up in a different place, considered by a different person.

"Dellie?"

Silence.

Lillian's hand reached out to gather back the papers. Dellie's voice, not a word, but a sound, stopped her.

—————

She smoothed the bedspread, lining up its tufts into even rows and assured that the white-work medallion was properly centered on the bed. She reached over and touched a saturated wick with a match before seating herself on the edge of the mattress amidst the steady pool of light cast by the kerosene lamp. Dellie steadied her hands. They quivered with some long frozen feeling as she sorted the letters by date. She placed the last one, dated November 11, 1918, at the bottom. She was ready to begin.

She tried to read deliberatively, but her eyes, ravenous, would not have it so and leapt from word to word, line to line, page to page. As she read each salutation, she heard Pendril's voice in her ears. *My dear sweet Dellie; Dellie, my own heart.* She heard his voice lift from the page, telling the stories collected as he crossed the globe.

The first letter had been written while at sea between Barbados and Liverpool. In it, he recalled himself as a boy—him and his gang, Coleridge, Lane, and Dite, down at the Careenage in Bridgetown. If a ship had just come into port, it was worth the Headmaster's lashes for skipping school. It was worth being chased by the Harbor Police to be a part of the pageant. He recalled how once they had made a few pence for delivering papers to a man standing behind the Customs House. They had bought some rum from Simon's Ned and made themselves tipsy. Another day, they had earned a few coins by coiling ropes and used the proceeds to buy some baker's paper to fashion kites with bones from the cane. They had caught some good breezes and the kites flew far out over the water on the air. Mostly though, they had just sat on the dock, staring out at the glistening water and at the ships coming and going, imagining, imagining, imagining.... He couldn't remember the day they had made the pact that took him and Lane off to sea.

The pages told of places he had been, dock districts in port cities that were peopled by men like him. His letters took her down labyrinths of winding, narrow streets with buildings and businesses crammed together cheek-by-jowl. He wrote of merchants plying goods and services—women, drink, cheap meals, lush fabrics. He described rich carvings of wood, ivory, or stone in fantastic shapes and expressions, man's gods and demons, a range of exotic goods bought or pilfered from ports across the globe by men traveling the invisible roads of the world's seas...searching, searching, always searching.

These men of the sea were of every color and language, he wrote. They prayed, each in his way. Some were from the lands of the colonizers, others, the colonized, but he described how each had the same look when his eyes were on the water. He had seen dozens of districts as he traversed the globe. He had gathered memories of people, smells, sights, tastes, for stories to be told when there was someone to tell them to. Each line of his letters bore the unspoken questions: Was she that person? Was it too late?

He had not pursued information about her since he had left. In the years since then, he had seen the Seychelles and while there bitten into the sweetest fruit on God's earth. He had been to Dublin and seen a nun drying the tears of a child. He had been to Edinburgh and in its winding streets had watched for nearly an hour as an old, old man walked up an endless hill. He had once docked in India, place of his ancestors, and touched the face of a blind man who could have been his brother. He had smelled spices that tantalized the nose, touched silk so light and fine you had to remember it was not air. He had seen shows in the sky from stars and planets and comets that left him breathless.

Once he had watched as a pod of whales surrounded a huddle of babies when his ship ventured too near. He and other seamen like him had marveled at God's creation and could see why there were so many names for that Majesty. Once he had seen the sea churning and in it arms, thousands of them, every shade of black and brown reaching out toward the sky while the wind carried a sound like wailing. Another time, as he sailed around the Cape of Good Hope, he had heard a beating like a heart and watched a group of women in white drum and dance on a pure stretch of beach. He had seen the endless pouring forth of forms reveling in life and its beauty and terror.

The pictures that Dellie saw through Pendril's eyes touched something in her, calling forth memories from before time. And then his letters began to tell of the war.

Pendril wrote of the talk of war that for a year passed from man to man along the docks. Talk about land boundaries. Seamen like him watching strange men lurking about and passing bulging envelopes hand-to-hand in consideration of loading crates without proper papers, or letting a group of men with hate-filled eyes slip on board in the dead of night.

He wrote of the words about war that passed among the men of the sea. They heard talk of killing societies—groups of men called the *Black Hand* or *Union or Die*. Killing societies: groups of nations called the *Allied Powers* or the *Triple Alliance*. Killing societies. Killing people. They heard that passenger ships would be fair game in the rumored war. They heard that steamers carrying goods—food, coal—would be fair game—the spoils of war. They heard that the shipping lanes would be mined, that German vessels would pose as ships under a neutral flag and that their *sea*, that God's *sea*, was to be a battleground in a war over land.

Dellie slid the paper from the envelope. The writing was barely a scrawl choppy, jagged like the writing of a child. She squinted to make out the words. *A strange ship changed flags and unfurled the German war eagle. It pulled alongside the Wellburn and started blasting and then it was like a dream. I saw myself lunging toward Lane to push him out of the way. And Lane was gone in a mist of red and heat. Gone, Dellie. Just like that, a person gone and me screaming"Lane! Lane! Lane! Lane, where you gone to?" How could a person with the vision of such a thing inside of him be in the world? Talk to another person? How can I be in the world among decent people?"*

He told her that he had loved her since they were in primary and that for all those years, plus nine years at sea, through thirty-three ports, he was still dreaming of her. The letter ended with a statement, *"It is time to come home now, I think"* and two questions, *"Was that place, was home, where she was? Was it too late?*

Dellie tipped her head back to stay the tears and stared at the ceiling. She wished that she were the woman the letters had been written to. A woman who lived in the world and didn't just take up space in it, a woman who immersed herself in things, who saw, who felt, who could afford the intemperance, the recklessness, of hope. A woman who could be comfortable among people. She wished she wasn't a "used to be" woman—used to be someone's mother, used to be someone's wife, used to not be just a spectator. She wished she wasn't a woman who endlessly and without purpose sewed scraps of fabric into fanciful handkerchiefs. She wanted to be a woman who could see color. That was what she wished. And she was ashamed for it.

She remembered the conversations from years ago and all that had happened in the nearly three thousand days since her ship had pulled back from the Pierhead in Bridgetown. And now Pendril needed to know "was it too late?" There was no beginning or end to that answer.

With no plan, no real thought of any kind, Dellie pulled her shoes from the closet—sturdy black leather, modest heels, thick laces. She slipped them on and tied them with precision. She gathered her hat and waistcoat and headed out of the house. Her feet touched the unyielding pavement as she headed toward the docks district and the address scrawled in the top left of the last letter.

She found herself in front of a rooming house. Her eyes scanned the structure, window shades uneven or askew. Voices of men, words slurred in drunkenness, spilled from behind them. She picked her way with care through a barren yard toward the front door, ignoring the lunging and snarling of a dog secured to a post and the crawling eyes of a huddle of men sharing something hidden in a tattered brown bag.

Pendril stood waiting in the doorway of a second-floor room as she rounded the landing. When her foot achieved the top step, she did not falter at the tremble that moved through her body from the center outward.

There he stood in a doorway, shirtless, hair disheveled, pants wrinkled, feet bare.

He moved aside and allowed her to enter his quarters. They mirrored hers—bed, small desk, chair, dresser. A worn green shade covered a window and obliterated any view of the outside.

They stood facing each other, wordless. Pendril's right arm crept up and crossed over his torso, an attempt to cover the shame of the scar that bisected his body from breast to navel.

"Pendril."

Her voice was barely audible as she stretched out her arm and moved his away from his chest. They each gasped as her fingers traced the dead, unfeeling rope of the scarred-over wound.

Dellie let Pendril move her hand away. The words hummed in each one's mind. "Is it too late?"

He breathed in—jagged, tremulous. She stood, still and firm in her crisp, pleated skirt, starched blouse, and orderly shoes. No spot or wrinkle or looseness—from a casual pose or perhaps from a knee crossed brazenly over its mate— nothing lay about her to indicate where life had intruded and left its mark.

She did not move as he stepped closer to her and closed his eyes. She breathed in his scent and touched his hair. She traced his eyebrows and they fell into each other. Wordless. Holding, holding, simply holding.

They walked. The moon, full, and round like a pregnant belly, hung over the three-story houses of lower Brooklyn. It poured out a cool white light onto the street before them. Its whiteness mixed with the deep, undulating shadows of branches and leaves dancing with the breeze.

And so they walked past parks and solitary trees with short, wrought-iron fences ringing their trunks to protect them from the distresses of the city. They traversed blocks of barricaded doors and shuttered windows, past newsboys bundling papers that broadcast the world's dramas as it shuddered through the end of a war and the end of an empire. They walked past various nightwalkers. The women looked them over, but said nothing, curious perhaps, for just a brief moment, of what the vital night errand of these daytime people could be.

Dellie and Pendril walked and heard snatches of conversation, duets, single voices, spools of lives organized neatly in the rows and rows of buildings that spanned the geography of Brooklyn.

"…slogging through the forests in Belgium…"

"The food is terrible and I can't wait for a taste of your…"

"…to save the carfare. If I do that everyday we'll be able…"

"Books are due. Don't forget to…"

The sash of moonlight pulled and pulled them past the cramped row houses of the new settlers, and into the areas peopled by those for whom they worked. A chorus of stray cats cried somewhere in a lot.

They walked and walked, passing through the clutter of civilization to where Brooklyn gave way to its ancestry, the houses sparse, the streets unpaved, and the smell of the salt sea sharp in their nostrils.

Dellie paused at the foot of a wooden walkway of weathered silver curling across the sand, luminous in a faint glow from the moon. She took Pendril's hand and they walked on, planting their feet just so, each step mindful of the obvious rough spots and places where boards had long ago gone missing. They avoided the spikes of beach grass that had pushed through with no concern for anyone's effort and imposition of order.

The air was still, the tide slack, poised between coming in and going out. The only sound was the soft hiss of sea foam as it melted into the sand. With the moon as their lantern, they took the six short steps down to the sand. Dellie shuddered at its chill, but it evoked no thought, no memory.

Dellie sat on the last step and removed her shoes, slid her stockings down over her feet, carefully placing each in a toe of her shoes. Without sound she stood and slipped out of her dress, then out of her shift. She folded them, smoothed them, and laid them on the sparse grass, bending the stalks in her work. A gentle tug removed her wedding ring, a slide shed her earrings, and a pull brought her bangles over her wrist. A neat pile grew at the side of the ancient steps.

She unfurled her hair and let it tumble down, a wild mass about her shoulders. The moon offered the light for her open-air boudoir and she examined herself — arms, legs, breasts. The chill air called up a pattern of small bumps on her skin that she regarded without interest, as if they had appeared on another. She gazed dispassionately at the water for a moment, noting the rhythm of the waves, not crashing, but gently lapping the shore. She walked toward the water.

Pendril fell behind. He paused and watched her, the coolness of the sand and the sharp scent of the sea pulling him, forcing his mind elsewhere, to places he no longer wished to go. He dropped his clothing and shoes into a rough pile.

"Pendril. Pendril, come." Dellie's voice moved through the night.

It was then they heard the sound, drums, like hearts beating in time. At the water's edge, where the sea met the sand, stood a host of people arrayed in white, women in cascading dresses, men in loose shirts and pants, clothing that shimmered in the moonlight. They beckoned to her — there were Cal and Henry. She could make out Palley, and then others whose faces, gestures, movements were familiar, but whose names she did not know. He saw before him the aunt who had raised him, his parents; there was Lane. And there were others, people that they had seen in their dreams, seen all their lives, but whom they could not name.

The crowd drew them into the water — the cold of it a shock that made them both draw breath inward and shake hard, rough trembles from within.

The hands of the people in white moved over them, stilling them, rubbing them, pushing them, pulling them, forming and re-forming them. Dellie and Pendril each cried, screamed, thrashed, now hot, now cold. The figures took them by the arms and legs and lay them back, back, back, till they floated and were enveloped by their lives. They saw things separately, then together, the memories of one mixing, combining, joining with the memories of the other and of all of the people surrounding them — a small island, the thick smell of hot sugar, kisses under a star-apple tree, cane, cane, cane, Cal, a scream and a flash of red, jars glistening in the sun, a riot of flowers, a row of brownstone houses, M'Ma brushing Maude's hair, walking, walking, barrels of sugar, rows of sewing machines, a husband, a child, Henry, Harrison's Line, breadfruit, kisses under a star-apple tree, a child sleeping, a child dancing, a child dying, a child, a child, a child, kisses under a star- apple tree.

They took to the water and floated gently, yes, they floated ever so gently and people — Cal, Mrs. Chandler, Lane, Henry, Palley, Pauline, and those whose names they did not know — encircled them. The vision of a ceremony, ancient, old as memory itself, passed before them. They watched a woman pounding a drum and changing form, formless, then a veil, a robe, a clay figurine, a smooth black stone, a spring. Back, back, they tumbled through the earth itself, through water, through air, time, memory; through thought and hope to the beginning where they heard all around the sound of a drum beating, echoing, sounding for depth, like the sound a child hears in the womb...

Then they were on the sand, the people around them dancing. Dellie and Pendril watched. The people in white whirled, torsos undulating, feet a blur, the ululations of their voices rolling across the silent dunes on an ancient spit of land in Brooklyn, on into the night and beyond. Dellie and Pendril hovered at the edge of the ring of dancers. Suddenly, Dellie's eye caught a movement at the center of the circle. A small boy, twirled, moving his legs, arms, and shoulders, doing a funny little bouncing dance. A voice made its way into her head.

"Dance Mama, dance! Just dance!"

And Dellie spun and dipped and moved, laughing and crying, singing and moaning. Pendril moved toward her and with her. His voice, his body, with her, apart from her. Their voices one, their bodies one. The sound of drums enveloped them, as did the life of the child, the lives of the women, the men, the dunes, the sea, the moon, the sky — everything. And Dellie and Pendril danced.

The incoming tide crept around them, and across the sand. The two lay linked on the gray grains like twin infants spent from bursting from the womb. Dellie roused first, the wetness of the sand and the lick of the waves pulling her awake. She stood, the first rays of the sun grazing her skin. She tipped her face to the sky and saw the few threads of pink and gray that embellished the swath where sky and sea were one. A smile opened her face as she admired the flecks of rosy light beginning their day's flirtation with the water. Pendril, behind her, moved, brushing the sand from his body. They looked out at the water and clung to each other. New, whole, clean, just born.

They turned together and followed their footprints back to the wooden walkway and began their walk home. It was not too late.

Afterword

To me she was ancient—gray hair in a bun, stockings knotted just above her knees, fingers bent with age. She always wore a pair of plain gold earrings, a modest gold band on the ring finger of her left hand, and an armful of silver bangle bracelets incised with intricate patterns. Except for the ring, her jewelry was from "home" and identical to that of her sisters, Lillian, Maude, and May in whose houses the whole extended family rotated for various celebrations and expansive meals. What I remember most clearly about my grandmother, however, is sitting on the floor; Nana's knees holding me firmly in place and her hands alternating the brush, the comb, and the pomade as she worked my hair from a wild mass into two respectable braids down my back and one near the front to contain the overflow. And while we sat, her hands brushing, smoothing, weaving hair in and out, over and under, she told me stories.

Nana was from Barbados, from a small village in the farming parish of St. George. She talked about "home" and about Brooklyn at the turn of the twentieth century, about a time before she was a grandmother, when she was a woman named Dellie with red hair, the daughter of a carpenter on a sugar estate. Her stories were filled with magic, strange places with names like Taborvilla, My Lord's Hill, Sweet Bottom; and extraordinary people—her parents Cal and Henry, her grandmother M'Ma, her bosom friend Winnie, and also a mad woman who practice *obeah*, a rude parrot, and a host of others.

My grandmother had an old, decrepit black leather handbag, a faded black flower crafted of ribbon fixed to it, that she kept wrapped in an old pillowcase and stored in her dresser drawer. She would take it out from time to time, consider its contents, and return it to its place. The children in the family were all afraid of it. Although we dared each other to touch it, none of us ever did. We knew some of the items in its pockets. A nut, light brown with dark brown circle that made it look like a cow's eye, that she had brought with her on the voyage to New York. ("The old folks back home said that these things washed all the way across the sea from Africa!")

A small carved ivory charm of a camel. ("Your grandfather brought that back with him from a trip to Morocco when he was a seaman.") And a lock of hair tied in the edge of a handkerchief. ("From my mother's head.") But there were things that she never spoke about--compartments never opened--at least not in front of us. It was with that bag and the contents of those closed compartments--the letters, the birth and burial certificates and faded photographs, a piece of pale blue beach glass--that the search for my grandmother's life, for the woman named Dellie that my grandmother was, began.

Not all of what I have written is factual. But all of it is true.

Glossary

About and abroad- far and wide

Bajan (bay jun) - a person of Barbadian ancestry, birth, or culture; of or having to do with the culture of Barbados

Bay rum- a distillate of alcohol and bay leaf scented with spices and citrus used as a men's cologne or aftershave

Bim/Bimshire- from the Igbo meaning my home or my people, a friendly name for Barbados

Chattel House- a moveable house constructed of 12 by 20 foot timbers. These dwellings have one, two or perhaps three roofs, depending on size and number of additions.

Chupse- a sound expressing derision or incredulity made by sucking the teeth

Cou-cou- a West Indian dish made of cornmeal, okra, and seasonings

Coolie- a derogatory term for a West Indian person of African and South Asian lineage

Duppy- a ghost

Doogla- a derogatory term for a West Indian person of South Asian and African lineage

Jump-up- a party

Knock-about woman- a woman of slim virtue

Mauby- an astringent beverage made from the bark of a tree

Marl- a crumbly mixture of clay, sand, limestone, and crushed shells

Obeah- a system of beliefs or actions used to harness or to defend against dark, supernatural forces

Own-way- stupid *and* obstinate

Shtetl- a diminutive Yiddish expression for a small town in Central or Eastern Europe with a large population of Jews

Sorrel- a drink made from the flowers of a hibiscus plant

Wall house- a permanent dwelling built on land owned by the occupant

Yu know nuh- you know; of course, obviously

Near the Hope
Discussion Questions

The story takes place in Barbados and Brooklyn. Is the author successful in contrasting those two settings?

To what extent, if any, are the settings also characters in the novel?

What images, people, settings, or objects are symbolically significant?

What are some of the themes of the novel?

How is Dellie's experience universal?

What are some of the folk practices that Dellie and her friends and family maintain? How do they relate to or complement other religious or cultural practices?

What passages did you find insightful? Funny? Poignant?

What are the main character's traits and motivations?

How would you describe the relationships and dynamics between the various characters?

What passages offer insight into the characters? Into setting? Into mood?

Why does Dellie flee the island without a word to Pendril?

What role does the New York Bajan community play in the lives of the characters?

There are elements of magical realism in the novel. What are they? Do they enhance or detract from the story?

How are Dellie's choices affected by her character, her culture, her social status?

About the Author

Jennifer Davis Carey has family roots in the Caribbean and the American south. A native New Yorker, now residing in Massachusetts, in addition to writing, her passions lie in education and public service. She has held numerous positions in both areas and holds undergraduate and graduate degrees from Harvard University. She has published opinion pieces in the *Worcester Telegram and Gazette*, and a short story in the journal *The Caribbean Writer*. She learned to appreciate the beauty of language by listening to her grandmother and great-aunts, and honed the craft of writing with Algonkian Writers, Sewanee Writer's Workshop, Hurston-Wright Foundation Writing Workshop, a residency with Voices of our Nation (VONA), and coursework at Grub Street in Boston. *Near the Hope* is her first novel.